WORLDS OF INK AND SHADOW

LENA COAKLEY

Worlds of Ink and Shadow

HarperCollins Publishers Ltd

Published by HarperCollins Publishers Ltd

First Canadian edition

The drinking song "Here's to the Maiden of Bashful Fifteen," which is quoted on pp. 171–172, was written by Richard Brinsley Sheridan and first appeared in his play *The School for Scandal*.

HarperCollins books may be purchased for educational, business, or sales promotional use through our Special Markets Department.

HarperCollins Publishers Ltd
2 Bloor Street East, 20th Floor
Toronto, Ontario, Canada
M4W 1A8

www.harpercollins.ca

Library and Archives Canada Cataloguing in Publication information is available upon request.

ISBN 978-1-44341-659-7

Book design by Maria T. Middleton

Printed and bound in the United States
RRD 9 8 7 6 5 4 3 2 1

For Clare

Are there wicked things,
not human, which envy
human bliss?

CHARLOTTE BRONTË

CHARLOTTE

C HARLOTTE BRONTË DIPPED HER PEN INTO the inkwell and dabbed it on a blotter. For a long moment she held it over the blank page, waiting. She was writing the final scene of a story, and she wanted it to be . . . transcendent.

On the other side of the desk, her brother, Branwell, was scratching away. His spectacles sat folded in front of him, and he was bent double over his paper, his eyes only an inch or two away from the words. When Branwell couldn't get a scene right, he simply went on to the next one—and the next, and the next. Half his page was covered already, she noticed with disgust, and he was writing with his left hand, too. Her brother wrote equally well with either hand, but he chose the left only when he was writing about Alexander Rogue, his magnificently wicked villain.

"Remember," Charlotte said. "You're not to kill off any of our characters without my consent." Rogue had a nasty habit of dueling with Charlotte's favorite people. "I had plans for Count Roderick."

Branwell shrugged, drawing a red blanket closer around his shoulders. "Pompous nincompoop. He deserved to die like a dog."

"He was mine! I was going to have him woo Lady Constance."

Her brother smirked. His pen hadn't slowed its speed throughout this exchange, and Charlotte felt suddenly daunted by the sheer volume of words it produced. *Scribblemania*, Branwell called it.

She got up and closed the window against the damp. Below her in the churchyard, the gravestones were vague and indistinct, coming in and out of view as gusts of wind swept the mist across them. Her father's church, which was just beyond, had disappeared, enveloped by the fog.

On her return to the desk, she tripped over the heavy muller Branwell used to grind his paints. She pushed it into a corner with her foot and sat down again. "Your attempts to annex this room for your own use have not gone unnoticed," she said.

They were in the children's study, as they had always called it, a small upstairs room with no fireplace. Half a dozen of her brother's unfinished paintings sat on easels or leaned against the walls, his bed was pushed up into a corner, and his wooden paint-box lay open by the desk, spilling out brushes and packets of expensive pigments ordered from Leeds.

Branwell gave a loud, barking laugh, slapping his hand on the desk, seemingly delighted by one of his own turns of phrase. Charlotte clenched her teeth, sure he was purposely ignoring her. She had missed her brother when she was away at school, had waited eagerly for his letters, but now that she was home for good, everything about him vexed her.

"Do you hear? The children's study has always been for all of us."

Branwell was beyond hearing. With a twinge of envy, Charlotte saw that his mind was in that place where the real world falls away.

All those words, she thought. *If someone straightened Branwell's writings into a single line of black ink, would it circle the globe?* She had written like that once, for the sheer joy of being in invented lands, not caring whether the words were good, whether they were *art.*

Her brother threw her a glance—such a strange, ecstatic look in his blue eyes. Charlotte sat up straighter in her chair. There was something feverish in that look, as if something were burning her brother up from the inside. It gave her pause. Like the gravestones coming into view when the wind tore the mist away, Charlotte saw her brother. Truly saw him.

The blanket he wore was an old ratty thing, but on him it looked dashing, like a bullfighter's cape. There were red wisps on his chin that a generous person might call a beard, and he was wearing his carrot-colored hair long and loose, in an artistic fashion that suited him. Branwell had turned seventeen that summer, and even Charlotte had to admit he was becoming rather handsome.

And yet . . . how thin he was, and pale, with something frenetic about those ever-moving fingers. Both he and Charlotte were ill more often than their sisters; they felt the cold more keenly; they tired more quickly. Charlotte knew why, but usually she was able to imprison the reason at the back of her mind.

The light changed. There was something in the room with them that hadn't been there a moment before, something bright. Charlotte would have seen it if she turned her head, but she kept her gaze on Branwell.

"What have we done?" she whispered.

Still writing furiously with his left hand, Branwell lifted his right, palm up.

"Banny, don't!"

Her brother's eyes were shut now, his face beaming with corrupted joy. His quill fell from his hand. Charlotte held her breath—and as she watched, her brother disappeared.

"Oh," she said. The sight still surprised her after all this time. She glanced to the study door, but they had been careful to shut it, as always. The light was gone. She was alone. "Reckless boy."

She leaned over to look at Branwell's side of the desk. Incredibly—miraculously—his words were still unspooling across the page. Charlotte took up her own pen with determination. In very small, very cramped handwriting, she began to write.

EMILY

MILY BRONTË OPENED THE STUDY DOOR A
crack, peering inside. "They're gone," she whis-
pered. She and her sister Anne slipped in, closing
the door behind them.

"Goodness, where is the floor?" Anne said.

Branwell's books and painting things littered the room, and his
bed was unmade. By mutual agreement Tabby, the Brontë family
servant, didn't enter the children's study, and so it was the only
place in the parsonage where untidiness was allowed a foothold.

"I was wondering where all our teacups had gone," Emily
said, looking around. "But for heaven's sake, Anne, you mustn't
get distracted and begin straightening things." She opened the
window to dispel the scent of linseed oil and turpentine. "Anne?"

Her sister was staring at the desk now, a mix of fascination and aversion on her face. "I shall never become accustomed to that."

Emily came up beside her. It was uncanny, she had to admit. Two papers sat on opposite sides of the desk, writing themselves. If their siblings had been present, Anne and Emily would have heard the scratching of their pen nibs across the pages—not to mention Branwell's nervous humming, mumbling, and foot tapping—but these words appeared in perfect silence.

"What should happen if the paper ran out?" Anne asked.

"Their writing is so small it never does." This wasn't entirely true. Once, Emily had seen a story of Branwell's write on top of itself again and again until the paper was black, but the sight had so unnerved her that she decided not to mention it to Anne.

"I don't like it."

"These are not the stories we've come to read," Emily said, turning away. With her foot, she pushed aside a braided rug and knelt down, lifting a loose floorboard. Underneath was a small space where Charlotte and Branwell kept their finished writings.

"Couldn't we simply ask to read their work?" Anne said. "They've always allowed it before. We don't have to steal."

Emily glanced again at the desk, eyes narrowing. Charlotte and Branwell were far away now, in fantastical worlds they refused to share.

"Admit that I'm willing to eat the crumbs from their table?" Emily lifted her chin. "Certainly not. And we're borrowing, not stealing."

CHARLOTTE

VERDOPOLIS. CHARLOTTE'S EYES WERE SHUT, but she knew she was no longer at her desk; the little parsonage in Yorkshire was far away.

A party. The final scene of her story would be a grand party.

The lovers had been tested. Insurmountable obstacles had stood in their way, but now their trials were over. They were married. All of Charlotte's characters, major and minor, would come together for a celebration. At a certain point, the new wife and the new husband would see each other across the room and share a knowing look, and anyone reading Charlotte's story would sigh with contentment, because that look would somehow contain all the couple's happiness, and prefigure all their golden days to come.

Yes, Charlotte thought. That was how it would be. She imagined room after dazzling room in readiness—fires glowing, silver gleaming, glassware sparkling on ornate tables. She opened her eyes.

A beautiful woman in gossamer silk floated through the fine rooms, making a last inspection before her guests arrived. It was Mary Henrietta Wellesley, the new bride. Shyly she nodded at the footmen in velvet and gold. Though of high birth, she had been raised modestly and was unused to having so many servants. Charlotte was no longer sitting. Instead she crouched behind a crimson curtain.

"Who's there?" Mary Henrietta cried. "Show yourself!" She turned to alert a footman.

Charlotte stepped out, and for one horrible moment she was herself, a plain girl in a mouse-colored dress, too small, too ill-favored to belong anywhere in this world. She looked down at her worn shoes on the gleaming marble, murmuring under her breath: "*Eager for the party to begin, Lord Charles had dressed early, and now had nothing else to occupy his childish temperament but to harass his poor new sister.*" Somewhere far away in Haworth, these words appeared across Charlotte's story paper.

"Oh, it's you, Charles," Mary Henrietta said with a merry laugh. "Don't frighten me so."

Charlotte, now a boy of ten in a blue velvet suit, capered across the floor. "Will the Duke and Duchess of Fidena be here? And the Earl of St. Clair? And the young viscount?" Her high boy's voice echoed in the enormous room.

"Of course." A shadow passed across Mary Henrietta's lovely face. "Unless they receive a better invitation."

Charlotte flopped down on a brocaded sofa as if she owned it, which, as one of the Wellesley heirs, she did. "Don't be foolish. You're a duchess now, and a Wellesley. There is no better invitation than ours."

"I suppose not." Mary Henrietta sat down on the edge of the sofa, careful not to wrinkle her gown. "I wouldn't mind so much for myself if no one came, but ... I'd like everything to be perfect for *him*."

Charlotte rolled her eyes, something she would scold Emily for doing back home. "Zamorna thinks everything you do is perfect. He is besotted with you, as well he should be."

"Perhaps." Mary Henrietta did not look reassured. "It's just ... he's had so many wives and lovers before me ..."

Charlotte sat up. She hadn't meant for the conversation to take this turn. "It's you he loves now."

"Yes." Mary Henrietta tugged at one of her chestnut curls. Her hair was not yet done for the party, and it hung prettily around her shoulders. "So he says."

A story's happy ending was no time for marital doubts, in Charlotte's opinion, but sometimes, in spite of her best efforts, her characters would drift away from the plot like recalcitrant sheep, as Mary Henrietta was doing now. She often felt that being an author was like being a sheepdog, always snapping at her characters' heels to keep them on track.

"*Mary Henrietta looked down to smooth her dress,*" she said, "*and when she looked up again, the troubled expression upon her face had melted away, replaced by a new bride's glowing smile. 'Of course he loves me,' she said, and Zamorna's sordid past was quickly forgotten.*"

Mary Henrietta neither noticed nor acknowledged these words, but she looked down to smooth her green silk, and when she looked up, her face did indeed glow with happiness. "Of course he loves me," she said. "Forgive my foolish talk, Charles."

"Milady! There you are!" Mina Laury, Mary Henrietta's faithful maid, burst in clutching a handful of ribbons in different lengths and colors. "We haven't finished with your hair, and your guests will be arriving soon."

Mary Henrietta glanced at the ormolu clock with jeweled hands sitting on the mantel. "Oh dear!" she said, leaping up. She gave Charlotte a kiss by way of good-bye and darted off with her maid.

Charlotte was left touching her cheek where Mary Henrietta's lips had been. One of the benefits of playing Charles Wellesley was that every time Zamorna married, she got to have an elder sister again for a little while. She laughed and ate a walnut from a cut-glass bowl, then sprang from the sofa, going out through the tall French doors and onto the balcony. A warm breeze washed over her, perfumed with jasmine. It was never cold in Verdopolis, never damp. The sun was setting behind her, and a sliver of moon was already rising above the magnificent Verdopolitan skyline.

I made this, she thought. *All this is mine.*

She said aloud: "*All the church bells in the city began to ring the hour, but loud as they were, they could not drown out the clatter of approaching wheels and the whinnying of fine horses.*"

Before she had even finished the sentence, the chimes of St. Augustin and St. Michael's began to ring in unison. Then, to her delight, the carriages arrived, gilded carriages decanting tiny-waisted ladies in brightly colored silks, frothy with lace. Golds, greens, and crimsons dazzled the eye: Colors were richer in Verdopolis than anywhere else. Charlotte caught glimpses of dainty, satin-sheathed feet as the ladies stepped lightly to the ground, assisted by handsome, slim-hipped gentlemen with piercing eyes and aquiline features.

She leaned over the balcony railing, waving and shouting with abandon at the guests. She didn't worry about falling, didn't worry about being unladylike. After all, she wasn't a lady; she was a ten-year-old boy.

She turned back inside and ran through room after room, stopping at the entranceway just as a pair of footmen in powdered wigs swung open the great doors. Up the staircase like a glittering tide, the party guests arrived. She stood aside and let them all go by in a swirling, chattering, laughing wave. Charlotte knew them all, but since she was a young boy, they took little notice of her, and that was as she wanted it.

A moment later, the party's host and hostess came out to greet their guests. All eyes turned to them, the wealthiest and most fashionable couple in Verdopolis: Lord Arthur Wellesley,

Duke of Zamorna, eldest son of the Duke of Wellington, and his latest bride, the incomparable beauty Mary Henrietta. Immediately Mary Henrietta was surrounded by admirers, and the duke was pulled to the other side of the room by his own coterie of friends.

"Stop!" Charlotte said. The room fell silent. All were still. Gentlemen were frozen in the act of bowing to young ladies or lighting their cheroots or accepting glasses of punch from elegant servants. Ladies were frozen as they blushed behind their fans or admired the fine paintings on the walls.

Charlotte, the only moving person in the room, wove through the crowd, adjusting a stray curl here, straightening a bow there. She stopped in front of Zamorna.

Her hero was as handsome as the statue of a Roman emperor—tall, with a high, noble forehead, loose curls, and arresting brown eyes. Even frozen, he took her breath away. He was so aloof, so arrogant, so aristocratic. Zamorna had been the main character of Charlotte's stories ever since she was a little girl. Whenever Branwell's villain, the wicked Alexander Rogue, tried to rob a bank or assassinate someone or kidnap a young lady, the Duke of Zamorna was always there to save the day. Women were his one weakness, but now that he had found Mary Henrietta, his days of ensnaring highborn ladies with his famous "basilisk gaze" were surely over.

Charlotte looked back at Mary Henrietta, trying to see her through Zamorna's eyes, trying to be sure she was flawless in every way. "The dress should be violet," she said. "And more . . . diaphanous."

Immediately, Mary Henrietta's dress changed from green to violet, the fabric so sheer and fine she seemed to be swathed in mist.

"Yes. Perfect."

Charlotte moved back toward Mary Henrietta and climbed up onto one of the high-backed chairs behind her, wanting to see every passion that crossed Zamorna's face.

"*The duke looked over at his wife, catching her eye,*" she said.

Immediately the scene began again with all its noise and bustle and laughter. Men finished their bows; ladies lowered their fans and smiled. Zamorna and Mary Henrietta both looked up at the same time. Charlotte held her breath in anticipation. Across the room, the husband's eyes met his wife's . . .

"*Mary Henrietta Wellesley radiated grace and beauty . . .*"

Charlotte kept her gaze fixed on Zamorna, waiting to see his face change, waiting for the vast depths of his affection to sweep over him. From her vantage point on the chair, she could almost pretend he was looking at her.

For a long moment Zamorna and Mary Henrietta regarded one another. Then the duke nodded to his wife and went back to his conversation.

No, Charlotte thought.

Mary Henrietta turned back to her companions. "Excuse me. What were you saying, Ambassador?"

Charlotte sat down on the gilded chair. A stiff breeze swept through the room, rustling the curtains and the ladies' gowns. Charlotte put her arms around her shoulders, chilled, as if the damp gust had come all the way from Yorkshire. Now when she glimpsed her hero through the crowd, his face seemed waxy and unreal, lacking any true life.

Over the years, Charlotte had given Zamorna many love interests, each more beautiful, virtuous, and devoted than the next. Once, she had been satisfied with these romances—thrilled even—but now . . . now she was beginning to see that she had never sparked true feeling in Zamorna, true fire. In fact, none of her characters came fully to life, not like people in a real book, not like—she hated to admit this—Alexander Rogue sometimes came to life on Branwell's pages.

But there was no wonder in her failure, she told herself. She was no author. She was simply an eighteen-year-old girl from Haworth, England, a girl who was destined to be a governess someday soon, and probably an indifferent one at that.

Perhaps I am only playing with the world's most exquisite set of dolls, she thought. Perhaps it was time to put her dolls away.

BRANWELL

BRANWELL BRONTË WAS IN A PART OF VERdopolis that Charlotte never wrote about, far from the Tower of All Nations and the Duke of Zamorna's mansion house. Here the shabby wooden houses were crammed together, and refuse lined the streets. He turned down a narrow alley where a rough-looking fellow with a clay pipe was slouched against a wooden door. The man tipped his hat to him, but there was something insolent in the gesture.

"In the secret meeting rooms of the Elysium Society," Branwell said under his breath, *"Alexander Percy, Earl of Northangerland, also known as Alexander Rogue, was plotting his latest outrage."*

He crossed to the wooden door, whispered a password to the man with the pipe, and entered.

In stark contrast to the outside of the building, the inside of the Elysium Club was splendid. The walls were covered with red velvet and gold. A fountain surrounded by ferns gurgled in one corner. There were no windows, and Branwell doubted any of the red-eyed men hunched over glasses of gin or sitting around the gambling tables knew if it was night or day outside. These were gentlemen of wealth—there were numerous silk cravats and gold-tipped canes in evidence—but many had a somewhat sinister air. To be a member of the Elysium Club, one needed to be worth at least five thousand a year—and to have slain a man.

Branwell handed his hat and coat to a servant and glanced around, the smoke thick enough to make his eyes sting.

"Lord Thornton," said the barman, sliding a glass of undiluted brandy toward him across a mirrored bar. Branwell gave a nod and drank it down. Here in Verdopolis he was no longer a poor parson's son; he was Lord Thornton Witkin Sneaky, rich young reprobate. Unlike Charlotte, though, Branwell didn't change his appearance when playing a character, and so Lord Thornton looked like himself—with a few slight differences.

"Have you seen . . . ?" he began. The barman jerked his head to the back of the room.

Alexander Rogue was draped lazily over a chair like a black lion, smoking a cheroot. He was long and lean and not particularly handsome—drink and evildoing had weathered his face, as had two years of piracy on the high seas—but he had a presence that commanded attention. As always he wore plain black, but the diamond earl's star at his breast marked his class—that and a certain haughtiness to his gaze.

"Thornton," Rogue called without getting up, "settle a bet. S'Death says I have orchestrated eleven kidnappings in my lifetime, but I aver it was an even dozen."

Branwell approached the table where Rogue sat with a fiendish-looking old gentleman. His name wasn't really S'Death. He was Mr. R. P. King, Rogue's right-hand man, but he gave off such an impression of wickedness that he was nicknamed for the blasphemy. He was very short and squat but rather spry for a man with such an ancient face. His twisted features were like something one would find in the bark of a tree or the grain of a wood panel, and yet his hair was flame red—obviously dyed. He was known to be one of the richest men in Verdopolis, though how he came by his wealth was a dark mystery. His accent proved he was not born to it, but no one dared ask.

"We count your wife in the tally, I suppose," Branwell said, as a servant brought him a chair.

"Zenobia? Of course. It's how we met."

Branwell sat down and rubbed his chin thoughtfully—one of the slight differences to his appearance was that in Verdopolis he had an excellent beard. "And do we reckon the Hawthorn sisters as one or two?"

"The twins!" Rogue said, and he brought his hand down on the table with a thump. "Ha! I do believe we forgot those harpies."

S'Death was jotting down names in his little black book. "Eight, nine, ten ... damn and blast! It is thirteen. Neither wins."

There was a pile of banknotes on the table, which Rogue divvied up between them. The older man seemed to watch a little sadly as Rogue's portion disappeared back into his jacket pocket.

"Is it kidnapping then?" Branwell asked. "Or shall we attempt another bank robbery?"

He could have made this decision himself, of course, but unlike Charlotte, he liked to let his plots go where they may. He found that if he stood back a little, Rogue almost seemed to choose for himself.

His villain took a pull of his cheroot. "Ah, the youth of today are so energetic, S'Death."

He snapped his fingers, calling for spirits, and at once a waiter appeared with a bottle of brandy and three glasses. Rogue poured two glasses and took the bottle for himself. "What's the use of coming up with a magnificently wicked plan when it is sure to be foiled by that Casanova in silk?" Branwell knew he was talking about Charlotte's hero, the Duke of Zamorna. "You heard he thwarted my scheme to fix the Verdopolitan horse races?"

Branwell nodded. This had been the plot of one of Charlotte's stories. "Perhaps an overthrow of the government then?"

"Been done," said Rogue with a sigh, taking a draught. One of his character traits was that he drank almost constantly but never appeared to be drunk.

S'Death made a clicking sound with his tongue, shaking his

head. "Such an excellent scheme it was, too, assassinating the entire Verdopolitan parliament at once." He put his hand to his breast. "It breaks my heart to think of them all downing glasses of punch at Zamorna's party tonight."

"Party?" Rogue and Branwell said at once.

"You hadn't heard? He's having a grand party at Wellesley House."

So Charlotte has finally managed to come up with an ending for her latest story, Branwell thought.

"Seems a bit of a snub that you and the countess weren't invited, Rogue," S'Death went on, "what with the hostess being your daughter and all."

"A snub indeed," Branwell said.

Mary Henrietta Wellesley was Rogue's child from a previous marriage, and many of Charlotte's recent stories had made great use of this. *I love you, Zamorna, but it can never be, for you are the enemy of my wicked father. Oh sorrow!* The couple seemed to be settling into the dullness of domestic bliss now. Branwell was tempted to enliven things by having Rogue break into the party uninvited, but Charlotte would be livid if her happy ending were spoiled. He needed a moment to think through the best course of action.

"*A cry of 'I'm ruined' rang out in the smoky hall,*" Branwell said under his breath.

"I'm ruined!" someone cried.

A man at the other side of the room lurched up from one of

the gaming tables, scattering a deck of playing cards to the floor. He pulled a gun from his jacket pocket. The barman ducked behind the bar, and all the gamblers hid under tables—all except Rogue and Branwell, who stayed where they were, and S'Death, who turned in his seat with interest. Great wealth was often won and lost at the tables of the Elysium Club, and the old black-guard liked to keep abreast of whose fortunes were high and whose had fallen.

Waving the gun before him, the man stumbled to the gentlemen's lounge in obvious distress. A moment later a shot rang out.

"Another suicide," S'Death said with a hint of repressed glee. He took out his black book, turned over a few pages, and shook his head. "Oh, but there's a pity. He owed me a thousand." He licked a stub of a pencil and carefully crossed out the man's name. "At least he didn't do it right in front of the bar like the last one. They were cleaning brains out of the chandeliers for days. Remember, Rogue?"

Rogue gave a bored shrug, then stubbed out his cheroot into a jade ashtray.

"You know," Branwell said, "the more I think of it, the more I agree with S'Death. Zamorna's snub must not go unanswered."

"I'm two steps ahead of you, boy," Rogue said.

"Ah," said S'Death, "I know that look. You intend to make another attempt on the parliament?"

"No," answered Rogue. "They're not the true enemy, are they?" He rose from his chair. "It's time we got to the root of the problem." A feral grin spread over his face. "I fear my poor daughter will have to buy herself some widow's weeds, for tonight we kill the duke himself."

Branwell struggled to keep the shock from his face. He did love to vex Charlotte, but he hadn't planned this. A nervous giggle escaped his lips. Rogue and S'Death were both staring at him, waiting for his opinion.

"All right," he said. "Let's do it."

EMILY

MILY," ANNE SAID QUIETLY, "WHY EXACTLY
do we *want* the crumbs off their table?"

Emily was rifling through the papers hidden in
the secret place under the floorboard, Charlotte's
tied neatly with ribbon, Branwell's in haphazard piles.

"What I mean is," Anne continued, "there is no shortage of
reading material in this house. Charlotte is an excellent writer,
but Mr. Shakespeare is better, and if it's Branwell's wickedness
you like, Papa says we may read Lord Byron in moderation."

Emily tried to keep her features motionless. She valued her
privacy, and Anne's ability to read a person's face bordered on the
uncanny. "I suppose I simply want to keep abreast of our people
in Verdopolis," she said. This grazed the truth, at any rate. "We

helped to create them—the older ones, at least—and I want to see what those two are doing with them."

Anne pursed her lips, but Emily, not as gifted at reading people, couldn't tell if her sister believed her.

Everything had been different when they were young. Once, all four siblings had crossed to the invented lands together. Together they'd explored worlds inspired by Aesop's Fables and *Gulliver's Travels* and *The Arabian Nights*. Who could have asked for a better childhood? By the time she was ten, Emily had visited islands inhabited by giants thirty feet tall and had traveled to the moon to speak to the gentle, blue-haired folk who lived there.

True, it was Charlotte and Branwell who created these places, but they'd been happy to take their younger sisters. In those days, they crossed over by acting out a story, not by writing. All they needed were a few opening words. A door of light would open, one of them would make that mysterious hand gesture, and they would all go through. Branwell and Charlotte never explained how it was done, but Emily had always believed that it was only a matter of time before the secret was revealed to her.

Then Anne and Emily were cast out. To this day, Emily couldn't understand why. It was around the time that Charlotte and Branwell invented Glasstown, and she supposed her older siblings simply wanted it all to themselves. By the time it became

Verdopolis—a more appropriate name for what was now a glittering city—Anne and Emily had to read their older siblings' writings if they wanted to know what was happening there.

"Look," said Anne, smiling. "One of our little newspapers." She reached into the spot under the floorboards and pulled out a miniature book. The Brontës had made dozens of such things when they were children—little newspapers where they recorded the doings of their favorite made-up characters. Tabby had helped them sew the bindings out of old sugar bags.

"We'd best hurry," Emily said, glancing at the desk. "There's no telling when they'll be back."

Anne sighed and replaced the little book with tender care. She never complained about their banishment from the invented worlds; now Emily wondered if her sister missed them as much as she did.

"Isn't it remarkable," Anne said, "how one can become attached to fictional people?" She looked at Emily with large violet-blue eyes. "The feeling might become quite strong, I expect."

The thought occurred to Emily that in some other, very different life, where Anne was not a virtuous parson's daughter, she might have told fortunes out of a gypsy caravan. "Mmm."

"We are so isolated here in Haworth, with no one of our own age to befriend, and the men and woman of Verdopolis are real, in a way. It wouldn't seem strange to me if . . . someone . . . might even fall in love with one of them."

Emily kept herself as still as a rabbit on the moor, knowing that a denial would give her away.

"And I suppose," Anne went on, "that Charlotte's hero Zamorna is very compelling to read about. He's so . . . dashing. Is that why we're going to so much trouble?"

Emily let out a breath, repressing the urge to smile. She replaced the board over the hiding spot and stood up, clutching a selection of Charlotte's and Branwell's newer writings to her chest. With her foot she kicked the rag rug back into place.

"Perhaps," she said.

ANNE

NNE BRONTË HAD A FANCY, SOMETHING too foolish to ever mention. Sometimes she imagined that there was a tiny mathematician in her mind. He was always busy, this little man, measuring the wideness of smiles, calculating the timbre of voices. He tallied his numbers on an ever-clicking abacus, and occasionally, to her great surprise, he would look up from his reckonings and tell her unknowable things. *This person is lying. That person is afraid.* Today her little man told her that Emily was keeping secrets.

"You're quite certain that all the story papers have been returned?" Anne asked as she laid out the breakfast things.

"Safe under the floor again," Emily replied without turning around. She was staring out the window, a bouquet of spoons in her hand. Grasper, the family's Irish terrier, had his paws on the sill, as if he, too, saw something diverting in the fog.

"Every page?"

"Every page."

The parsonage was so small that it had been difficult to find a place to examine their stolen property. In the end they had spent the previous afternoon reading stories in Papa's study, where the family piano was, taking turns at playing scales so that no one would become suspicious.

Anne set the family's plain white china around the little table. One bowl was chipped, and she put it at her own place, turning the flaw toward herself. "And the animals. Have they been . . . ?"

"All fed."

Anne watched as Emily ran a hand over Grasper's ears, noticing that her sister's skirts were wet with dew; she must indeed have been outside this morning, feeding Jasper, the tame pheasant they kept in the yard.

"I didn't see Snowflake," Emily added. "But I expect he's still out murdering things."

"And did you . . . ," Anne began.

"And, and, and," Emily repeated. "Don't we get enough scolding from Charlotte?"

Anne held her tongue. Emily didn't deserve harassment; her older sister might be dreamy, but she didn't shirk her chores. Still, Anne liked to be assured that everything was perfectly in its place. The Brontës had nothing fine—everything was plain and functional—but Anne loved how neat and orderly their home was, especially on mornings like this one, when the fog surrounded them like an endless, gray sea. Somehow order made her feel that no matter what dangers lurked outside, the parsonage was their snug little fortress, where nothing evil could touch them.

Finished with her work, she looked at her nearly perfect table and refrained from mentioning the missing spoons. Emily seemed to have forgotten she was holding them.

"What exactly is so interesting out there?" she asked instead, coming up behind her sister.

"The fog. It's like a living thing this morning. See how it pours itself over the stone wall?"

Anne could barely see the wall, though there was only a short stretch of green lawn between it and herself. The churchyard beyond, with its small monuments and crooked gravestones, was all but lost.

"It makes me think of the gytrash," Emily said.

The gytrash. The ghost dog of the moors, who tore out the throats of unsuspecting travelers. Anne had always hated that story. She frowned and peered out into the grayness. It had been foggy for so many days that there *was* a sort of unreality descending on the parsonage. The town of Haworth, which lay beyond the church, was beginning to feel like a fairy tale, while the stories Tabby told of fairy hobs and ghost dogs seemed as near as they had in childhood. Anne put her hand up against the cold glass, her breath fogging the pane. "Yes. I think I see what you mean."

Crack! Something sounded just above their heads. Anne jumped, making a little scream, and Grasper yelped. A second report split the air.

"It's only Papa," Emily said, laughing. Their father slept with his pistols loaded, and they must be discharged for safety, or so he said. He shot them out of his bedroom window every morning. "Did you think it was the spectral hound?"

Anne tried to laugh, too, but her heart was beating fast.

"Oh, heavens, the spoons." Emily looked at her fist as if the spoons had just appeared there. Quickly she dispensed them around the table. Grasper followed, getting underfoot. In name he was their father's dog, but, like all their pets, he circled Emily like a planet around a star.

Emily moved to the birdcage in the corner of the room. "You should make a remark today, Anne."

Anne stayed at the table, aligning cutlery and making final adjustments to a vase of wildflowers. "Oh. I don't know."

"Try. It could be something very simple."

Though her conversations with Emily were easy and natural, with others Anne could only manage a few stilted words—and at meals with Charlotte and Branwell bickering, and Aunt Branwell scolding, and everyone talking at once, even those few words seemed to dry up and blow away.

Emily put her fingers through the bars of the birdcage, making *tutting* noises. Rainbow and Diamond, the tame finches she had raised, fluttered and chirped. "Tell them we saw the gytrash in the fog. That would make for wonderful conversation."

Anne blushed at the idea. "I wouldn't have Papa think I still believe in such things."

"Who saw a gytrash?" Tabby bustled in carrying a tray. She was a large woman of about sixty, with a wide, red face and a stomach that enveloped the cords of her apron. Tabby was the family servant, but to Anne, who had known her all her life, she was more like a member of the family.

"We did," Emily said. "Right outside."

Tabby set down her tray and put her hands on her hips, taking in Emily's wry smile. "That's nowt to make fun about." She picked up a spoon and waved it at Emily to make her point, disturbing the lovely order of Anne's table.

"The Heatons at Ponden Hall were quite bothered by a spirit a few years back." She put a finger to her chin. "Not the gytrash, though. This'un came as a headless dwarf, I believe. Or were it a burning barrel rolling down t'ill?"

Emily giggled. "If I were a thing of fog and shadow and could take any form I wanted, it would not be a barrel rolling down a hill."

Tabby pursed her lips. "Now you mind me, young miss. These things are not t' be mocked. Old Tom sends out his minions in many forms—the white lady dragging her chain, the dusky calf, the ghost of a loved one. It's the see-er who chooses the appearance, not the spirit. Whatever you're fearing most, that's the form it takes." She began to take things off her tray—a cone-shaped loaf of sugar, a saltcellar, a pitcher of cream—each one landing with a thump on the table. "Is ther making a remark this morning, Anne?"

Anne looked shyly to the floor. "I'm not sure what I'd say."

Tabby thrust the empty tray under her arm. "How's about: The porridge is 'specially good today."

"Is it?"

"What a question. It's 'specially good every day."

Anne was saved from arguing the grammatical sense of this by a series of bumps and scrapes from upstairs—the unmistakable sounds of Branwell moving his easels about. He must be inspired to paint today.

"Ee 'eck!" Tabby said. "Are both t' men up already? I mun get that porridge off the fire." She smiled. "Or I'll make a lie o' your remark."

When she was gone, Anne gave a semblance of order to the things Tabby had deposited so haphazardly onto the table, and then she joined Emily, who was standing at the window again.

"I used to long to see the gytrash," Emily said.

"Surely not."

Emily's hand found hers and squeezed. Her fingers were ice cold. "I would ask Charlotte to tell me the story again and again, though it always terrified me."

"I can't imagine why you'd want to hear it," Anne said.

Emily looked at her with a frown. "Haven't you ever wanted to be devoured?"

The chill in Emily's hand seemed to travel through Anne's blood and across her body. Of course she hadn't. "No." She let her sister's hand go.

Just then, the little mathematician in Anne's mind looked up from his clicking abacus and blinked.

"Oh," she said. "I got it wrong, didn't I? We didn't steal those papers to read about Zamorna, did we? It's the villain. It's Alexander Rogue you love."

Emily made no answer, but Anne knew she was right. What she didn't know was why the idea should disturb her as much as it did. Rogue, Zamorna—they were both only fictional characters, weren't they? But in his stories, Rogue had done such cruel and terrible things. He was chaos. He was the black hound, tearing out throats on the moor. What sort of person could love that?

CHARLOTTE

CHARLOTTE SAW IMMEDIATELY THAT PAPA was troubled about something. Normally he spent the pre-breakfast bustle looking over his spectacles at his children with benevolent satisfaction, as if pleased, and just a little surprised, that they had made it safely through the night. Now he sat ramrod straight at the head of the table, a stony look on his face. With his flashing eyes and snow-white hair, he looked like an Old Testament prophet. Charlotte could see why some of his parishioners were afraid of him.

She set a steaming teapot on the table and sat down. Something was not quite right with her sisters, either. Emily was gazing off at nothing, while Anne made minute adjustments to the dishes and cutlery within her reach. These things in themselves weren't unusual—Charlotte sometimes wondered if Anne might like a compass to orient the butter dish—but she could detect some tension between them. Perhaps they'd had an argument, though how one could argue with Anne, who was so mild and quiet, was a mystery to her.

Branwell and Aunt Branwell were the same as always. They sat on Papa's right and left, oblivious to his mood, chattering across the table. Or rather, Branwell chattered. Aunt Branwell only nodded in rapt attention, as if every word out of his mouth was worthy of embroidering on a sampler.

"I hope you are all aware of the honor your brother does you," Aunt Branwell said, turning to Charlotte and the girls, "by choosing you as his models."

Charlotte smiled tightly at this. "I had an excellent lesson planned for Anne and Emily today. I hope the 'honor' of sitting for this portrait is worth postponing their education."

"Why, Charlotte," Aunt Branwell said, "I'm surprised. Your brother is an artist, and inspiration has struck. We ordinary folk must bend to his muse."

"Do forgive me, sister," Branwell said, a twinkle in his eye. "My muse is such a tyrant."

Charlotte gave him a glare.

Aunt Elizabeth Branwell had come to help with the children thirteen years ago, when their mother died, and had never left. She'd been an invaluable help over the years, but now that Charlotte had been to school and seen a bit of the world, she couldn't help but notice that her aunt was a bit of an embarrassment. The false curls she wore on either side of her head didn't match the rest of her hair, and her old-fashioned dresses were stretched too tightly across the bosom. She took snuff and made her own beer and insisted on wearing her pattens inside, claiming the stone floors of the parsonage were too cold, even in summer, and so her feet clomped and clattered everywhere she went.

"You *will* be combing your hair a little more nicely for the picture, won't you, Emily?" Aunt Branwell asked.

Emily had a way of coming up out of a daydream with a peevish look on her face, as if disgusted to discover she was in the world again. "Yes, Aunt," she said. Charlotte was certain her sister had no idea to what she'd just agreed.

Aunt Branwell gave a frustrated hiss. "Why, you girls are very cavalier, I must say. I've never had my portrait done in oils, and I'll warrant there are few in Haworth who have. You might all be hanging in a gallery one day." Getting no response from the Brontë sisters, she turned to Papa. "I say, your girls are very cavalier. Don't you agree, Patrick?"

Papa grunted in agreement, but he was as oblivious as Emily. He was marshaling his words. Charlotte had seen him do it often enough. Every Sunday morning before church, Papa would sit alone in the vestry for a minute or two, frowning to himself. Then he would stand before his congregation, set his pocket watch on the lectern, and speak extemporaneously for exactly one hour. *Someone is going to get a lecture over breakfast*, she realized. *Please, God, let it be Branwell.*

Tabby bustled in with a tureen, took one look at Papa's face, and began to serve the oatmeal porridge with twice her usual speed. She'd been known to fuss around the table for the entire meal, listening to conversations and offering up opinions asked or unasked, but now she dashed back to the kitchen as if she'd left something burning on the stove.

When she was gone, Papa gave a small cough. It was enough for everyone, even dreamy Emily and self-absorbed Branwell, to snap to attention and sit straighter in their chairs. Usually he would say grace now, but instead he pulled a small piece of paper from his breast pocket. Charlotte's heart sank.

"I have in my possession a mysterious document," Patrick Brontë said gravely. "And I'm curious to know what you will make of it." He displayed the small rectangle of paper, back and front, to show that it was covered on both sides with tiny writing. "Had I happened upon it in any other context but this house, I would have assumed it a missive of the fairies, the writing is so small and cramped. To whom does this belong?"

The siblings glanced around the table at one another.

"It's mine, Papa," Charlotte said. It *was* hers, one of her many story papers, but it should be safely under the floorboards. Had their father found the secret hiding place?

"I thought as much."

Aunt Branwell pulled her spectacles out of an embroidered case and put them on. She took the paper from his hand. "But it's unreadable."

"I rather wish it were," Papa said, "but look at this line here. It clearly reads: *The Duke of Zamorna kept a mistress in seclusion, fathered numerous illegitimate children, and drove two of his wives to suicide.*"

"Good heavens!" Aunt Branwell cried, dropping the paper as if she'd been burned. Branwell reached across the table to pick it up.

"Who is this duke, may I ask?" Papa asked Charlotte. "And what has he to do with a parson's daughter? More of your stories, I expect. Look how you've made your sister blush." He gestured to Anne, who blushed now at being singled out if she hadn't before.

Charlotte fought the urge to leap to her hero's defense. Why couldn't Papa have found a story that outlined Zamorna's bravery? His nobility?

"What do you think, Branwell?" Papa said. "What is your opinion of your sister's endeavors?"

Branwell held the paper at arm's length and squinted at it. "Shocking," he said finally. "Tut-tut. Really, Charlotte. We must set an example for the younger ones."

"Ha!" Emily barked a too-loud laugh, then lowered her head.

Papa ignored this. "I thought that sending you away to school had cured you of this childish habit."

The word *childish* made Charlotte wince. She had to bite her lip to keep from protesting.

I should feel ashamed, she thought. *Why don't I?* A proper daughter would be mortified to have disappointed her father, yet she found herself feeling more annoyed at his interference than remorseful for her actions.

"I have tried to stop writing stories," she said, keeping her eyes downcast. "I know it is a poor use of my energies."

"Stories are not wicked in themselves," her father said, more gently now. "I myself have written them, but always to instruct my flock. They have a moral lesson. What moral lesson does your dissolute duke teach us, Charlotte?"

"None at all, Papa."

"None at all," he repeated, looking around the table. "The purpose of art is to elevate the mind. This is why I have surrounded you children with all the books I can afford"—he lifted a hand to the walls—"why I have purchased so many of Mr. Martin's biblical engravings to better our souls. Has it been in vain?"

"I hope not, sir," Charlotte said.

He took a handkerchief from his pocket and wiped his spectacles. Charlotte noticed that his high collar, though spotlessly clean, was beginning to show wear, and his jacket was frayed at the cuffs. Every spare penny Papa had went to his children—Charlotte's school fees, the piano for the girls, Branwell's painting materials. What was wrong with her?

"You are not ashamed," Papa said, as if reading her mind.

Charlotte's mouth opened, then she shut it again quickly. "I assure you that I am, sir," she said. Had she been sullen or surly? She hadn't meant to be.

"Oh, fear not. Your imitation of contrition is very convincing." Charlotte felt the heat rise to her face. "Would you like to know why you feel less than you think you ought?"

Charlotte raised her eyes to his. "Yes. I would."

"Because sinning frequently inures one to the shame of sinning, and you have been sinning for a long time." He put a hand over hers and continued, not unkindly. "You are a liar. An inveterate one, I think."

She heard Anne give a little gasp.

"Oh," Charlotte said, tears beginning to smart behind her eyelids. She felt suddenly exposed, as if her father could see down to the very bottom of her.

"Why, Patrick, surely that is too harsh," Aunt Branwell interjected.

"Is it too harsh?" Papa asked, not taking his eyes from his daughter's face.

"No," Charlotte breathed.

"I don't know exactly what my children lie about," Patrick Brontë said, "but I feel them—all the little lies of this house. They are beginning to take their toll."

Around the table Charlotte's siblings sat frozen, as if captured in one of Branwell's portraits, guilt stamped on their features. The shame Charlotte hadn't been feeling now stabbed through her like a knife. It was true that the Brontë children had told many lies over the years. Once, they had thought themselves so clever to deceive their father, to cross to other worlds right under his very nose without his ever knowing. Now she wondered if every falsehood wasn't a little chip from her soul—and not just her own, but from her siblings' as well. Branwell had joked about setting an example for the others, but he was right. She was the eldest. She should have set a higher standard.

"I wonder what Maria and Elizabeth would have made of this," Papa said.

"Oh," Charlotte said again. This was the coup de grâce that made her vision blur with tears. It had been years since she had heard those names on her father's lips. "My sisters would be very ashamed of me, I'm sure."

What clean, white souls they all would have if Maria and Elizabeth had not died, she thought. They should have been the ones to set the example, not her.

Papa ran his fingers over his mouth, looking suddenly tired. It had cost him to say those names. He didn't invoke his dead children lightly. "Well," he said, forcing a smile, "I have pontificated long enough for a day that isn't Sunday, and I fear our porridge will turn cold. Shall we bow our heads?"

"Wait," Charlotte said. "I'd like to say something, if I may, Papa." He nodded, and Charlotte stood. Her siblings were still looking very grave. She hoped they were in the proper frame of mind to hear what she had to say, especially Branwell. "I have been thinking a great deal about . . . my stories." She nodded significantly to them, willing them to understand that she was not talking about writing so much as about crossing over. "Papa was very wise when he called my writing a childish habit, and I think he understands that, for me, it's a dangerous one as well."

The small square of paper that had caused such consternation lay in front of her on the table. Now she took it up and held it out, looking at each of her siblings in turn. "Emily. Anne. Branwell." She ripped the paper in half. Emily gasped. "I am renouncing my invented worlds and all who live there. If any of you are in the grip of a similar childish habit"—she raised an eyebrow at her brother—"I challenge you to do the same."

ANNE

THE PAIN THAT FLASHED ACROSS CHAR-
lotte's face at breakfast had made Anne's breath
catch. *Why did she do it?* she wondered. *Why renounce
her stories when they obviously meant so much to her?*

"Stand there, Charlotte," Branwell said, waving a hand distractedly. "And pinch your cheeks—you're pale as milk. You too,
Anne. It's lucky you both had your curl papers in this morning."

Anne dutifully squeezed the flesh under her eyes as Charlotte
took her place beside her. They were in the children's study, pos-
ing for the group portrait.

"I don't think a gentleman should display such familiarity
with a lady's morning toilet," Charlotte said.

Branwell was busy scraping freshly mixed paints onto his palette, and he answered without looking up. "If you don't want me

to know you use curl papers, then don't burn them at the dining room grate where anyone can see them."

The room felt terribly cramped. Anne couldn't imagine how Branwell slept with all the clutter and with such a strong smell of linseed oil. She and Charlotte were in front of the door where the light was best, while their brother and his easel were next to the window.

Branwell shook back the too-long sleeves of his painter's smock and took stock of the room. "Now, where the devil is Emily?"

"Here I am," she said, squeezing through the door.

Oh dear, Anne thought. There was anger in the tightness of her sister's face, in the hardness of her eyes.

Like Charlotte and Anne, Emily had changed into her best dress—plain green with a wide, white collar and large gigot sleeves. Anne's was almost identical but dark blue, while Charlotte's was lower cut and worn with a fichu around her shoulders. All the dresses were silk. Poor as they were, the girls owned only silk dresses, as their father believed that cotton could too easily catch fire.

"Now, there's a fine complexion," Branwell said, oblivious to the anger in Emily's face. "Comes from all those long walks on the moor. You look like a corpse by comparison, Charlotte."

Anne glanced at Charlotte, but her sister only pursed her lips and ignored the slight. She was very sensitive to comments about her appearance.

There are too many emotions in this small room, Anne thought. *Too many barbed little words.*

When they were all in place, Branwell picked up his brush. "I feel I must mention that nonsense at breakfast, Charlotte." He tried to make his tone light and conversational, but Anne didn't miss the strain in his voice. He made a few small marks on his canvas. "Is it safe to assume that your claim to be quitting Verdopolis was a falsehood for Father's benefit?"

Charlotte took a moment to answer. "I assure you, it was no falsehood."

Branwell feigned an indulgent smile. "You won't do it."

"My decision is made."

A look of panic crossed his face, but it was gone in a second. "No," he said. "This is another one of those resolutions that you'll go back on a week later. I recall a pledge to speak French for two hours every day, and another to give up sugar in your tea."

Charlotte shrugged as if to say, *Think what you like.*

"But you can't stop!" Branwell said, his voice rising in pitch in spite of himself. "Verdopolis is ours—yours and mine. It would fall apart without either of us."

"It's yours now," Charlotte said.

"I don't think you understand. Our worlds aren't so easily abandoned. You forget, I tried once. I tried . . . They don't . . ." Branwell lowered his voice as if someone might be listening. "They don't let you go."

"What on earth are you talking about?" Charlotte asked. "Who doesn't let one go?"

Branwell stabbed at his palette with a brush. "We'll discuss this between ourselves," he said, looking pointedly at Anne and Emily. "Later."

"My answer will be the same."

"Are you planning to paint at all today, Branwell?" Emily interrupted. Anne looked to her in alarm. Was she the only one who could see Emily was practically quaking with rage?

"Quite right," said Charlotte. "Do begin, brother. The girls and I are being held hostage by this wretched painting. I'd planned to teach them some new irregular verbs today."

I must say something, Anne thought, *suggest we do this another day.* She didn't understand all the emotions smoldering in the room, but she felt sure they would burst into flame at any moment.

Branwell held up his brush. "Well, I'm sorry, but I must paint today." A cruel smirk crossed his face. "As you know, *Mr. Robinson* comes at the end of the summer." He elongated the syllables of the name. "And *Mr. Robinson* is very eager to see my new work."

Charlotte's face turned stony, and Anne felt the tension in the room rise even higher. Usually Branwell had the sense not to mention the man's name.

Earlier that summer, two of Charlotte's pencil drawings had been chosen for inclusion in the exhibition of the Northern Society for the Encouragement of the Arts. It was a great honor, and the whole family had traveled to Leeds by carriage to marvel at the works on display. They had met Mr. Robinson there and seen his portraits. Branwell had shown him some of his work, and it was Mr. Robinson who convinced Papa that Branwell could be a professional painter—with a few private lessons, of course. There was simply not enough money for Charlotte to have lessons as well.

"Father is paying *Mr. Robinson* two guineas a lesson to teach me to paint in oils. He must have a large body of work to critique. Do you know what *Mr. Robinson* said the other day?" Branwell asked. "He told Father I had a prodigious talent. That was his very word: *prodigious*."

"I expect he only said it to get some drinking money," Charlotte replied, mimicking Branwell's false smile. "Rumor has it that *Mr. Robinson* has a prodigious appetite for alcohol."

Anne could see that this taunt hit the mark. They had all noticed that Mr. Robinson smelled of whisky.

Don't let's fight, Anne tried to say. *Please*. The words tangled in her mouth.

Branwell slammed his palette down onto his desk and turned to point at Charlotte with a paintbrush. "You can't stand the fact that if future generations remember you for anything at all, it will be for being Branwell Brontë's sister."

Charlotte sputtered. "What did you say?" She left her place, navigating around the easel. On her toes, she looked over Branwell's shoulder at his canvas, though he tried to prevent her by moving his body back and forth in front of her.

"It's not finished!" he complained.

"How exactly do you intend to bestow immortality on the Brontë family, Branwell?" Charlotte asked. "With this? You haven't even given us hands. Has *Mr. Robinson* not yet covered the extremities?"

Stop now. Do stop.

"Jealousy makes you very unattractive, Charlotte," Branwell spat. "Or should I say, more unattractive than usual."

The room fell silent. Branwell looked guilty as soon as the words were out. Charlotte went bright pink. Anne could see that she was fighting to keep her face fixed, trying desperately to show that Branwell's comment had had no effect.

Charlotte was not a physically attractive person; there was no getting around it. Her complexion was poor, her lips were thin, and her hair was stringy—and on top of this she was so very small, almost doll-like, that she was always being mistaken for the youngest. Her one beauty was her large, gray eyes, but these were hidden by her thick spectacles and by her unfortunate habit of squinting at everything.

"They were *my* sketches," Charlotte said icily. "We only went to Leeds because my sketches were chosen, but somehow *you're* the one who ended up with the great painting teacher." Anne was certain she was about to sweep out and slam the door.

"Stop it!" Emily cried. "Why are the two of you talking about such inanities?"

Charlotte and Branwell shared a confused glance. Even Anne was surprised by her vehemence.

"The very future of Verdopolis is hanging in the balance, and the two of you are arguing about nothing!" Emily's words came tumbling out. "You mustn't stop writing, Charlotte. You mustn't! Branwell's right. Verdopolis is both of you. I . . . I couldn't bear to see it diminished in any way."

Charlotte shook her head, trying to make sense of Emily's abrupt reversion to the topic of her writing. "I fail to see how this is any of your concern."

Emily's face grew red with rage. "You're so selfish!" Her voice was a high-pitched shriek. "I hate you both with the hottest passions of hell!" And then it was she, not Charlotte, who swept out of the room.

"What the devil?" Branwell said when she was gone. "You women are all mad. Was she in earnest or was she acting out a scene from *Udolpho*?"

"Please do not judge all women by *that*," Charlotte said with a forced laugh. "What is Verdopolis to her, I ask you?"

Isn't it enough that it is something? Anne wanted to ask.

"I suppose I must go after her," Charlotte said, leaving Anne and Branwell alone in the room.

Branwell threw his brush in frustration. "Damn and blast!" Anne winced at his anger and at the mark of paint the brush left on the floor.

I could have prevented this, she thought. *I saw it coming and said nothing. Why didn't I talk about the weather or pretend to be ill?*

"I suppose I'll have to work on the Martin copy now." He gestured to another canvas leaning up against a wall, but he made no move toward it. Instead he stood with his hands on his hips. "I'll tell you, Anne. Somewhere on the other side of the world, there is a man whose three sisters dote on him. They bring him his tea and soothe his brow and listen to his cares. They realize that it's their duty to support him. Their duty!"

Anne wanted to remind Branwell that she had brought him tea only the day before and that she was more than happy to listen to his cares, but she was too demoralized to try to form the words.

"That paint won't keep now that it's mixed," Branwell said. "None of you understands how much these pigments cost." He took off his smock and hung it over a chair. "I'm going out for a smoke."

And then Anne was alone. The wind gusted through the window, knocking a canvas that was leaning against the wall to the floor. She propped it up again and shut the window. Then she bent to pick up the fallen brush.

"The oatmeal porridge was especially good today," she said to no one at all.

BRANWELL

"NANNY DEAR! ARE YOU THERE?"

Branwell wheeled around, paintbrush in one hand, palette in the other. There was no one in the room. He went to the window and looked out—his friends from town were sometimes too shy of his father to knock on the door. No one. The fog was finally lifting, and above the church, a stiff breeze was pushing clouds across the sky. Branwell was used to the Yorkshire wind and its tricks: Sometimes it seemed to speak, sometimes it sobbed and moaned. He told himself that this was all he'd heard and went back to his canvas.

The room was neater than it had been in a long time—Tabby never entered except to change his bedding, but someone had swept and dusted, cleaned his painting knives, and grouped all his brushes into jars in order of size. What a dear little mouse that Anne was. Heaven forfend Charlotte would ever show him such support. Charlotte insisted on calling this "the children's study" and invaded it whenever she pleased, but it was *his* studio, and his bedroom, too—at least it was during the warmer months. The room had no fireplace, and by December it was so cold that his wash water would freeze solid in the basin overnight. Still, he would stuff rags into the window cracks and shiver in his blankets, delaying the night when he would finally have to relent and go back to sharing a bed with his father.

God almighty, he thought, *I cannot wait to leave this place.*

He put a pea-sized dab of bone black on his palette and mixed it with a dot of white. Since his models had abandoned him, he had switched to another painting, a vast biblical scene with marble staircases and stone columns and dozens of gaudily dressed sinners swooning. It was a copy of *Belshazzar's Feast* by John Martin, an engraving of which leaned on a chair beyond his easel. Branwell was working on the central figure, Belshazzar, the Babylonian king who points in alarm as he sees God's writing on the wall. Tentatively Branwell dabbed at the king's flowing robes, but his fingers were stiff and the paint smeared.

He sighed and wiped the paint away with a rag, wondering where inspiration had gone. Why was this so difficult? He had copied *Belshazzar's Feast* before. Of course, that was in pencil, not in oils. And it was when he was younger, when art was just a pleasant pastime, before it was decided that painting would be his profession. How strange, he thought, that the moment his father agreed to support his painting career, laying out vast sums of money for Branwell's pigments and his canvases and his lessons, all the joy drained out of the activity, like blood from a slaughtered lamb.

He closed his eyes. "I call forth Inspiration," he said aloud. "Guide my hand, sweet Muse, and . . ."

"Banny!"

Branwell jerked around, and again found nothing. The wind rattled at the window. He tried to shake the feeling that he was not alone.

"I haven't done anything," he said aloud. "It was Charlotte. I learned my lesson before." No one answered, of course.

He chose a new brush. There were already flesh tones on his palette; he'd mixed a lot of those for the group portrait. Perhaps he could try to capture Belshazzar's face. After a while he began to paint in earnest, loathing every stroke, but pressing on. He hated that difference, that horrible difference, between what he wanted to make and what he was able to make, but he told himself that this was simply how it was: The more he worked, the further his creation would get from his ideal. In Verdopolis if he wanted to make something, all he had to do was imagine it, but it was no use wishing that painting could be like that.

Then, suddenly, there it was. A face. King Belshazzar's face was looking at him from out of the canvas. The king was only a small part of a much larger work, and his robes were still a little stiff, but the face . . . the face was good. Branwell had made something that had life.

Behind him, someone coughed.

Branwell froze, brush in hand. It was such a dreadfully familiar sound, the cough of someone who is dying. This time, he didn't dare turn around.

"I don't believe in ghosts," he said to the room.

Two more long coughs, wet and painful, closer now. Branwell shivered as if a breath had touched the hairs on the back of his neck.

"Banny," said a voice, a child's voice. "Could I have a glass of water?"

He shut his eyes tight. "Don't. Please."

"Branwell!"

He turned to find Charlotte standing in the doorway. There was no one else in the room. They were alone.

"Are you all right?" she asked. "I heard . . . something."

"Blast, Charlotte!" he shouted, letting his fear escape as anger. "Can't a man have a scrap of privacy in this house?"

The concerned look on his sister's face turned sour. "Man? What man? I just see a carroty-haired lump of boy!" She slammed the door again.

Branwell turned back to his painting and cursed. Belshazzar's face was gone, ruined. He must have brushed it with the sleeve of his smock when he turned around.

He lifted his brush and began again.

EMILY

MILY BENT OVER THE DRAWING IN HER LAP, a pencil clutched tightly in her hand. She was sitting on a favorite stone, feet not quite touching the ground. The cold and damp seeped through her petticoats, but she was used to that. Behind her, Sladen Beck gurgled pleasantly. A low mist clung to the ground. It hadn't rained, but droplets of water weighted the tall grass, and the lichen-spotted boulders that jutted up out of the heath were all glazed with dew.

With precise strokes she formed the cheeks of her subject, smudging with a finger to shade the cheekbones. She sat back for a moment to examine her work, but the portrait wasn't right yet. With her pencil, she darkened the whiskers, adding a crueler turn to the lips, a wider flare to the nostrils. There. There he was.

"Rogue," she whispered.

Charlotte had once let it slip that creating a story—either by writing or by telling—put her in the right frame of mind for crossing over. Did it work for drawing, too? Was Emily in the right frame of mind now? She held out her hand, palm up, as she had seen her brother and sister do. There was no question of where she would go. Emily had been dreaming of the world she would make for practically her whole life. Gondal. A mysterious island in the middle of a dark sea.

"A door," Emily said, squeezing her eyes shut. "I call for a door to Gondal."

Sound carried far across the moorlands, but all she could hear were the bleatings of a few sheep and the distant call of a curlew.

"Please. I've been waiting so long."

Emily thought that she could feel how close Gondal was, how close it always was. She could nearly see it. She was nearly there. Gondal yearned for her just as she yearned for it. The only thing that separated them was a gauzy film, so thin she could almost pierce it with a fingernail.

"Hello!" a voice called over the hills. Emily winced. Grasper had been sitting quietly by her feet, but now he ran a circle in the wet grass, barking a greeting.

"Hush," Emily cautioned. Grasper cocked his head at her, then shook the water from his coat. Emily squealed and drew her notebook up out of the way of the blast.

"Emily!" The voice was closer now. "I know you're there."

Emily blotted the portrait with her sleeve and sighed. She loved her family dearly, but she'd often thought that if she could see Charlotte and Branwell once a day for an hour, Papa and Tabby once a week, and Aunt Branwell at Christmas, she might be much happier. Usually Anne was the exception.

"Hello," Emily called reluctantly.

"There you are!"

She watched as Anne picked her way down the path that ran along the water. She had changed back into her everyday dress, and her skirts were wet to the knee. All around her, purple fox-glove swayed on long stalks. As she drew closer Emily could see that her cheeks were rosy, and the strands of hair escaping from her bonnet were curled from the damp.

"You look like a heroine out of a book."

Anne smiled shyly at this and looked to the ground, making her even prettier in Emily's opinion. She gave the dog a pat on the head. "Charlotte is quite vexed with your mistress, Grasper."

"Irregular verbs?" Emily asked.

"Of course. We couldn't find you."

"I couldn't face lessons today. I'm sure I would have said something very rude. Did you hear her? She and Branwell think they can simply stop writing—but they mustn't! All their characters would wither and die. It's murder!"

Anne hesitated. "I'm not certain it's exactly murder . . ."

"It's the next thing to it!" Emily edged over, letting Anne sit next to her on the stone. "Those two are so irritating. I've tried to forgive them for keeping us out of Verdopolis—you know I have—but every time something new happens, like today, I grow angry with them all over again."

Anne smoothed her skirts, then clasped her hands over her knees. "They must have their reasons. You mustn't let anger get the better of you."

"Reasons," Emily scoffed. "You are far too charitable."

But she took Anne by the arm and looked out over the hills, trying to let their beauty soothe her, give her the same calm grace that seemed to be her sister's natural state. For a while they sat quietly, feet dangling. Grasper capered around them, snapping at underwings in the grass.

"I miss crossing over, too, sometimes," Anne said. "I miss being able to talk to other people as easily as I talk to you."

Emily had always suspected that the reason Anne was able to speak to people in Verdopolis was because she never quite believed they were real, not the way Emily did, but if this were true she didn't want to know. She gave her sister's arm a squeeze. "We'll get there again. I promise."

"Goodness!" Anne said, noticing the notebook in Emily's lap. "Is that Rogue? You've made him look like Lord Byron."

Emily had drawn *her* Rogue, not Branwell's. He had the same face, but it was younger and rougher, and he was burly instead of lanky, with jet-black curls. "Wonderfully wicked, isn't he?"

"How ever did this happen?"

Emily knew what she was asking. "I don't know, exactly. I've always liked Rogue as a character—he's much better than Zamorna—and then one day I began to make up stories about him in my head. And then . . ." She smiled at her own foolishness. "Before I knew it, the arrow had struck."

"I suppose it's your age," Anne said sagely. After a moment, they both burst into laughter. Now that Emily had turned sixteen, "I suppose it's your age" was Aunt Branwell's response to any moodiness or forgetfulness on Emily's part. "If we knew any gentlemen outside our own family, I expect you'd fall in love with one of them instead."

"No. I wouldn't," Emily said, turning serious again. "No one's like Rogue."

"Thank heaven!"

Emily shifted on the stone to face her. "Anne, if we could make Gondal, then Rogue could live there, even if Verdopolis were left to ruin."

Anne pursed her lips. "But Gondal is just a game, something we made up. It's not a real world like Verdopolis and the Glasstown Confederacy."

"It's more than a game," Emily insisted. "It was meant to exist. They've tricked us out of our world by hoarding their secrets for themselves, but before you got here, a door was about to open—I'm sure of it! Hold out your hand and we shall try together. Come, Anne."

"No."

Emily took her hand and tried to hold it out with her own, palms upward. "I know we shall be able to now."

"Stop it!" Anne pulled her hand back so forcefully that Emily's notebook fell onto the grass.

"What is the matter with you?"

"I don't want to cross over—not to Verdopolis, not to Gondal, not to anywhere!" Emily was surprised by the intensity of Anne's words. "I miss the invented worlds, yes, but . . . I don't want to go back."

"I don't understand."

Anne slid down from the rock. "At breakfast, when Charlotte said she was renouncing her worlds, I felt . . . relief."

"What? Why?"

"I felt that we had escaped something. Narrowly escaped." She bent down to pick up Emily's notebook, brushing it off as she spoke. "Emily, if Tabby were telling us a fairy tale about some parson's children who could make the worlds they imagine become real, do you know what I'd ask myself?" She didn't wait for an answer. "I'd ask myself, what price did they pay? In all the tales, when people are given such gifts, there's always a price."

"If there's a price," Emily said firmly, "I shall pay it."

CHARLOTTE

ALL HER STORIES WERE FINISHED NOW. ALL Charlotte's beautiful characters were to be put away in a box like toy soldiers—the lords, the ladies, the innocent maidens, the heroes, and the villains. Mary Henrietta. Zamorna. She sighed.

"Stop," she said aloud, as if she could halt a scene in real life the way she could in Verdopolis. "You are falling prey to self-pity, Charlotte."

She pushed up her spectacles and tried to concentrate. She was sitting on the sofa in the dining room, knitting a stocking for Anne. Knit, knit, purl, purl, making ribbing. Usually she found the clicking of the needles and the complex movement soothing. Knit, knit, purl, purl. Snowflake, Emily's evil cat, purred at her side.

A hundred new ideas flew through her mind, a hundred new stories for Zamorna. Her poor hero. He deserved better than to be abandoned. She could cross over to him now without anyone knowing. Emily and Anne were still out walking, Papa was at a baptism, Aunt Branwell was in her room. All Charlotte had to do was write or speak a few sentences, and then reach out her hand when a door appeared.

"No," she said aloud. "No, no, no. I promised Papa."

Scents from the kitchen wafted in. Beef, potatoes, apple pudding—all the things she liked best. More temptations. Emily ate all she wanted and never grew stout, but Charlotte had to be vigilant. Knit, knit, purl, purl. Being plain was bad enough, she reasoned; she would *not* be plain and plump.

"No temptation has seized you except what is common to man," she said, quoting from Corinthians. "And God is faithful; He will not let you be tempted beyond what you can bear." She couldn't help but wonder if the temptation to cross to magical worlds was truly "common to man."

At that moment, Branwell flung open the door like an actor making an entrance, his red blanket around his shoulders. Charlotte felt she could almost kiss him for taking her mind from her troubles, but she didn't intend to show it.

"There are things we must discuss," he said portentously. He came up in front of her as she knit, bending to give Snowflake a pat on the head. The cat snarled and raked at Branwell with his claws. "Ow!"

"That always happens," Charlotte said, not looking up from her work, "and yet people continue to do it."

"That thing will kill us all someday!" Branwell cried, clutching his hand.

"Yes. And leave our bodies on the doorstep as little presents for Emily." She came to the end of a row and put her knitting aside. "What did you wish to speak about?"

Branwell eyed the white cat, which was now slouching off toward the kitchen. "Read this," he said, sitting down. With a flourish, he handed over a page of his work.

Charlotte scanned the page, squinting at her brother's appalling handwriting. The scene took place in the secret meeting rooms of the Elysium Society. At first it seemed like Branwell's usual fare—Rogue . . . S'Death . . . drinking . . . a suicide—but when she reached the end of the passage, she frowned. "What's this? A plot to murder Zamorna?"

Branwell slapped his bony hands on his bony knees, appearing pleased with himself. "That's right. And he won't die a heroic death, either. He'll die like a dog. He'll . . . he'll beg for Rogue's mercy."

Charlotte dropped the paper in his lap with what she hoped was an air of scorn. "Is this some ridiculous attempt at blackmail? Are you trying to tell me that if I quit the invented worlds, you will kill off my favorite character?" She was tempted to take back the page and tear it into tiny pieces, but instead she shrugged. "Do what you will. The Duke of Zamorna's legacy will live on."

"I think not," Branwell said. Was he chortling? "In my story, it will be revealed that Zamorna is not really the Duke of Wellington's heir, as everyone thought, but the son of a poor tailor. All will come to light. It was *Zamorna* who tried to assassinate the parliament and rig the Verdopolitan horse races."

"That's absurd. He thwarted those schemes!"

"And . . . and . . ." Branwell was obviously making up the plan as he went on. "The famous diamond bandeau he gave to Mary Henrietta?" He lifted a finger into the air. "Paste! And all the portraits he claims to have painted? Forged! Or . . . no . . . they were actually painted by Rogue! Zamorna's entire legacy will crumble to dust."

Charlotte felt her face grow hot, though she tried to sound unconcerned. "What do you want, exactly?"

Branwell grinned, rocking back and forth in his seat. He could sometimes become overwrought in a way that Charlotte found unseemly. Under all his pomposity, there was something delicate about his nerves. Charlotte suspected this was why their father had never sent him away to school.

"One more story," he begged, clasping his hands. "Please."

"Stop bouncing. I'm becoming seasick on my own sofa."

"What harm could it do? A final farewell to Verdopolis, written by us."

He really did look absolutely beside himself. She set a hand on his knee to stop him from being so agitated. "I'm sorry, Banny,

I truly am, but I've decided. I'm giving up writing, crossing over, Verdopolis—all of it."

Branwell's face fell. "You're serious."

"I am."

He sat back on the sofa, deflated. Then, as if just taking in something she'd said, he sat up again. "If you give up writing, how will you ever become an author?"

Charlotte was taken aback. She had never told him that she wanted to be an author, had never mentioned it to anyone.

"If you don't write, then you'll have to become a governess." There was genuine concern on his face. "You'd hate that life."

"Y-yes," she said, unable to hide her surprise at his knowing things she had never confessed. There was little else a poor woman of her class could do to earn her way, but she had never relished the idea. If it weren't for the necessity of teaching her sisters, she would be out of the house and working as a governess now. Her secret hope had always been to write for a living instead.

"It was a childish idea," she said. "The truth is, my writing . . . it simply isn't good enough."

Branwell waved a hand dismissively. "Nonsense. It's quite adequate."

"*Adequate* is not good enough for today's publishers, I'm afraid, and it's not good enough for me."

Branwell scowled. "Well, if you're determined to wring a compliment out of me, then you are more than adequate. You are approaching good. You are an approaching-good writer."

She smiled. "It's no use, Banny."

"Devil take you! I won't say more than that."

"I'm not asking you to!"

Branwell crossed his arms and puffed out his cheeks. "The fact that you've decided not to pursue a career as an author—a decision I think is highly premature, by the way—doesn't mean you can never write again."

Charlotte sat back on the sofa and tried to gather her words. She felt sorry now for tearing the story paper at the breakfast table without a word of warning to her brother. It had been cruel. She was turning her back on something they'd shared for a long time.

"Branwell," she said gently, "when we write, doors appear. We can't stop that. I have simply become unwilling to pay the toll for going through. You and I pay too heavy a price for crossing over."

They both looked to the open door leading to the hall. They rarely spoke about the price they paid to get to their worlds, and they were scrupulously careful about keeping the secret from their younger sisters.

"I don't know why you have to bring that up," he said. He slouched in his seat and pulled the ridiculous red blanket closer around his shoulders. Branwell was always cold—either that or he thought the blanket's flamboyant color suited him.

"If I continue to write," Charlotte said, "I don't think I'll have the strength to resist crossing over. I must give up the whole idea of authorship."

"You're determined to make a martyr of yourself."

"Oh, I suppose I might write essays—but absolutely nothing imaginary." She felt her shoulders slump. "The price would have been worth it if I had become a writer, if I could have made something great and beautiful . . ." She straightened up again and took her knitting into her lap, handing her brother the ball of yarn. "But I must simply face the fact that in all our years of writing and crossing over, I have never been able to create anything better than a melodrama—and, Banny, if crossing over is only an escape, an amusement, I cannot justify it."

Branwell didn't have an answer for this, but she didn't expect him to. For a while she sat in silence, knitting and purling, while he let out yarn as she needed it. Their aunt would say that a lady shouldn't work a stocking in a man's presence, but Charlotte didn't think Branwell counted.

"I know you love him," her brother said.

Her fingers stopped.

"You pretend it will be easy to cast him aside, but I know you. It will be like losing a limb to leave Zamorna."

Something tightened in her chest. "No one can love a made-up person."

"It's obvious from your writing how you feel. I don't blame you."

She let out a hiss of breath. "Now you've made me drop a stitch."

"Admit it, Charlotte. If you could write Zamorna's greatest story yet, wouldn't that be worth the price?"

EMILY

"I'D LIKE TO SPEAK TO YOU." CHARLOTTE'S VOICE was stern.

"Certainly," Emily replied.

"Put on your bonnet, please. We'll take some exercise."

Emily winced. In their small house there were few places to have a private conversation, and so the siblings sometimes used long walks or invented errands as a means to be alone. Charlotte evidently wanted to have a lengthy talk.

Emily put on her bonnet and lightest cloak and waited for Charlotte in the hallway. The Brontës had finished their midday meal, and Papa had gone out again to visit parishioners. Branwell had disappeared upstairs. Anne and Aunt Branwell were sewing in the dining room.

"In Penzance one could tell the difference between summer

and winter," Emily heard Aunt Branwell say with a long sigh. She came from the south of England and had been grumbling about the Yorkshire climate for as long as Emily could remember.

"Yes, Aunt," Anne replied. Emily felt a little guilty for abandoning her.

Charlotte came down the stairs tying her bonnet. Usually the younger girls would be free in the afternoon to follow their own pursuits, but of course Emily had disappeared to the moor that morning and couldn't very well assert her freedom now. Charlotte ushered her toward the door.

Whatever Aunt Branwell might say, summer was at its peak in Yorkshire. The fog had finally lifted, and the patch of lawn between the parsonage and the churchyard had turned a lush green from all the wet weather. The flowers Charlotte had planted along the cemetery wall were lifting their heads to the sun.

Charlotte led Emily through the cemetery gate, striding with businesslike efficiency along the narrow path. Many of the local women had taken advantage of the break in the clouds to lay their laundry over the tombstones to dry. Charlotte shook her head at this and tut-tutted as they passed.

"If we see anyone we know, don't stare into the void like a sheep. Try to smile. We've got Papa's reputation to uphold."

Emily bared her teeth at her sister's back. When had Charlotte become this person? It seemed to be Aunt Branwell's voice coming out of her mouth. Emily missed Charlotte Brontë, friend and confidant. Charlotte Brontë, teacher and chaperone, she didn't like half so well.

They rounded Papa's church and came out onto Haworth's noisy main street. A horrible stench hit Emily like a blow, making her eyes sting. There were no sewers in Haworth, and many of the houses had muck middens at the back—fenced enclosures where the contents of the privies were kept until they could be removed. The one at the back of the Black Bull Tavern was particularly bad, and the price of warmer weather was an increase in the smell. Charlotte covered her nose with a handkerchief and hurried them down the steep road toward the center of town.

"Why are we going this way instead of walking the moor?" Emily asked, still blinking from the stench.

Charlotte took a moment to answer. "This is Haworth," she said. "This is where we live. I needed to look the real world in the eye today."

Emily lifted her skirts to avoid a mound of rubbish at the side of the road. "The moor isn't any less real than this," she grumbled.

As they descended, Haworth became poorer. The houses were built right up against the street, and they were all begrimed with soot from the factories. These were workers' cottages mostly, built to accommodate the families of mill employees. Nearly all the inhabitants of Haworth were in the wool trade in some way or other. If they didn't work at a mill, they combed wool at home or farmed sheep—though a few cut stone in one of the nearby quarries.

Haworth is an ugly place, Emily found herself thinking, and she gazed up longingly at the glimpse of green hills still visible above the blackened chimney pots.

"Yesterday when Branwell and I were writing," Charlotte said, "I clearly remember closing the window, and yet when I returned from Verdopolis it was open." *How like her to notice a detail like that,* Emily thought. She and Anne were similar in that way.

"I opened it," Emily confessed. "And it was I who left that paper for Papa to find. I'm sorry, Charlotte. It was an accident. I thought I'd returned all the stories to the place under the floorboards."

Charlotte nodded as if she had gathered this already. "Why didn't you simply ask to read our writings? I thought you'd lost interest in the invented worlds. At least . . . I hoped you had."

Lost interest, Emily thought. *Did she truly believe that?*

They reached the bottom of the hill, and Charlotte led them onto a wide stone bridge, where they stopped and looked out over the parapet. In front of them was Bridgehouse Mill. The humming and clattering of power looms and spinning jacks and other machinery could be heard through its open windows, and smoke from its tall chimneys spread across the sky like a stain.

"Marvelous view," Emily said, raising her voice a little to be heard over the machines. "I can see why you wanted to come!"

She looked down at the river below. Effluence from the dyeing process had turned the water a sickly blue color, and skeletons of dead fish littered the banks, their odor mingling with the distinctive muttony smell of washed wool.

"Honestly, Charlotte, is this our destination?" Her frustration was getting the better of her. She was certain now that her sister had brought her here to be scolded. "You thought this was a congenial place for a conversation? It's disgusting."

"It's life," Charlotte said, peering up at Emily with frank directness.

There was something arresting about being looked at by Charlotte Brontë. She was very small, under five feet, and yet Emily often found her quite intimidating. Her large gray eyes seemed to pin Emily to the spot. An angel would have a gaze like that—a rather terrible angel who could see all one's sins. Emily shifted her feet, bracing to hear some uncomfortable truth about herself.

"I'm sorry," Charlotte burst out suddenly.

Emily was taken aback.

"I'm sorry that everything I teach you, everything you learn, can only lead to one dreary profession. I wish . . . I wish I could have saved you from that."

That's a wicked trick, Emily thought. *Leading someone to believe they are about to be scolded only to make an apology. It leaves one quite unprepared.* "We don't blame you. Anne and I have always known we would have to be governesses."

Charlotte nodded and turned to look down at the river, though she was so small she had to stand on her toes to see over the parapet. "We'll be quite miserable, you know," she said to the water.

"Oh. Yes, I suppose we shall."

Charlotte peered at her again. "You know?"

Emily gave a short laugh. "That we shall make terrible governesses? Certainly." Her own personality, she knew, was entirely unsuited to such work, though she could imagine Anne succeeding, if she could ever overcome her shyness.

"I've been to school, you see." Charlotte's gray eyes seemed to plead with her, but Emily didn't know for what. "I've socialized with other people. They're not like us. We're odd. We have opinions. We've been overeducated in some things and undereducated in others. Once we leave the parsonage, we'll never truly find another home."

Emily's heart sank at these words, though she knew they were true. The idea of leaving the parsonage and the moor had always been a chilling one for her. "Is this why you brought me here? To tell me things I already know?"

Charlotte frowned. When she spoke again, her voice was hardly audible above the factory din. "Emily, knowing what's ahead of us, how do you bear it all?"

Emily felt a chill of annoyance filter through her. "How do we ordinary folk, with no fantastical worlds to escape to, manage to survive the banality of daily life? Is that what you are asking?"

Charlotte cast her eyes to her feet. "Yes. I suppose it is."

"Anne and I survive because daily life is all you left us with," Emily said crisply. "You banished us, as I recall."

Charlotte looked up. "Banished? Is that how you feel?" She seemed surprised, though Emily didn't know how she could be.

A horse-drawn wagon came rattling toward them, and the girls had to squeeze up against the stone parapet to let it pass. The driver raised his hat to them as he went by.

"Keep that little lass out of trouble now, miss," he said to Emily with a wink.

She was mortified to be winked at by a stranger, but the fact that he had obviously mistaken Charlotte for a small child made it much worse. She glanced at her sister, but Charlotte only set her face to stone, as if her outward appearance was just another cross she had to bear, and not the heaviest one at that. Emily felt a sting of pity for her. The wagon turned into the mill yard, joining others bringing raw wool and lumber or leaving with dyed cloth and yarn.

"It was for your own good," Charlotte said. "Keeping you from the invented worlds."

The warmth Emily had been feeling for her sister iced over. "My own good. Is that so?"

"How bitter you sound. I always hoped you would find other pursuits to take the place of crossing over with us."

Emily's anger rose. "And what pursuits do you think could

take the place of going to the moon, Charlotte? Or to Ali Baba's palace, or Lilliput? I was one of the Genii, flying over the land on my satin pillow, and now I'm . . . I'm nobody."

Charlotte shook her head. "I'm sorry. I truly am."

"Don't apologize, teach me. Show me. How can I make a world of my own?"

Charlotte's eyes widened, and she grasped Emily by the arm. "Don't even say that. It would be the greatest mistake of your life!"

"You may think you are acting in my best interest," Emily said, pulling away from her touch. She turned away so as not to see Charlotte's face as she went on. "But a part of me will always loathe you for keeping the invented worlds to yourself."

There was a long pause. It was a shocking thing to say, but Emily fought the urge to take it back, fought the urge to look over at her sister. She felt a hand touch her arm gently.

"It wasn't an accident that Papa found that paper, was it?" Charlotte asked quietly. "You left it for him to find."

Emily continued to stare fixedly at the water, knowing that if she met her sister's gaze she might start to cry, and then all her anger would dissipate. She wanted to keep her anger a while longer.

"Yes. I did." She had wanted to see her sister scolded but had gotten no satisfaction from it. "I did, and I'm not sorry."

"I suppose you felt I deserved it."

Emily bit her lip. Guilt was such an inconvenient emotion. "Oh, why won't you at least do me the courtesy of losing your temper?" Tears did come to her eyes now, just as she'd known they would. "It was a wicked thing to do. I know it was."

"It was for the best," Charlotte said. She was being maddeningly calm. "It did me good to see my writing through Papa's eyes."

"How can you say that? He thinks your stories are childish, and they are anything but. Now they are coming to an end, all your beautiful words, and it's my fault!"

"It's not," Charlotte assured her. "I think I would have stopped writing at any rate."

Emily pulled a handkerchief from her pocket and noticed that it was one of the ones Charlotte had given her for Christmas with little roses embroidered on it. "Oh! I'm a terrible person, I know I am." She used the handkerchief to blot the corners of her eyes. "It's only . . ." She considered telling her sister about Gondal, about how she longed for it, but she was afraid words could never do her world justice.

Charlotte gazed at her in silence for a while. She wore the same puzzled expression that she did when trying to translate a particularly complicated passage from the French. "Would it help if you were allowed to say good-bye to Verdopolis?" she asked finally.

Emily froze. "What do you mean?" Hope fluttered in her stomach, but she couldn't allow herself to believe that her sister was talking about letting her cross over.

"The truth is that Branwell wants me to write one more story. An ending. A final farewell. I think perhaps I should accommodate him. And . . . it occurs to me that since you and Anne were there at the beginning of that place, you should be there at the end."

Emily felt her heart lurch. "Do you mean . . . Are you saying that you will let us go with you again?" *I'm going to see Rogue*, she thought, and for one moment her whole body seemed to float.

"Don't excite yourself, now, for heaven's sake! It's only the one time."

Emily tried to make her face as serene as her sister's, terrified lest she change her mind. "Don't excite myself," she repeated. "How can I not?"

Charlotte took her hand and squeezed it, and Emily felt the warmth of her through their thin summer gloves. "Listen to me, Emily. This is important. If the four of us cross over again, I need you to promise that you will be content with the ending I create. I need you to promise that you will not beg for more."

"Anything," Emily said, a giddy laugh escaping her. "Anything, anything!"

"And most of all, I need you to promise you will not try to discover how Branwell and I are able to cross over. That is a secret that must be left alone."

"Of course," Emily said quickly. "I promise."

CHARLOTTE

FTER MONTHS AT SEA, TWELVE ADVENTURERS were shipwrecked on the coast of Africa. The land was beautiful and fertile, and so they planted flags and claimed it for England. With the help of the four Genii, they built the city of Glasstown on the very spot where their ship had come to rest.

I hope I'm doing the right thing, Charlotte thought.

She was sitting on a chair in the bedroom she shared with Emily. Her two younger sisters sat on the bed, holding hands, unable to hide the excitement shining in their eyes. The Brontë siblings had waited three days for the perfect time to cross over. It was rare to have the house to themselves, but today Tabby was visiting her sister and Papa had taken Aunt Branwell into

Keighley. Branwell was writing his own story in the next room, but, by mutual agreement, the two stories would converge at the party.

"Now remember," Charlotte said, "no event can be revised in Verdopolis—no dead characters resurrected, no ruined ladies unruined. Branwell and I have tried many times but to no avail. The plot can be directed, of course—must be, in fact—but once an event happens, it has happened for good and all."

"We know," Emily insisted. "We've been to the worlds before, remember."

"Ah," Charlotte said. "That brings me to another point."

Emily groaned. Charlotte knew that she was being a bit insufferable, but she couldn't help it. Now that the moment had finally arrived, she was feeling protective of Verdopolis. She felt as if she were letting a precious glass bauble into the hands of two children who wanted to play catch with it.

"As I was saying. The last time you were in Verdopolis, you were there as one of the Genii, the great creators, but magical entities don't figure in Verdopolis anymore, except as part of ancient history. Now our stories are more realistic, and we must play characters. The two of you will need to decide who you might be. Take some time now—"

"I know who I will be," Emily interjected.

"As do I," Anne said quietly.

Charlotte hoped they'd given the matter enough thought. "I see . . . There are only a few more things . . ."

"For heaven's sake!" Emily cried. "Papa and Aunt Branwell will be back in a few hours."

"I'm sorry," Charlotte said. "It's just . . . I've loved this world. I want to give it a perfect ending."

"You will," Emily assured her. "Your stories are always perfect. Isn't that right, Anne?"

For a moment Charlotte thought Anne could not have heard, for she only stared straight ahead, frozen, like Jasper Pheasant when he's seen the cat.

"Isn't that right, Anne?" Emily repeated, poking her sister in the side.

Anyone else would simply nod her head, but Charlotte saw that for Anne this would be a falsehood. She did not think Charlotte's stories were perfect.

"I see," Charlotte said, trying not to sound icy. "Well, I hope I shall always welcome literary criticism."

Anne glanced around the room as if looking for an escape. Finally she fixed her eyes to her knees and whispered, "It's nothing, really. It's just . . . I suppose I've always wished your writings were a little more . . . true, Charlotte." She was blushing very red now.

This came so close to Charlotte's unspoken fears about her own work that she felt her eyes widen in surprise. "What do you mean by true?" she asked, but Anne's only answer was to shake her head.

"Anne has mentioned that she wishes your stories took place

closer to home," Emily said hesitantly. "After all, we don't actually know anything about Africa, and it doesn't figure much in the story, except that it never snows and there are palm trees."

"I know one thing about Africa," Anne said, finding her voice. "There are Africans in it—but in Verdopolis they only appear when Branwell wants to have a war. That seems . . . well, I can't put my finger on it, but it doesn't seem . . . Oh dear, I wish I hadn't begun this line of thought." She dropped her head again. "Please ignore me."

"You shouldn't have mentioned it," Emily hissed. "What can Charlotte do about it now?"

"Not at all. The point is well taken," Charlotte said, but her little sister's words rankled. She herself had chosen Africa as a location long ago, mostly because it was far away and warm. She'd been a child then and had given little thought to it, but it occurred to her now that perhaps she had no business writing about a place she'd never seen and knew little about.

She stood up and inserted herself between her two sisters on the bed, cutting off any further discussion. "Very well, then. Are we ready? Each of you hold onto an arm." She forced a brightness into her voice that she didn't quite feel. Her sisters took her arms.

"At last," Emily said.

"You won't be able to get home by yourself, of course. You'll need Branwell or me to cross you over again—and we must be touching you."

"We know. We know everything. Hurry!" said Emily, bouncing a little with barely contained glee.

Charlotte closed her eyes, trying to push aside a feeling of unease. She had said she wanted the end of Verdopolis to be perfect, but now, after Anne's criticisms, she had a strange presentiment that it would not be. She reminded herself that she was the world's creator; its ending would be what she willed it to be.

"*All the party guests had arrived,*" she murmured. "*Young Lord Charles moved from group to group unnoticed, listening to men talk about Verdopolitan politics, admiring the ladies' clothes, their long necks, the nets of jewels in their hair.*"

Without opening her eyes, she knew that the room had grown brighter. The door was here—at least, she and Branwell had always called it a door. It wasn't something they went through, though; it was something that went through them. She held out her hand, palm upward. Immediately she knew that it was coming, and she braced herself. It always felt as if some great maw was rushing toward her, to swallow her up. *This is the worst part,* she thought.

"This is the best part," she heard Emily whisper.

Charlotte felt a moment of sheer terror, knowing it was upon her, and then—*whump*—it was over.

"*He slipped into a small salon decorated in green and gold,*" she said, "*where a fire danced in a carved malachite fireplace. Two guests came in with him to take refuge from the noise and bustle of the party.*"

Charlotte opened her eyes. A thrill ran up her sides and

all the way down her arms. She was here. She was home. She examined her boy's body, smoothing down the blue suit and touching the lace frill at her throat. Charles Albert Florian Wellesley, her other self. Everything seemed to be right. Next to her was the Countess Zenobia, Alexander Rogue's wife, which was rather odd. She wouldn't have been invited to the party.

"Why, it's young Charles," the countess said, setting a gloved hand on the fireplace and looking down at Charlotte with a bored smile.

She wore a velvet gown in her signature color—blood red. A black feather drooped from her pert French chapeau. Charlotte's eyes widened as the realization dawned: This was Emily.

"Absolutely not," Charlotte said.

Everything about the Red Countess—from her bare white arms to her tiny corseted waist to her seductive, heavy-lidded gaze—seemed to radiate a knowledge of things a sixteen-year-old parson's daughter should have no knowledge of.

"What's wrong?" Emily asked. She looked in the mirror above the fireplace, shaking her head to make her dangling earrings dance.

Charlotte turned away, wishing she had a fichu with which to cover her sister's voluptuous bosom, and noticed Anne, who was sitting demurely on a sofa. Anne was not playing a character with her own face, like Branwell's Lord Thornton. She was herself. Her hands were folded in her lap, and she wore the same blue silk dress she wore every Sunday. *What a prosaic child,* Charlotte thought. Did she have no imagination at all? Whereas Emily seemed to have too much.

"For heaven's sake. The both of you—"

"I've always thought Zenobia was very underdrawn," Emily interrupted quickly. "Rogue's wife should be more than a red dress. She should be . . . extraordinary. Don't you think? She could be a woman of letters who speaks five languages and has affairs like a man."

"Perhaps, but, Emily, this isn't how things are done. You should play someone on the fringes of the story, not a major character."

"Why? I'd much rather be someone interesting. Wouldn't you? Wouldn't anyone?"

The door opened and Zamorna's friend, the Viscount Castlereagh, entered the lounge, a glass of whiskey in his hand. When he saw Emily he choked, then recovered himself and made a short bow. "Countess," he said.

Emily blinked languidly at him. "Viscount."

He mumbled an apology and left. Even this short exchange seemed inappropriate to Charlotte somehow.

"There," Emily said. "The countess is here, and she has been seen." Emily glanced at herself in the mirror again, yanking up the top of her dress in an unladylike fashion. "You said no event could be revised. I'm part of the story now, and there's nothing you can do."

"*The countess* is a part of the story," Charlotte said. "And you're correct, there is nothing I can do about that now. However, *you* will not be playing her."

"What?"

"If you can't invent suitable characters for yourselves, I'll have to do it for you." Charlotte closed her eyes. *"Lady Anne and Lady Emily, cousins of Charles and the duke, were visiting from the provinces."*

"Oh!" she heard Emily cry.

"These naive young sisters had never seen anyone like the countess, whose blood-red velvet contrasted greatly with their simple but elegant, and perfectly appropriate, attire."

Charlotte opened her eyes warily. The Countess Zenobia was still in front of her, looking exactly as she had before, but now, to her relief, there were two young ladies on the sofa instead of one. Emily was looking down at her body in disgust, her face pink with anger. Anne was frowning, too, which struck Charlotte as ungrateful. She had a lovely dress now—tiered blue muslin trimmed with flowers. Emily wore the identical ensemble in yellow. Granted, their dresses weren't as revealing as the prevailing Verdopolitan fashions, but Lady Anne and Lady Emily were from the provinces, after all.

The Countess Zenobia looked around the room as if wondering how she got there. She blinked disdainfully at the three of them. Then, seeming to realize that they were nobody in particular, she swept out of the room.

Emily stood. Her hair, Charlotte had to admit, might have been a mistake. It was intricately done in plaits that circled back on themselves in six or seven loops, each loop affixed to her head with a large yellow bow. One of Charlotte's friends from school had described this style in a letter, but Charlotte had never actually seen it.

"Come, Lady Anne," Emily said darkly. "We've monopolized our dear cousin Charles for long enough." She pulled Anne toward the door. "I believe we will find more engaging company elsewhere."

BRANWELL

RANWELL STOOD ON THE BALCONY OF Sneaky Hall in his evening clothes, looking out at his beautiful city. All was well again. Charlotte's threat to quit Verdopolis was an empty one; he'd seen to that. He didn't believe that this would be their last story. She'd find some reason to keep coming back. She always had. The setting sun tinted the towers and the church spires, and the colors reflecting off the buildings reminded him of something. When he recalled what it was, he smiled.

One of Branwell's earliest memories was of colored light playing on a white wall. His sister Maria knew the trick of it. If he cried or if anything upset him, she would sit him on her lap and take out a little looking glass that had been their mother's. Then she would shift it back and forth to catch the window light, making the reflections dance. The beveled edge of the mirror acted as a prism, turning the white light to garnet and blue and amethyst. Maria could always enchant him this way. It was his first experience of beauty.

When he and Charlotte created this world, Branwell had insisted on calling it Glasstown. He told her it was because the great bay was like a looking glass, but it had been another mirror he was thinking of. In truth he wanted his city to be named for that first perfect memory of color and light—and for Maria, who shared it with him. When they were older, he and Charlotte rechristened Glasstown with its more elegant name, Verdopolis, but Branwell never forgot that his sister Maria was at his city's heart.

"Thornton!" a voice called. Rogue was standing at the gate, a black carriage behind him. "Ready for a night of crime and mayhem?"

Branwell raced down the stone steps and crossed the gravel drive at a run, letting the iron gate bang behind him. It wasn't until he was in the carriage and it had started moving that he noticed Rogue's appearance. "What in Lucifer's name . . . ?"

Rogue raised an eyebrow. "Explain yourself."

Branwell hardly knew where to begin. It was undoubtedly Rogue who sat across from him, wearing his typical black, but he was too young, too handsome to be the callous scoundrel who had wasted his best days with drink and debauchery. "You're . . . you've . . . gained weight."

"Have I?" Rogue shrugged languidly and stretched out on the seat. "It's the high Verdopolitan living."

It was more than that. Branwell himself was thin and slight, and he'd always liked the idea of such a powerful man as Rogue being built the same way. This Rogue was positively strapping—not fat, but burly as a black bear.

"Your . . . curls," Branwell said.

Rogue touched his hair. "What the devil is the matter with them?"

"You look positively windswept. You look . . . like Lord Byron."

Rogue frowned darkly. "Intolerable. Has my appearance truly changed?" He patted his upper body, looking down at himself. "I can see no difference."

Branwell's fists tightened in anger. If Charlotte was responsible for this, he would turn the Duke of Zamorna into a ninety-year-old man with false teeth and a digestive disorder. She must know that. What was she thinking?

"This is *their* work, of course." Rogue stared out the window of the carriage with a furrowed brow. They had entered the most fashionable part of the city and were passing the main square. "Never a good sign when *they* show their hand."

"They?"

"You know." Rogue glanced around as if someone might be listening. He lowered his voice. "Them. The Genii."

Branwell started. Rogue was talking about his siblings and himself. *The Genii* was what they called themselves in the old stories, back when all four Brontës used to walk through the invented worlds as little gods, creating and destroying. At one point—it was in their *Arabian Nights* phase—they flew about on satin cushions solving disputes and passing judgments. But when they got older, he and Charlotte decided it was better to hide themselves more deeply in the story, to play characters. They hadn't used the term *Genii* in a long time.

"Oh, one doesn't hear so much about them anymore," Branwell said with forced casualness. "I expect they've gone away."

Rogue leaned forward. "Don't be fooled. I see evidence of their meddling occasionally. I tell you, Thornton, the very idea of them chills me to the core."

"You sound as if you're afraid of them."

"Who wouldn't be?" Rogue idly rubbed his whiskers. "Sometimes, after a hard night of drinking, I have a moment where everything becomes clear, and I realize we are nothing more than puppets dancing on their strings." He slapped his hand down on his thigh. "Oh, to cut those strings, Thornton."

This was very strange. Branwell had long believed that Rogue was more than just a character in a story. In point of fact, he considered Rogue his dearest friend and had confided many secrets to him over the years. But now Rogue was exhibiting a self-awareness that Branwell never could have guessed at.

"Have you always thought this?" he asked. "Why have you never told me?"

Rogue stood, holding onto the ceiling of the moving carriage to balance himself, and pulled thick curtains across each window. He sat down again on the edge of his seat, knees touching Branwell's, and crooked a finger, beckoning him close. Branwell leaned in.

"This is something I've never told another living soul," Rogue whispered. "Two other times in my life I've felt their interference. You know that I sometimes feel . . . confined by Verdopolis. I'll warrant you've heard me say a hundred times that I was happier in my pirate days."

Branwell nodded.

"But here's the strange thing. A part of me knows that I have always been Alexander Percy, Earl of Northangerland, and that I only became a pirate to escape my debts, and yet . . . another part remembers a time when I was not a nobleman, when S'Death and I were cutthroats and nothing more. Does that not seem odd to you?"

"Indeed it does," Branwell breathed.

Odd and very close to the truth. Rogue had started out as a pirate, but as Glasstown grew and became Verdopolis, and as Charlotte and Branwell's plots became more and more about the highest tiers of Verdopolitan society, Branwell had decided to make Rogue a nobleman. It wasn't a revision, more a filling in of backstory, one that allowed Rogue to fit with the glamour of his new setting.

"Are you saying that you were changed? Altered by the Genii?"

Rogue nodded. "A terrible thought, but one I've come to believe." He pulled a cigarette case from his breast pocket, lighting a cheroot.

"What is the second incident?"

Rogue puffed thoughtfully, taking a while to answer. "You will think me quite mad."

"I'm sure I won't."

"Do you recall the time when I stood before a firing squad for plotting against the government? It was a few years ago."

"Of course."

Three and a half years earlier, Charlotte and Branwell had decided to end crossing over for good, as they had always promised to do someday. Charlotte was leaving for school, and it seemed the perfect time. They devised a long, convoluted plot that took all of Charlotte's last months at home to play out. The firing squad was to be their final scene.

"I was meant to die that day."

Involuntarily, Branwell gave a little gasp. It was true. Rogue had been meant to die. The scene was to have ended with three words: *Ready. Aim. Fire.* Branwell wrote the first two, but he could never bring himself to write the third. Charlotte left for Roe Head School, and still he could not write it.

In the end, Branwell was very glad he hadn't killed his hero. Charlotte broke her promise. At school, she began writing sugary love stories about Zamorna before the month was out. Rogue had come a hair's breadth from being dead for good. Branwell and Charlotte had tried many times to resurrect a character, but they had never succeeded.

"I heard the last words that I would ever hear," said Rogue, staring straight ahead as if he saw the scene before his eyes. "*Ready. Aim.* And then . . . nothing. The world stopped. I seemed to hang for an eternity between the words *aim* and *fire*. Days, it seemed. Weeks. Oh, how I longed to break free of that moment that held me like a bug in amber. I swear I almost did. I swear that in that strange dream I became aware of some other place where time was passing, some place where the Genii lived. I knew that if I were only a little stronger I could go there—and I swore that if I ever did, I would tear those gods apart with my very teeth."

Rogue shook himself from his reverie and looked down at his cheroot, seeing that it had burnt down unsmoked. He crushed it under his shoe. "Then, all at once, the world began again. My sentence was reprieved at the last moment, as you know—but no one will ever convince me that the Genii did not have me marked for death that day. Why they changed their minds I cannot tell you, but I'm damned if I'll be beholden to them."

The carriage came to a halt, and Branwell drew back the curtain on his side, happy for an excuse to look away from Rogue's dark and brooding gaze. "This isn't Wellesley House," he said.

Rogue shook his head. "No. We're picking up S'Death." Branwell hadn't planned on this, but he told himself that that's what came of letting his plots wander where they would.

The carriage door opened and the old man entered. He was wearing a suit of mossy green, which made his wrinkled face look even more like the knot of a tree. Obviously he had taken trouble with his appearance, in honor of the grand party, and his out-landish red hair was smoothed down with grease.

"Those are some dark expressions," he said. "What have the two of you been plotting?"

"Discussing the Genii," said Rogue.

S'Death looked from one to the other, and if he noticed any difference in Rogue's appearance, he didn't mention it. "Genii? Don't believe in 'em. Mythical beings riding around on pillows? What sort of mode of transport is that, I ask you?" He banged his cane on the roof of the carriage. "Drive on, Bertram!"

"I expect I've sounded very foolish, preaching my sermon against the old gods," said Rogue, when they were once more bumping over the cobbled roads. "In fact, most days I am able to convince myself it's all in my imagination. Other days, of course . . ." He broke off and suddenly—inexplicably—began to smile.

Something in the pit of Branwell's stomach knotted in fear. Rogue's teeth were far too white and too plentiful, like an ani-mal's, like a wolf's. No. Charlotte was not responsible for these physical changes in his favorite character. She was far too sensi-ble for this, too prudent.

"Other days?" Branwell asked.

"Other days I hope the Genii do exist—because if they do, it is not the Duke of Zamorna who is my true enemy." Rogue sat back, his jacket opening so that Branwell could see the revolver at his waist. "Mark my words, Thornton. If I ever meet those cursed beings, I shall paint this city red with their blood."

ANNE

SOME TIME BEFORE THEY WERE BANISHED from the invented worlds, when Anne was about eight and Emily was about ten, Charlotte invented a game for them. It had been to get rid of them, Anne now realized, something to occupy the younger ones while Charlotte and Branwell created their Glasstown adventures without interruption—but Anne had loved it anyway. After helping them to cross over, Charlotte would make Anne and Emily a room with nothing in it but a window and an empty wooden chest.

"This is a magic chest," Charlotte told them the first time. "It will give you anything you want." She closed the lid. "Like this: One, two, three . . ." She opened the lid again, reached inside, and pulled out two crowns, which Anne and Emily dutifully put on their heads.

When she was gone, Anne had no trouble making the chest work. She asked for a pencil to draw with and got it; she asked for thread to sew with and could make whatever color she pleased. But when Emily asked for emerald thread, she got a chest full of emerald green beetles that swirled around her when she opened the lid and then flew out the window. When Emily asked for a pencil, she got a long, red snake—pencil thin—that coiled around her wrist and up her arm. She called the snake Jack and cried when she realized she couldn't bring him home.

After a while they learned not to ask for anything, but to see what gifts the chest would give to Emily on its own—brass door-knobs of different shapes and sizes; a pair of lime green gloves, both for the left hand; chipped teacups with scenes from their favorite books painted on the sides; a beautiful set of mourning jewelry made from the braided hair of a dead person. Anne and Emily had played with that last gift a long time, marveling at the intricacy of the fine plaits and trying to imagine who the dead person might have been.

Anne had known from the start that the "magic chest" wasn't truly magic—or at least it was no more magic than anything else in the invented worlds. She and Emily themselves created what was inside. It was odd, though, that Emily never knew what would be there before she opened the lid. Anne reasoned that there must be a part of Emily's mind that Emily herself was unaware of, a part of the mind that flowed unseen like a subterranean river, thinking its own thoughts and making its own decisions without consulting Emily at all. Anne wondered if she, too, had such a river inside her—but whenever she asked the chest for nothing, counted to three, and opened the lid, nothing was exactly what it gave her.

"Look what she's done to my hair!" Emily exclaimed, looking in the mirror. "She obviously hates me." She lifted a loopy plait and let it fall. "What other explanation could there be?"

She had pulled Anne through room after room of Wellesley House—galleries and gaming rooms and salons—until the noise of the party was far behind them. Finally she must have decided that they were far enough away, and they had stopped in what seemed to be a lady's private sitting room.

Emily flopped down on a plump sofa. "Do you think we made this little chamber, or did Charlotte?"

Anne looked around. It was a comfortable room—smaller and slightly less ornate than many of the others they had seen. There was a chair by the window for sewing and a desk in the corner for writing. The sofa sat in front of the fire—fireplaces were always lit in Verdopolis, she had noticed, regardless of the weather. "Why, Charlotte made it, of course. She makes everything in Wellesley House."

"Yes, but she can't be imagining all of it at once, can she?" Moments earlier Emily had been livid, but now she seemed quite at ease, with her arm draped over the sofa's back. Perhaps she had decided not to ruin what might well be their last visit to Verdopolis.

Anne sat on the sofa's edge. It was so overstuffed that it seemed to sigh underneath her, a disconcerting feeling. How strange, Anne thought, that Emily should be so accustomed to luxuries she had never known in life.

"Are you suggesting that we made this room without realizing it?" Anne asked.

"Well . . . perhaps Charlotte makes the room, but we fill in the details based on our ideas of what Zamorna's mansion should look like."

Anne's eyes fell to the mahogany claws on the feet of the writing desk, the green tassels on the curtain sash. She remembered that they had always been able to make small changes in the invented worlds, and there did seem to be a little bit of Emily in these things. The pattern on the wallpaper, when she examined it closely, was one of heather and foxglove.

Abruptly, Emily sat up. "And here's another question. That hall we just came down." She pointed to the closed door. "Is it still there?"

"Of course it is." Anne stood and opened the door, revealing the rather nondescript hallway.

Emily turned her eyes to the ceiling. "Well, of course it's there now, but perhaps it simply appears when you open the door and will disappear the moment you close it."

Anne laughed. "That is an unprovable hypothesis."

"In fact, all those rooms we passed—do they exist when no one is there, I wonder? Does Verdopolis itself?"

Anne had always thought of the invented worlds as places to be visited, but of course they were made by her siblings and wouldn't exist without them. She looked around, seeing the room anew.

"I wonder how much power we have to change this place," Emily mused. "I wonder if she banished us so we'd never find out the scope of what we can do."

A thought occurred to Anne. "Scissors, please," she said. She counted to three and pulled open the drawer of the nearest side table, smiling as she took out a pair of scissors. "Look, Emily. We can still change some things, just as we could before." She sat down again on the sofa and began to cut the silk flowers from her dress, tossing them one by one into the fire.

"Oh," Emily cried. "Don't ruin your dress. It looks so lovely on you."

Anne snipped the head off a flower with a bit too much vigor, leaving a small hole. She'd expected Emily to understand. "I wanted to be exactly myself, not Lady Anne from the provinces. It's what I chose."

Emily frowned. "I thought you simply couldn't think of a character to play."

Anne shook her head, trying to find the words. "It's foolish . . . but you know that I wish Charlotte's writings were more true.

I suppose I thought a plain Haworth girl might be just what Verdopolis needed."

"I see."

"And a muslin dress, too." Anne looked up at her sister. "They can catch fire, you know. I feel quite in danger."

"Oh, Anne, that's just an eccentricity of Papa's," Emily said, sitting down again. "But I'm very sorry, at any rate. If I'd chosen to play a character Charlotte approved of, she might not have changed either of us."

Anne couldn't help but smile. "You were so wicked, Emily. I don't know how you dared. The Red Countess, of all people!"

Emily smiled, too, but then leapt up again with an "oh" as if struck by lightning. "I have an idea," she said. "If you and I *do* create these rooms without realizing it, do you think that if we closed that door, counted to three, and opened it again, we could make any room we wanted?"

"Haven't we just determined that it's a hallway?"

Emily made a frustrated hiss. "For heaven's sake, Anne. It could be anything. It could be a magical door. To Gondal."

Anne doubted this was possible. There were unwritten laws and rules to Verdopolis set down by Branwell and Charlotte. Occasionally characters had visions or saw ghosts, but Anne had read enough about Verdopolis to know that there was no fairy-tale magic like what Emily was describing.

"I don't . . ."

"There's no harm in trying, is there? Stand here with me."

Anne joined Emily in front of the door. "Very well, but don't say what you wish for aloud. Remember when we used to play with the wooden chest that Charlotte made for us? Things were always more interesting when you asked for nothing and then opened the lid."

"Splendid idea," said Emily. She put her hand on the door handle, giving Anne a nervous glance. "One. Two. Three." She threw open the door.

It was still only a hallway, just as Anne had imagined it would be. However, it wasn't empty now.

"Ladies," said a deep voice. Into the room stepped Alexander Rogue.

CHARLOTTE

WAS IT CHARLOTTE'S IMAGINATION, OR was the room different in some inexplicable way? She was still in the green and gold salon, and the malachite fireplace was still exquisite, but the paintings on the walls were all of shipwrecks or storms raging over jagged mountains. Hadn't they been tranquil landscapes before?

This was Emily's doing, somehow. Even as a child, she had ruined stories with her strangeness. Charlotte should have remembered how, in the old days, her plots had veered off in odd tangents when Emily was around, and even her own characters became unpredictable. At least Charlotte's collaboration with Branwell allowed for each of them to have their own particular stories—whereas Emily's imagination seeped into everything like strong dye, changing what wasn't hers to change.

"Did you hear? Zenobia Percy is at the party," a woman said.

Charlotte was alone in the room, but the double doors were open. She could see the party guests gliding by in their finery and could hear snippets of their conversations.

"The Red Countess?" a man answered. "Why would she be here? Her husband is the duke's deadly enemy."

Why indeed. What in heaven's name was Charlotte to do with this plot development? Truth be told, Emily was right about the character's potential. Zenobia could be the Verdopolitan Madame de Staël. The modern Cleopatra. *Perhaps she plays the mandolin and speaks fluent Chinese*, Charlotte thought.

"*All covet an invitation to her salons,*" she said under her breath, "*where the greatest politicians, the wittiest authors, and the most talented artists gather around her like moths to a flame.*"

Yes. She liked that. But still, why would the Red Countess come to the party?

"A love affair," she breathed aloud as the idea struck. "A love affair with the Duke of Zamorna."

Now, that was interesting.

Not only were there hundreds of dramatic possibilities to such a romance, but it would also mean that Branwell's character, Alexander Rogue, was a dupe and a cuckold. Charlotte grinned, thinking how vexed this would make her brother. He deserved it. Hadn't he threatened to kill off Zamorna?

Charlotte felt a twinge of guilt for what this would do to

Mary Henrietta—she'd be devastated to learn that her husband was having an affair with her own stepmother—but then, she would be so beautiful in her melancholy. Besides, her noble and virtuous love hadn't set Zamorna's heart on fire the way Charlotte had hoped it would. Perhaps forbidden love—guilty, tortured love—with the Countess Zenobia would finally bring him to life.

Charlotte ducked behind a sofa and squeezed her eyes shut, ready to take hold of the story. In a singsong voice, she murmured:

"The young lord Charles, though intelligent beyond his years, was not above the games and japes to which all boys are prone. After being abandoned by his rude cousins, he fell to playing with a ball, which bounced under the legs of a silk-upholstered sofa that had once belonged to Louis the Fifteenth. It was for this reason that when the Duke of Zamorna and the Viscount Castlereagh entered the room and shut the door, they believed themselves to be alone, not noticing Zamorna's young brother behind the sofa. Dear reader, do not blame young Charles for not admitting his presence, for otherwise how would we know of the conversation that ensued?"

"I did not ask her to the party," came Zamorna's voice. "You must believe me. She took that upon herself. But now that she is here . . . I must dance with her, Castlereagh. By God, one dance is all I ask."

Charlotte opened her eyes. The Duke of Zamorna stood by the fire with his friend, the Viscount Castlereagh, a handsome, fair-haired gentleman of twenty-one. Both held glasses of sherry in their hands. In past stories the young viscount had idolized the duke, but now he looked at his mentor with shock and disappointment in his eyes.

"Zamorna, you are mad. You have married the most beautiful woman in Verdopolis—a paragon of virtue and loveliness. Why throw away your happiness for a dance with another man's wife?"

"*Zamorna hurled his glass into the fire*," Charlotte said, "*making the flames dance.*"

Zamorna hurled his glass into the fire. "Damn it, Castlereagh! I tell you, I must! She and I have a history—one that I cannot forget."

"I would think a face like Mary Henrietta's could make you forget all else."

"A man such as I can never be content with one woman." Zamorna looked into the distance, his face twisted with strange passions. "It is my curse." He grabbed his friend by the hand. "I beg you, find some pretext for keeping my wife away from the ballroom, for if she sees me dancing with . . . her . . . she will know all."

Castlereagh shook his head. "I can refuse you nothing, my friend." He drank the remains of his sherry in one swallow to brace himself for what he was about to do. Then he gripped Zamorna's shoulder in parting, smiled grimly, and left the room.

EMILY

MILY STOOD WITH HER HAND ON THE door. Her mouth was dry and blood throbbed in her ears. It was Rogue. Her Rogue. How real he was—exactly like her portrait of him, only more vivid, more vigorous. *I wanted to meet him dressed in red*, she thought, *not with these ridiculous bows in my hair.*

"What an unusual gown," he said. "It changes color with the light." He took a step forward and seemed to fill the room.

Emily looked down. Her dress was the one that Charlotte had given her, but now it was a deep scarlet, and the roses trimming the bottom were real and in full bloom. She touched her head, hoping her hair had changed as well. It hadn't, though a glance to the mirror told her the bows had also turned red.

"I'm afraid I am lost," he said. "Is there a party somewhere in this rabbit warren?" When no one spoke he gave a small bow. "Alexander Percy, Earl of Northangerland. Also known as Alexander Rogue."

"We know who you are," Anne said, backing away. He raised an eyebrow at this.

Emily curtsied, though her body didn't feel her own. She was sure her face was as scarlet as her dress. "I am Lady Emily, and this is Lady Anne," she said. "We are cousins of the Duke of Zamorna."

"And these are private rooms," said Anne. "Please begone."

Emily turned and glared. Her sister had retreated behind an armchair and was gripping its back with tense fingers. Emily turned back to Rogue and smiled what she hoped was a sweet smile, but it felt insipid on her lips.

"Forgive my sister's rudeness. Do sit down, Rogue . . . your lordship."

"We must not detain you," Anne said.

Rogue glanced at Anne, then back at Emily. "I do have business at the party." His hand went briefly to his waist, where Emily knew his pistol was hidden.

He mustn't go yet, she thought. She caught a hint of his scent— like horses and tobacco—and had the strongest urge to lean into his chest. *Emily Brontë. Take hold of yourself.*

"Before you go, do have a look at . . ." She wracked her brains for something that would keep him. "This."

She leapt to the drawer where Anne had found the scissors. "One, two, three," she said under her breath, and she pulled the drawer open.

"Good heavens," he said. "Is that an antique stiletto?"

"Yes," she said, surprised as he, but pleased with her result. "Indeed it is."

Carefully Rogue took the long, thin dagger out of the drawer and held it up. "Beautiful. Look at the workmanship on the hilt. I collect these, you know."

"I know."

"For heaven's sake, Emily," Anne hissed. "Now you've armed him."

"He was armed already," Emily retorted. "He has his pistol." Rogue started at this, and she smiled sweetly at him again. "One assumes." She sat down and gestured to the place next to her on the sofa. "Do make yourself comfortable. I'm sorry we have no refreshments to offer you. All the servants are occupied with the party."

He sat down. "Cousins of Zamorna, you say? I'm surprised to find the duke has such amiable relations. You'll forgive me. He and I are not exactly friends."

"Oh, that's all right. We think our cousin Zamorna is the most colossal ass. Don't we, Anne?"

Anne glowered, and Rogue barked a laugh at Emily's candor. "I can't say that I disagree."

He toyed with the stiletto, trading it from one hand to the other. Then, as if coming to a decision, he gripped the handle and pointed the tip toward Emily. "I suppose he'd pay a high ransom for you girls, should you go missing."

Emily's heart leapt. "Oh," she said. "Are you going to kidnap us? What a wonderful idea!"

Rogue frowned. "I can't say that anyone has ever reacted that way before—and I've carried off a dozen women."

"Thirteen," Emily said. "If you count the Hawthorn twins as two."

He looked at her now, and his wide smile was a beautiful surprise, piercing her heart as surely as the stiletto. "What a strange young lady you are. I'm beginning to wonder why I've never been to the provinces."

She stopped breathing. *Oh,* she thought. *This is how I'll die. From a look.* It wasn't a handsome face by most standards—his brow was too heavy; his eyes were too wide-set; his whiskers and eyebrows were too bushy—but in that moment she couldn't possibly look away.

Lightly he brushed her cheek with his finger, making a chill run down her spine. Somewhere Anne began to cough, but it seemed far away.

"You're not one of those women who screams all through an abduction, are you? I find that very trying."

"Screaming is a very sensible response to kidnapping, in my opinion. But no, I'd be meek as a lamb. I'd faint a lot and sigh like a bruised flower. Then, when you least expected it, I'd stab you in the eye with your own knife and steal your horse."

"Marvelous," he said.

"I know!" Anne's voice punctured the moment. "Perhaps the earl would like to help us wind our wool into balls while we tell him all the gossip of the provinces."

"Pardon?" he said.

Emily blinked as if awakening from a dream.

"We country girls would find such an evening a thrill, I dare say," Anne went on. "And—goodness!—if we are kidnapped, we shall have many such evenings in front of us. We may bring our knitting with us, mayn't we? Lord Percy, my sister tells the most amusing story about a vicar's cat getting caught in a tree." She feigned a laugh. "Wait until you hear it."

Rogue was looking around the room as if wondering how he got there. Emily flushed, suddenly aware of her youth, her scarlet dress, her ridiculous plaited hair.

"But I hope we are not keeping you from other engagements, Lord Percy," Anne continued. "Didn't you have someone to meet? An evil plan to put in motion? I feel you mentioned something along those lines."

Rogue felt again for his hidden pistol. "Yes." He stood. "I don't know why . . . I really ought . . ."

Emily stared daggers at Anne. "Before you go, you must see what's in *this* drawer," she said to Rogue. She stood, reaching for the table on the far side of the sofa.

"It's yarn," Anne said. They both made a dash for the knob,

counting under their breath, but Anne was first. "I was right. A drawer full of yarn." She pulled out a tangled, multicolored mass and waved it at Rogue. "Winding this will take all night. I *do* hope you'll stay."

"Oh, no. Thank you," Rogue said, backing away from them. The stiletto was still in his hand, but he set it on the sofa cushion.

"That is not what I wanted to show his lordship," Emily said through clenched teeth.

"It's been a pleasure," Rogue said at the door.

"Stop!" Emily said, and Rogue stopped, frozen and unmoving. She hadn't known she could do that.

Emily went to him and took his hands in her own, though they seemed cold and inhuman now. She didn't like him this way. His hands should be warm. "This is what I wanted to show you," she whispered, and she squeezed her eyes shut. "One. Two. Three."

When she opened her eyes, Rogue was frowning into them. Anne was gone. Wellesley House was gone. They were outside under a gray sky, a strong wind whipping their hair. Where was she? She wanted to look around, but Rogue's black eyes fixed her to the spot. She could smell moor and damp, and she heard, somewhere close, the mournful call of a curlew.

"What witchery is this?" he said, and pulled his hands away.

Immediately they were in the sitting room again, and he was backing away from her across the floor. Emily hardly knew what had happened. It must have been Gondal, she realized with a stab of regret. She'd done it. She'd been there for a brief moment—far too brief. Her very own world.

Rogue was pressed against the wall now, pointing at her, terror in his eyes. "Genii," he breathed.

CHARLOTTE

CHARLOTTE WAS INDULGING ONE OF HER secret Verdopolitan passions. She knew it was unseemly, but she told herself that, after all, it was the very last time. She had gone to the grand ballroom, weaving her way in and out of the dancers to stand at one of the heavily laden refreshment tables at the far end of the room—and there she began to eat. She ate the way a ten-year-old boy would eat—without worrying about manners or growing fat. She ate marzipan and bonbons and sugared limes. She ate miniature oranges and tiny cakes that looked like musical instruments or crystal flowers or horses' heads with spun-sugar manes. She ate walnuts and glazed pecans and fruits that only grew in Verdopolis but that tasted like a spiced candy someone had given her once, a long time ago. No one dared to scold her. She was Lord Charles Albert Florian Wellesley, after all.

"Too sweet," someone said next to her, just as her mouth was full of cake.

Charlotte turned to see her brother leaning casually against a pillar. She swallowed quickly and brushed the crumbs from her velvet suit. "If you don't like the confections, may I direct you . . . ," she began. "Well, may I direct you anywhere but here, Lord Thornton?"

"I'm not referring to the confections," Branwell said, waving a hand over the assembly. "Or rather, this whole affair is a confection. Too sweet. It's all spun sugar, Charlotte."

His criticism slid off her. She had only to look around to know she had outdone herself with this scene. The mirror-paneled walls reflected a hundred glittering chandeliers; the orchestra never missed a note; the swirling dancers never missed a step. Perfect.

"The name is Charles," she corrected. "And I know jealousy when I hear it."

"What have I missed? I saw Mary Henrietta in the conservatory. She looked more tragically beautiful than usual—if that's possible." A footman with a gilded tray bowed his head and offered them refreshment, but Branwell waved him away.

"She's had a presentiment," Charlotte said. "The suspicion that Zamorna loves another gnaws at her heart like a worm."

Branwell frowned. "I hope she's not going to waste away from his neglect like his other two wives."

"I haven't decided."

"Don't kill her, Charlotte." She was surprised by the emotion behind this request. "She's too lovely to die. She's . . . well . . . you've turned her into someone rather luminous." The idea that Branwell admired the character more than he'd been letting on brought a smile to her lips, but he seemed to realize he had accidentally paid her a compliment, and the haughty tone returned to his voice. "Besides, it would be too similar to your previous plots, and you would begin to bore me."

Charlotte was about to reply with a cutting remark but then remembered what was to come and repressed a smirk. "I think that as the story progresses, you will find it original enough."

She looked out at the dance floor. Branwell hadn't noticed yet, but the Countess Zenobia and the Duke of Zamorna were already dancing together. It was a lively quadrille, and the partners did little more than hold hands as they performed the intricate steps, so there was nothing scandalous about their pairing. Not yet. She had to admit they made a handsome couple. Zamorna was magnificent in his short jacket and silk crepe breeches, and the countess's raven locks looked stunning against her scarlet gown.

"How could you call this a confection?" she asked. "When have I created a lovelier scene?"

Branwell shrugged, to her great annoyance. "You hardly let them breathe."

"Who?"

"All of them. Those dancers—they're like clockwork. I think you control every step. You're frowning with the effort."

What's wrong with that? she wondered.

"And what's the Red Countess doing here?"

Now Charlotte allowed herself a wicked smile. It was time to advance the plot.

"*The quadrille ended and Zamorna made a gesture to the orchestra,*" she said. "*A waltz began to play. He put his arm around the Red Countess. There were gasps from the crowd as they began to dance.*"

"What are you doing?" Branwell asked.

There was something truly shocking about Zamorna and Zenobia waltzing together. They were altogether too close—and too at ease in their closeness. Neither took their eyes from the other. Dancers left the floor, but Zamorna and Zenobia didn't seem to notice. No one who saw them could have any doubt: They were lovers.

"Charlotte, you can't," Branwell said. "The Red Countess is Rogue's wife."

"It makes perfect sense. Rogue only married her for her money. He doesn't love her."

"But you can't make my character a cuckold! Take it back."

"You know I can't," she said. "*At that moment, a pair of high doors* burst open, and Mary Henrietta came rushing through, ribbons fluttering, a vision in violet and green."

Mary Henrietta burst in just as Charlotte described. She looked at the dance floor, and a little moan escaped her. She put her hand to her heaving alabaster breast. Young Lord Castlereagh followed quickly after and was there to catch her when she fell into a graceful swoon.

"I thought you weren't going to write any more melodramas," Branwell sneered.

His words hit their mark. For the first time, Charlotte wondered if she'd made a mistake with this new pairing.

Out on the floor, the duke and the raven-haired countess waltzed on. They hadn't noticed the stir they had created, though many of the guests were murmuring loudly to one another. Mary Henrietta lay across a velvet sofa, a tear running down her cheek. Mina the maid dabbed at her face with a handkerchief.

Was this love? Charlotte wondered. Was this passion? Anne had said she wished Charlotte's writings were more true, but how was truth achieved? And if neither Zenobia nor Mary Henrietta had the spark to feel true love and to make Zamorna truly love them in return, then who did?

Perhaps I should dance with Zamorna myself.

The thought appeared as if from nowhere, but the picture it immediately conjured up in Charlotte's mind—of Zamorna reaching down to waltz with a tiny woman in spectacles—made her blush hotly. How the guests would laugh. Even the servants would hide their smirks behind white gloves.

"I shan't watch any more of this," said Branwell. "*Rogue entered and challenged Zamorna to a duel.*"

Nothing happened.

"Where's Rogue? What have you done with him?"

"I haven't done a thing!" Charlotte insisted. "I think it's a splendid development." In fact she was very glad that Branwell had thought of some action to distract her mind from its strange meanderings. She looked around the room. "Try again."

Branwell drew himself up and took a deep breath. "*Rogue entered, pistol drawn. 'Unhand my wife, you villain,' he cried.*"

They waited. Zamorna and Zenobia danced. Mary Henrietta moaned softly. Rogue did not appear.

"I suppose he's somewhere else," Branwell said sheepishly.

"You're his author," Charlotte said. "How can he be somewhere that you didn't put him?"

Branwell didn't seem to know what to say to this and looked defensive when he answered. "I don't keep so tight a rein on my characters as you."

"Looking for the earl?" said a voice.

S'Death, Rogue's frequent partner in crime, was so close at Charlotte's elbow that she started backward. "Mr. King," she said, recovering herself and giving a short bow. She'd never liked the man, and at that moment she liked him even less than usual.

With his flame-red hair and his asymmetrical face, he was a blot of ugliness on her brilliant party.

"Allow me to find him for you. I believe I know where he is." S'Death bowed deferentially, but Charlotte had the distinct feeling she was being mocked.

"Thank you," she said stiffly, watching him go. "I don't know why you ever invented that character, Banny."

"I didn't," Branwell said. "I thought you did."

EMILY

TRANGE," SAID ROGUE. "WHEN I WAS COMING here, I told a friend I'd like to meet one of the Genii— but you are not what I imagined."

He seemed to have lost some of his fear, and he stepped toward Emily, deep suspicion in his eyes. Anne had retreated behind the armchair again. Emily swallowed, wondering how much Rogue understood about who the Genii truly were.

"For one thing, I never imagined an omnipotent being wearing so many ... ribbons."

Emily touched her hair, silently cursing her elder sister.

"Why such an unassuming guise, I wonder? Would I melt to see your true forms? Would I go mad? Take off your masks, ladies—or I will deduce that you are harpies with pointed teeth and eagle wings and bare alabaster breasts."

"Sir!" said Anne.

Rogue smiled at the reaction. "You are the good and modest Genius, I see, unlike this other witch." He pointed at Emily. "Are you the one who changed my appearance? Made me younger?" Emily kept her expression fixed, but he seemed to divine an answer. "You may change my face, but I'm damned if you will change me." There was a mirror over the dressing table and Rogue bent to peer into it, rubbing his whiskers. "Why did you do it? The ladies will mistake me for the romantic hero."

She laughed at this, though it was a little forced. "Romantic hero? You look like the wolf in a fairy tale."

He turned and narrowed his dark eyes at her. "There is a certain sort of girl who wants the wolf to eat out of her hand. If you are such, I'll warn you, she doesn't keep her fingers long."

Emily met his gaze. "Some wolves can be tamed."

"Then we call them lapdogs, my dear—and you'll put no leash on me."

He stepped forward again, and Emily realized he was edging toward the stiletto on the sofa. She made a grab for it, but was too late.

"Ha! Now we'll find out if the gods bleed!" he said, brandishing the knife.

Emily moved to stand between Rogue and Anne's armchair. "You cannot hurt us." She tried to sound certain as she said this, to *be* certain, and make it true with the force of her will.

"Why not? Will I turn to stone?"

"Why would you want to do us harm?" Anne asked. "We are not your enemy."

"Why?" Rogue tried to step around Emily to speak to Anne, but Emily moved with him, and so he directed his words to her. "I have been meddled with! Tampered with! Do you deny that the Genii have a hand in all my failed schemes? Do you deny lifting up that fop Zamorna at every turn, while I am constantly struck down?"

"Zamorna has a noble heart despite all his flaws," Anne said. "Perhaps you fail because evil will always fail when faced with good."

Rogue raised an eyebrow at Emily. "Is she quite serious?"

"I'm afraid so."

He lifted the stiletto's blade so that it was at Emily's throat. "Make me a king. Make Zamorna drop dead of an apoplexy."

"I can't," Emily said. She struggled to keep her voice calm, forcing herself not to step back, though the blade was cold as ice. "I didn't make this world. We are . . . younger Genii, and not very important, if you must know. Our elder siblings made Verdopolis."

"If that is so, I might as well kill you now."

Emily took a deep breath, steadying herself. With one finger, she pushed the blade away. "I told you. You cannot. Though you might be wicked, your one redeeming quality is that you would never harm me."

Rogue scowled, gripping the knife more tightly. "I believe I must make one thing clear." He spoke the next words slowly and distinctly, each word as precise as a hammer hitting an anvil. "I decide what my qualities are, and I do not choose to have any redeeming ones."

He lunged toward her, and Emily couldn't help but flinch, but she didn't shut her eyes. The knife froze. Rogue struggled against himself, his face reddening. Finally he lowered his arm.

"Devil take you! It seems I can't kill a young lady in cold blood—though I deny it has anything to do with my *redeeming qualities*."

"I told you," Emily said, breathing heavily in spite of herself. "You can't harm a hair on my head."

His eyes narrowed. "That sounds like a challenge to me."

Again the knife shot out, lightning quick. Emily gasped, feeling a tug at her hair—and the next moment Rogue was dangling something in front of her eyes, a wild grin spreading across his face. It was one of her own plaits. He shook it, making its red bow dance.

"Perhaps I only need to work up to drawing blood."

Emily stepped back, her hand at her head. For the first time since he'd arrived, fear flooded through her. Could he harm her?

The door flew open. "What the devil are you playing at, man?" It was S'Death. "While you're here chatting, the Duke of Zamorna is seducing your wife!"

"What?" Rogue cried. "Damn his eyes! It's time for that man to die."

CHARLOTTE

OGUE ENTERED, PISTOL DRAWN. "UNHAND my wife, you villain!" he cried.

"At last," Charlotte muttered.

The musicians stopped their playing as he strode out onto the dance floor, boot heels clicking. The Duke of Zamorna stepped protectively in front of the countess. "We all know who the true villain is here, Rogue."

Zenobia shrank back behind her lover. "Be careful, my darling," she said. "He's a mad dog when he's angry."

"You dare call him *darling* in my presence, woman?" Rogue shouted. "Have you no loyalty?"

"What did you ever do to inspire it?" the countess spat. "You never loved me. You've never loved anyone."

"This is very good," Charlotte whispered to Branwell. "But

what have you done to Rogue's appearance? He's far too young and dashing."

"It wasn't me," her brother hissed back.

"If you mean to challenge me, I am at your service," Zamorna said. "Name your seconds, and I will meet you at dawn."

"A duel?" Rogue scoffed. "You mistake me for a man of honor, sir. Why should I allow you to arm yourself?" With that he cocked his pistol, aiming for Zamorna's head.

"Branwell, don't!" Charlotte said, grabbing her brother's arm, as if he were the one who held the gun.

The sound of a shot split the air. The countess screamed. Partygoers fainted or cried out. Mary Henrietta, still on her sofa, put a hand on her brow. "Oh, is my faithless husband dead, Mina? I cannot bear to look, for still I love him so!"

To everyone's surprise, Zamorna was still standing, though a star-shaped crack had appeared on the mirrored panel behind his head.

"No, milady, no," murmured the faithful maid. "He is not dead. Do not distress yourself."

"Damn and blast!" shouted Rogue. "I could not have missed at this range. It's unbelievable. You truly are protected by the Genii."

Zamorna touched his ear and blood came away on his fingers. He laughed wildly at the sight. "Perhaps I am."

Having had only one ball, the pistol was useless now, and Rogue tossed it to the floor, where it skidded toward the fireplace.

He scanned the room. Partygoers backed away at his fierce gaze, but he seemed to be looking for someone in particular. "You," he said, pointing into the crowd. He grabbed a girl in a blue dress and pulled her by the wrist onto the dance floor.

"It's Anne!" Charlotte said.

Rogue wrapped his hands around her little sister's neck. "Genii!" he called. "I know you are here. I know you are among us. I'm told this girl is a minor goddess, that she has little power in this world. I call on her betters, the elder Genii, to show themselves. Otherwise I shall strangle her before your very eyes."

"Stop it!" Emily pushed her way onto the floor. "You will not harm her." Charlotte was surprised to see that her dress was a lurid red.

"Branwell, what is this?" she said. "Why are Anne and Emily in the story? What's this talk of Genii?"

Her brother began to mumble words furiously, though she couldn't hear what he was saying. "It's no use," he said finally. "I can't change anything. The story is . . . I don't know . . . it's happening on its own!"

This must be Anne and Emily's plot, thought Charlotte, though it was strange that Branwell could not direct it. Those girls were always getting their sticky fingerprints on everything she and Branwell did. Charlotte had to admit, though, the story was unique.

"Rogue, you're mad," Zamorna said. "This young lady is my cousin from the provinces—not some mythical deity from our ancient past. Genii? Are you a believer in fairy tales now? Unhand the poor girl!"

Charlotte couldn't help admiring the straightness of Anne's posture and her bravely jutting chin. It made for a dramatic tableau—the small, slim girl with the dark figure of Alexander Rogue hulking behind her.

"I rather like him burly," Charlotte said. "Look at the size of his hands around her neck!"

"Stay back," Rogue said to Zamorna. "Stay back or I'll wring the life out of her. You!" He nodded to Emily. "Look through the crowd and point out the other Genii, the ones you say have made this place—if you don't, I swear, I'll turn this girl as blue as her gown."

"I tell you, you will not harm her. You cannot!" Emily said. She looked genuinely afraid.

Rogue's voice lowered to a growl. "Oh, I feel your will, little goddess, but I have a will, too. I don't know what I am exactly—a figment, some made-up thing—but I know that I am ungovernable by any man or god."

"Emily," Anne said, her voice ragged. "Do as he says."

Emily turned, catching Charlotte's eye. She seemed to be asking for help. Fear began to seep into Charlotte's mind. If this were Anne and Emily's plot, why did they look so afraid? She stepped onto the dance floor and clapped her hands twice.

"Stop," she commanded.

Nothing happened, though a few of the party guests looked

at her askance, as if wondering what the young lord could be thinking. She clapped her hands again. "Stop, I say!"

"Charles," Zamorna hissed. "Don't be a fool, boy. Stay out of this."

Why couldn't she take control of the story? Why couldn't Branwell? Whose plot was this?

"I'm waiting," Rogue said to Emily as Charlotte stepped back sheepishly. "Who are the elder Genii?"

Emily made a show of looking through the crowd. "I don't . . . see them."

"Branwell," Charlotte whispered. "Something's happening. Something I don't understand. I think we must go home—now!—even if it means we disappear in the middle of the party. If you can get to Anne, I'll cross Emily."

"Yes, yes, but how can I get to Anne before Rogue strangles her?" Branwell asked, his voice high with tension. "And . . . do you think . . . ?" He took her by the hand, something Branwell never did in Verdopolis or in life. It alarmed Charlotte as much as anything else that had happened. Her brother may have been playing Lord Thornton, but the fear in his eyes was all his own. "Do you think that if we die here, in Verdopolis, we die in the real world? Charlotte, could Rogue kill Anne?"

Charlotte felt the breath go out of her. She had always held such tight rein over her stories that she'd never thought to wonder about this. She'd never felt any danger. What if Anne . . . ?

"I have something to say," Anne said, interrupting her

thoughts. She was firm and loud in a way that was unfamiliar to Charlotte, commanding the attention of the room.

"That's better," Rogue said. "Name your coconspirators, girl."

"What I have to say is . . . is . . . Wellesley House is on fire!"

For a moment nothing happened, though Charlotte thought she saw Anne mouthing something else. Was she counting? Then the curtains behind Charlotte and Branwell burst into flame.

"Fire!" a servant screamed, dropping a tray.

In seconds the flames had risen up the curtains and were blackening the ceiling. Someone pushed Charlotte, and she fell. She looked around for Branwell, but she didn't see him.

"Fire! Fire!" The word was shouted on every side. Panic coursed through her. Charlotte was afraid she would be trampled. *Could we die?* she kept thinking. *Why haven't I ever asked myself that before?*

She managed to stand up again and look around, but her siblings were lost in the crowd. The party guests had spilled out over the dance floor and were swarming around Rogue and Zamorna, their drama forgotten as everyone pressed toward the double doors at the far side of the room. Rogue towered over most of the guests, so Charlotte could see him scanning the crowd just as she was. He seemed to have lost Anne and Emily in the confusion—that was one blessing, at least.

"Stay calm! Stay calm, everyone!" Mary Henrietta had risen from her sofa and was directing people to the door. "Are you hurt?" She put her hand out to a young woman cowering under a table. "We must away. Mina, help me with her." Mina and Mary Henrietta coaxed the young lady from her hiding place and shepherded her away. A moment later they were lost in the crowd. It had been a small exchange, but it amazed Charlotte. She hadn't orchestrated it, and she was sure her siblings hadn't, either. In fact, if she had, Mary Henrietta would have been saved by her husband, or by Castlereagh, but Mary Henrietta had acted on her own. It was in her nature to help people, to be kind, but Charlotte had kept her passive. And here she had taken action—done something noble. Even in the midst of the chaos, Charlotte found this extraordinary.

"Branwell!" she cried, catching sight of her brother in the middle of the dance floor. "Branwell! Here! Where are the girls?"

He didn't turn around. For reasons Charlotte didn't understand, he had a large punch bowl in his arms, red liquid sloshing onto the floor as he pushed his way through the crowd.

"Oh, help!" someone called. Charlotte recognized Anne's voice but couldn't see her. She climbed up on a nearby chair to look over the churning bodies. To her horror, she saw her youngest sister near the fireplace, the bottom of her lovely blue dress in flames. This must be why Branwell had the punch bowl. He had grasped what was happening and was trying to get to her.

He won't make it, Charlotte thought. *She's burning!*

Anne was trying to beat out the fire with her hands to no avail. "Emily!" Charlotte cried, looking around. "Where are you? Someone help!"

She noticed that Zamorna was very close to Anne, standing by the fireside looking distraught. *Oh, why doesn't he do something!* Charlotte thought. *Why doesn't he save her?* Mary Henrietta acted on her own; why didn't he? She tightened her fists and took a deep breath, willing the story to come back under her control.

"Zamorna, with no thought for his own safety, tore a tapestry from the wall and smothered the flames," she said.

Immediately Zamorna sprang to a large tapestry on the wall and ripped it down.

"Oh, hurry," Charlotte said. She got down from the chair and began to push through the crush of people to get to her sister. She lost sight of her again, but when the crowd thinned, she saw that Anne was sitting on the floor, her bottom half covered by the tapestry. The flames were out.

"Oh, thank heaven," Charlotte breathed.

Zamorna had a hand on Anne's shoulder and was leaning over her. A moment later Branwell got to them both and tossed the remains of the punch over Anne's legs. Charlotte almost laughed with relief.

She caught sight of Emily and grabbed her by the hand without a word, pulling her toward Anne and Branwell.

I'll never put them in danger again, she vowed.

CHARLOTTE

"WE SHOULD TELL THEM EVERYTHING," Branwell said. They were in the children's study. A mirror was propped up against a chair, and he was working on his own face in the group portrait, eyes moving back and forth between the reflection and the painting.

Charlotte sat at the desk. She had been working on a sketch of Anne, but now she set her pencil down. "No," she said. "I'm sure I'm right. What good would it do to stir up old mistakes? We must make a clean break—never go to Verdopolis again, never write about it again, never think about it, never talk about it." She looked down at her drawing, and a wave of guilt swept over her. "Especially after what's happened to Anne."

Anne had come back from Verdopolis burned, not on the

legs, as it happened, but on her hands and fingers from where she'd tried to put out the fire. They'd made up a story about her burning herself on the stove, but it hadn't been very convincing.

"She's not so badly injured," Branwell said as he dabbed his brush on his palette. "Even Papa says we needn't call for the doctor, and he always errs on the side of caution in such matters."

"Anne is so stoic. He doesn't realize—"

"Charlotte, you must stop torturing yourself."

She rubbed her forehead with her fingers. "How could we have exposed them to such dangers?" she asked, more to herself than to her brother.

Branwell set down his brush and came over to her. She could see that he wanted to comfort her, but instead of putting a hand on her shoulder or saying something kind, he only made a show of inspecting her drawing. "Not bad. A better likeness than the sketch you did in June."

"Thank you," Charlotte said. She nodded to the easel. "You are showing improvement as well." She picked up her pencil. "Although you've made your head too big."

Branwell's face soured, but he went back to his work without comment, taking up the brush again. For a while they worked in silence. Anne's likeness *was* rather good, Charlotte allowed herself to admit, though the nose was a little too sharp. She had drawn her sister in profile, eyes downcast, hair around her shoulders. This was the quiet Anne, the Anne she knew—but who was that girl who had been so brave when Rogue's hands were around her neck? Who was the girl who had set Wellesley House on fire?

"Whatever will you say to Emily?" Branwell asked. "She wants to know why we're leaving the story unfinished."

The tip of Charlotte's pencil broke, leaving an ugly streak across her drawing. "Isn't Anne's injury explanation enough?" she said, more sharply than she meant. "And can't you and I find some new topic of conversation?"

"There is no need to snap." Branwell drew himself up. He had his smock on and there was paint in his hair, but he had a way of making himself as imperious as a young emperor when he wanted to. "Anne's injury is not my fault. We should never have allowed the girls back into Verdopolis in the first place. Or rather, *you* shouldn't have allowed it. Why were they with us at all?"

"Why were any of us there? Why did any of us cross over again? Because of you, Branwell! Because you begged and blackmailed until you wore me down!"

"Wore you down? It was surprisingly easy."

"You were desperate! You had that . . . that mad look in your eyes. I made a vow, a vow to Papa not to go back, and you made me break it!"

"Spare me, Charlotte. I know what your vows are worth." He said this very smugly, with a superior look in his eye that infuriated her. Then he lifted his brush and pretended to turn his attention back to the painting—but Charlotte had no intention of letting him get the last word.

"Explain yourself! I am not in the habit of going back on my promises."

"Aren't you?" He came to the desk now, leaning against it until he was very close to her face. "We quit Verdopolis once before, you and I. Do you remember? When you went away to school?"

"Oh. That." Charlotte picked up a wadded piece of bread and carefully began to use it to erase the pencil mark on Anne's portrait.

"Yes. That."

She brushed tiny breadcrumbs from her page. It was all she could do not to shrink away from him, to pretend his closeness didn't bother her.

It was true that they had pledged to quit the invented worlds when she went away to Roe Head School. Branwell had been terribly upset when he learned she was writing there in secret, snatching moments to cross over when she could, always having to come back too soon. She didn't understand why he was still angry about it. It was all so long ago, and he'd started writing again himself soon enough, sending her Rogue's adventures by post, sometimes twice a week.

"So this is a true resolution?" he asked. "You're serious this time?"

"Of course. I've said I am."

Branwell took a step back and a joyless grin spread over his face. "Then you will have it, too, soon enough. That mad look in the eyes, as you called it. You'll see what I went through when you were at school."

"What do you mean?"

Branwell made his eyes wide and began to flap his arms like a bird. "Mad, mad, it's a family trait." He began to dance around the room, his long, thin legs jerking out from under his smock, making him look like a scarecrow.

"Stop it! You're acting like a fool."

Branwell laughed, and Charlotte was alarmed by the edge of hysteria in his voice. "You're the fool. Do you think we can simply stop? Do you think he'll let us?"

"Shh!" Charlotte hissed, eyeing the door.

He spun across the floor, arms wide, knocking over a stack of books. "Two little fools made a bargain, and now their lives are lost!"

"Branwell!" There were certain words they never said to each other, and *bargain* was one of them. "Hush! Honestly! I thought I heard something." She rose and opened the door, but no one was there. She looked both ways down the hall. There had been something—the creak of floorboards—but the parsonage was old, and it made all sorts of sounds.

Branwell stopped his capering and came to stand behind her. "Was it Emily?"

"Perhaps. Our voices were raised, and it's not above her to eavesdrop." She went to the desk and took up her sketchbook and pencil box.

"Where are you going?"

"I'll work in my room."

"Oh." Branwell looked genuinely disappointed. "You don't have to do that. I enjoy your company."

Charlotte could only gape. "I really don't understand you at all, Branwell," she said, and she nudged past him out the door.

EMILY

ARGAIN, EMILY THOUGHT, HER CHIN IN HER hands. She was sure her brother had used that word. *Two little fools made a bargain.* What bargain? And with whom?

"Tabby," she asked, straightening up, "didn't you tell us a story once about a pact . . . between some wicked thing and . . . someone you knew? Was it your mother?"

Tabby squinted at her for a moment, then pushed a knife toward her across the kitchen table. "Pilloputate!" she said.

What she meant was: "Peel a potato." And what she meant by *that* was: "If you want a story, you are going to have to work for it."

Emily pulled a very large bowl of potatoes toward herself. The old wooden table where she sat took up most of the small kitchen and was scarred from many years of slicing and chopping.

"My mother would never make a pact with Old Tom, I'll have you know," Tabby said, after Emily had begun to peel. "No more'n I would."

Old Tom. Emily had heard of him, of course. Whenever anyone claimed to see something strange on the moor, be it the ghost of a loved one or a brownie or the spectral hound, Tabby always said that they must have displeased Old Tom. Depending on which story she was telling, either these creatures were mad visions sent by him or they were his "minions" taking revenge.

"But she saw him?" Emily asked, frowning as fragments of the story came back to her. "And there *was* something about a bargain, wasn't there?"

Tabby gave a stir to the stew she was keeping warm on the hob, then fetched a large bunch of carrots from the sideboard and sat down next to Emily. "What made you think on that story?"

Emily kept her eyes on her potato. Eavesdropping was wrong and beneath her, and it was Charlotte's fault for making her stoop to it. "Nothing."

Tabby gave her a sidelong glance but didn't challenge her. She picked up a carrot and began to scrape. "Folks saw a lot of things afore the factories come. Haworth was a different place then. Why, when I was a young'un, our only tie to the outside world were the pack horses that come through town once a week." Her fingers paused as she remembered. "How I listened for the bells on those harnesses. 'Twere an event, their coming. They brung us our needles and our apples and our sugar, and took away our packets of wool. Even Leeds was worlds away t' me then. And London might as well have been the moon."

"But what about Old Tom?" Emily asked, trying to keep any impatience out of her voice. Getting Tabby to talk wasn't difficult, but sometimes steering her toward a particular topic was like steering a wayward sheep toward a pen.

"Harken her grilling me like a magistrate," Tabby teased. "Must be some important information you're wanting me to impart." She smiled and pushed her carrots over to Emily. "Worth scraping these, I expect. Once you've done with the tayters, of course."

Emily nodded without a word.

"Maybe I was wrong to tell you childer such stories," Tabby said, standing again. She could no more stop telling stories than a skylark could stop singing, but Emily didn't point this out. "You were such sweet little motherless waifs, the four of you. You'd gobble up me ramblings like they were food and you were starved for 'em, and then you'd look up at me with big famished eyes, wanting more."

She smiled at the memory, idly wiping her hands on her apron. Emily had to practically bite her own tongue to keep from hurrying her. There were beets on the sideboard, and Emily hated peeling those.

Tabby took a jar of flour from a high shelf. "Well, I'll tell you what happened exactly as me ma told it to me." She opened the jar and began to scatter flour onto the table. "She and her sister were coming home one night, all alone. They were going along that path in the valley that goes along Bridgehouse Beck, and they'd just reached that place where the water turns toward Stanbury—you knows it." Emily nodded. "The beck wasn't like it is now, of course—stinking o' mutton and rotten fish. 'Twere once quite a bonny place—had a sort of magic to it, if you can imagine, especially on a summer night, such as this was, with the moon glinting off t' water." Emily stopped her potato peeling and leaned forward.

"Now, they had some very good reason for going without a chaperone, I expects," Tabby said. This was as close as she ever came to suggesting Papa was lax on this point. "Only I never asked what. At any rate, there he was, Old Tom, sitting on a rock in the middle of the beck. He lifted his hat and greeted them very pleasant-like, me ma said, though he seemed to be paying most of his attentions to her sister Tabitha. I never did meet the woman, though I was named for her—beautiful and wild, by all accounts. Aye, Old Tom took a fancy to her."

"But who is Old Tom, exactly?" Emily asked. "Or what?"

Tabby shrugged and took a bowl of risen dough from the sideboard and turned it out onto the table. "Some folk say he's a devil, a sly old devil that somebody missed when they were all getting swept down to . . ." She nodded to the floor. "Others say he's Robin Goodfeller, the fairy, but he's no Puck like in your Shakespeare. I even once heard someone say that his name is Janus, and that the Romans brung him over in their boats, but I figure he was playing tricks on Yorkshire folk long afore that."

She pushed her sleeves above her elbows and began to work her dough. "So this Old Tom says to me Aunt Tabitha, 'What is your pleasure, my dear? A girl such as you is too beautiful for this little village. I expect you've a mind to see Paris or Venice or Rome.'" Tabby was kneading vigorously as she spoke. "Old Tom, he's standing on a rock in the middle of the river, and me ma can see right away there's sommat wrong about him. He's nobbutt Charlotte's height, and he's got yellow eyes and he's dressed all in furs, though the night were warm. Are you going to peel those tayters or not?"

"Yes, yes," Emily said, taking up her knife again.

"Well, me Aunt Tabitha was a vain thing, according to Mother, and so instead of ignoring him, she replied . . ." Tabby stopped kneading, put a hand on her chest, and batted her eyelashes. "'And will you take me to these places, sir?'" Emily laughed at the imitation.

"Old Tom grins like a fox and says"—Tabby lowered her voice to a growl—"'For a price, my dear. For a price.' But me Aunt Tabitha only tosses her pretty hair and says: 'I will marry a rich man, and he will take me to Paris and Venice and Rome, old man. You will get no price from me.'

"Now this was a foolish notion, o' course. The chances of a Haworth girl finding a rich feller to take her away was even less likely then than they are now. Still, Old Tom says: 'True that may be, true that may be. But could he take you here?'

"Then Old Tom give a sweep of his hand, and what does me

ma see but a strange scene just 'cross the beck. Folk are dancing on the grass—the strangest, most beautiful folk she's ever seen. Some have animal faces, and some have insect wings, and some have long blue hair the color of sky, and they're all dressed for a grand party. 'Come dance with the fairies,' Old Tom says. 'The price is the blue o' your eye. The blue o' your eye for a night o' dancing.'

"Well, it took a moment for them to understand what he was saying, but the long and short of it was, he was asking for Tabitha to give up one of her God-given gifts. Not her sight, mind, but the beauty of her eyes. Would you bargain that for one night o' frolic?"

Emily shook her head.

"Nay. Nor would me mother, but Tabitha had so many gifts, and she'd always loved tales of the fey folk, so she were sorely tempted. Luckily Mother had more sense. She picked up a rock and threw it at Old Tom. 'Gerraway, old devil!' she cried, and she hurried her sister away as the man in fur yelled blasphemies after 'em."

Tabby wiped her brow, leaving a smear of flour on her forehead. "And that's all," she said, beginning to knead again. "Me mother said she often dreamed o' those beautiful folk, but she never saw them nor Old Tom again."

Emily sighed at the potato in her hand, looking at the large pile she had still to skin. It was an interesting story, but she wasn't sure it had been worth the price. Old Tom might have something to do with Verdopolis and crossing over—or he might not. "I must have been very small when I heard this story," she said.

"Branwell used to love that one," Tabby said. "Once I caught him near t' wall out back, holding out a bonny shell someone had given him." She mimicked a high, little boy's voice: "'Old Tom, Old Tom, show me Paris, show me Rome. I'll give you this shell!'" Tabby laughed. "I gave him a swat, I don't mind saying— not that I think Old Tom is a danger in Haworth now."

Emily stared. Tabby had acted out the little scene, and when she'd gotten to the part where Branwell had offered up the shell, she had held out her empty hand, palm upward, just as Charlotte and Branwell did whenever they crossed over.

CHARLOTTE

LOOKING AT HERSELF IN THE MIRROR WASN'T usually something Charlotte did any more than was necessary, but now she forced herself to stare. She had finished her drawing of Anne and was sitting at the dressing table in the bedroom she shared with Emily. There was nothing more starkly real than her own pinched features in the glass; examining them kept her mind from wandering back to Verdopolis.

There were many things she could be doing—starting another drawing, planning tomorrow's lessons, helping Tabby in the kitchen—but a heaviness in the air and in her heart kept her from acting. She got up and opened the window, but there was no breeze. Emily was in the backyard. She was gazing out across the moor, where storm clouds were gathering. As

Charlotte watched, Emily climbed the low stone wall and set out toward the darkening horizon. Foolish girl. She was sure to get caught in the rain and miss her tea, but Charlotte found she didn't have the will to call her back.

"I seem to be made of sorrow," said a voice. Mary Henrietta's voice.

"No," Charlotte said out loud.

There would be no more hearing the voices of her characters, no more writing down their words. Writing would keep them alive for her somehow, and if they lived she would eventually cross over to them. It was inevitable. She must turn away from her beautiful people forever.

She sat back down in front of the mirror and sighed. Her hair was particularly limp this afternoon, and there was an angry red blemish in the center of her forehead, but there was something strangely steadying in the plainness of her own face. Nothing so ill-favored could ever exist in Verdopolis. From the mirror came an answering sigh.

Charlotte's stomach tightened. The sound hadn't been in her head; she'd actually heard it. She looked around, thinking something might have fooled her senses—a piece of paper falling to the floor, perhaps, or a bird fluttering past the window.

"Why does tragedy hang around me like a shroud?" said Mary Henrietta. "It is the truest thing about me."

This time Charlotte knew what she heard was real. The voice had come from the mirror, she was sure of it. She leaned forward. There, in the mirror's depths, was an image. It was blurred and dark at first, but it soon began to coalesce. An elegant jaw. Rose-petal lips. A sadness around the eyes. Mary Henrietta, the beautiful duchess, turned her head this way and that, oblivious to Charlotte, examining her perfect complexion.

"All Zamorna's wives and lovers end this way," she said. "In sighing."

Mina Laury was behind her, working through the duchess's chestnut curls with a silver comb. Though less refined, the maid was almost as pretty as the mistress, with her bright blue eyes and buxom charm, but now those eyes were dimmed and her brow was creased with worry. "Do not trouble yourself with such unwholesome thoughts, milady. I pray you."

Charlotte blinked, expecting this vision to disappear at any moment, but everything was perfectly clear now. Beyond the two women, a lady's dressing room was visible, ornate with lace and frills and dainty furnishings. It was not the dressing room of Wellesley House, but of course it wouldn't be, Charlotte thought with a pang of regret. Wellesley House had burned.

"I feel that I have been all Zamorna's loves," Mary Henrietta said. "Lady Helen Victorine, poor Rosamund, Marion Hume— they are all me. We are all the same idea, and we all die."

"Die! Sweet lady, do not speak the ugly word! I cannot bear it."

Charlotte had no sense that she was creating this conversation, and yet Mary Henrietta was voicing a truth that sometimes troubled her. All her heroines died, though she never intended it when she created them. Each time, she believed that Zamorna and his new love would live happily ever after—but this never came to pass. Now it seemed to Charlotte that all his lovers had been doomed from the start, that their deaths had always been there, overshadowing them—and she found she didn't want this for Mary Henrietta. Branwell had been right when he said that there was something luminous about her.

A thought sprang to her mind. Not only did Zamorna's lovers die, but there was often some loyal friend or servant who followed her mistress to the grave. With a sickening feeling in the pit of her stomach, Charlotte realized that Mina Laury might be doomed as well. Branwell was right about that, too: Charlotte's stories did repeat themselves.

"Why, Mina," Mary Henrietta said, "you're crying."

"I'm not." The maid bent to the mirror, blotting her eyes with a handkerchief. "It's only . . . I'm sure I would not wish to live without you, milady."

"Oh, my dear, sweet girl. You must not take my foolish talk so seriously. I have had such horrible dreams of late—I'm certain they are to blame for my dark mood."

Mina sniffed. "You have told me nothing about your dreams."

"I did not wish to trouble you—and you have no right to scold, my dear. I hear you calling out at night, and yet you do not confide in me." She patted her maid's hand. "Our nightmares are not so remarkable, I suppose, considering the upheavals in our lives. Let us blame my wicked father. I know that Zamorna blames him for all our woes. How strange that Rogue has set the whole city buzzing about the Genii. Do they exist or don't they? Is he mad or isn't he?"

Mina laughed through her tears and picked up the comb again. "He is a fool, I say."

Mary Henrietta smiled up at her. "Get my other comb, will you, my dear? This one pulls my hair."

As soon as Mina turned away, Mary Henrietta's smile fell, and sorrow returned to her face. "I wish the Genii did exist," she said softly. "I would ask them why death pulls at me so."

"And I wish I could save you," Charlotte whispered to the glass, but she somehow felt it was beyond her power. Her story was progressing without her now—but perhaps that's what stories always did. Perhaps the control she'd always thought she'd had was an illusion. She and Branwell created characters with needs and desires and flaws and then set them on their paths. Everything that happened afterward, all the collisions and disasters, were inevitable as clockwork, and even the Genii couldn't stop them.

"Oh, strange gods," Mary Henrietta said, "if this mirror were a portal to your world, I would smash through and make you answer me." There was a hint of anger in her voice that surprised Charlotte.

Mary Henrietta leaned toward the mirror, her brow furrowed, and Charlotte thought she must have found some minuscule blemish, but then a look of dread struck her face. "Oh, Mina, come look! There is something in the glass. Something hideous."

Charlotte put her hands over her mouth in surprise, afraid that they could see her, afraid that her own face might seem hideous to such perfect people.

Mina reappeared, bending over her mistress's shoulder. "But there is nothing, milady."

"You do not see it?" Mary Henrietta's eyes widened. "Oh, heavens. Am I going mad?" She touched her cheeks, her hair.

"See what?"

"It is . . . myself," Mary Henrietta said, peering close. "But I am so changed. Oh, Mina. Is this some harbinger?"

"There is nothing. Come away. Come away now." Mina put her arm around her mistress and tried to get her to rise from her chair.

"Oh, tell me this face is not my own."

"You are becoming overwrought. I beg you, come away!"

Charlotte stared into the glass, and for a moment she seemed to catch her heroine's eye. Then all at once Mary Henrietta began to transform, the perfect symmetry of her face twisting to irregularity and ugliness. Her cheeks grew gaunt and hollow, her lovely hair matted and uncared for.

"I have nightmares of this face," said Mary Henrietta's voice, but it was faint and fading, and the words didn't match the lips of the woman who now grinned at Charlotte from the mirror.

"Who are you?" Charlotte breathed. She felt sure that this new person could see her, could see *into* her. "What are you?"

The woman only smiled wider, showing a blackened bottom tooth. There was something terribly unnerving about her expression, something wrong and broken in her eyes, and yet there was something familiar about her, too.

She began to laugh—a low, slow "ha . . . ha . . . ha"—and Charlotte felt a shudder go through her body. She knew that sound, had heard it once long ago. She put her hands over her ears.

The strange woman lifted her fist and began to knock at the mirror glass, so hard it set the dressing table vibrating. Beyond her, the dainty frills and furnishings were gone, replaced with unpainted walls and a single candle guttering on a plain table.

"Go away!" Charlotte said. She stood, knocking over her chair, and shrank back into a corner of her room. She was afraid of this creature, afraid that there was only a thin sheet of glass between them.

The woman's laugh was loud now. It seemed to echo through the parsonage—a mirthless and tragic cackling. She knocked harder and harder upon the mirror. Charlotte's dressing table rocked back and forth. Then—*crack!*—the mirror broke outward, scattering shards of glass onto the bare floor all the way to Charlotte's feet.

EMILY

WHEN EMILY STOOD IN THE FRONT YARD she was in town: The graveyard, the church, and the Sunday school were straight ahead, and beyond them were the tavern and the main road leading down to the center of Haworth. Guests and parishioners saw the front yard. When Emily stood in the back, however, she was on the moor, with nothing beyond the low stone wall but rolling heather and heath. The only guests who came here were the wild moor sheep that sometimes wandered in through the wall's gap, leaving behind little tufts of wool caught on the shrubbery. It made sense that Tabby had seen Branwell standing at the wall trying to bargain with Old Tom. For the Brontë children, this was the place where civilization ended and wilderness began.

Emily stood there now. The air hung still and heavy. Even if she hadn't been able to see the dark clouds gathering over the moor, she would have known a storm was coming. The whole world seemed to be waiting for it. She closed her eyes and held out her hand, feeling as foolish as a child. Was it as simple as this? Had her brother and sister simply held out their hands, making offers to Old Tom until one was finally accepted? And if so, what had they given?

Perhaps Charlotte had offered up her beauty. But no, she had been plain for as long as Emily could remember; beauty was not a gift she had to bargain with. What then? Not cleverness. Neither Charlotte nor Branwell would ever give up that. Their health? Branwell and Charlotte *were* rather prone to illness. Emily shivered at the idea. That was a terrible bargain, but it was one she would give to see Gondal again. And Rogue.

Emily glanced behind her and saw Charlotte at an upstairs window. Quickly she looked away so as not to catch her eye. Emily was too close to the parsonage here, too close to town, to her sister's watchful eye. This might have been the right place for Branwell and Charlotte, but Emily had another place she'd always gone when she wanted to feel close to wildness. Without looking back, she climbed over the wall and set out quickly across the hills.

It wasn't until she slowed her pace and began to pick her way down the steep gully of Sladen Beck that she noticed the silence.

The wind was almost always blowing on the moor, and so its stillness seemed eerie. Never before had she been so aware of the sound of her own breath and of the grass brushing past her legs. Around her, purple foxglove drooped, the flowers too heavy for their stalks. In his novels Sir Walter Scott called these deadman's bells, and Tabby said that if you ever found a white one it meant there would be a death.

When she got to the beck she found the water strangely dark, reflecting a sky that was nearly black. She sat down on her favorite stone and looked out across the rolling landscape. Everything was so still. She loved the way the crevasses between the hills grew so green this time of year, hiding secret valleys, but the darkened sky made everything ominous and dim as twilight. Above her a hawk screamed, but somehow it was just a part of the stillness. She could hear its wings beating the air—*whump, whump, whump.*

Something bright caught her attention—a smudge of rust against the green. A fox. He came toward her, bushy tail held straight behind, eyes scanning the ground for movement. How long and sleek he was, what luscious fur, what perfect and precise movements. He seemed to be a visitor from an even wilder place than this.

The fox came within a few feet of Emily's stone, and she held her breath. She could see his sharp needle teeth, his twitching whiskers; she even caught the scent of his musk. Suddenly he leapt, all four feet leaving the earth. Something squealed. Emily gasped.

A moment later the fox was staring at her, a dead vole hanging from his mouth.

"How beautiful you are," Emily whispered. "I'd give anything to make a world as beautiful as you." She squeezed her eyes shut. "*Once there was an island in the middle of the sea. It was called Gondal, and it was a harsh and lonely place.*"

She clasped her hands together. "Old Tom, Old Tom. Everything my sister Charlotte and my brother Branwell have given in their years of crossing over, and everything they will give in years to come, this I offer, all at once, for one passage to my beautiful world."

She opened her eyes. The fox was gone, with nothing to prove he was ever there but a stain of blood on the ground. Beyond where he had been there was a strange blurriness, a slight warp in the light as if she were looking through a lens. It looked like a rip in the world. She stood up and held out her hand to the rip in the world, palm upward. It hurled itself at her, swallowing her whole.

At first everything was dark, and then a dim light appeared in a great, gray sky, illuminating a flat and empty world. "*The island of Gondal was full of wind and weather,*" Emily said. A wind blew up, and dark clouds poured into the sky. "*Heather and hills.*"

She smiled as what she invoked appeared. She'd had years to

imagine what she'd make, a place like her own moor but wilder—more beautiful and horrible. A warm rain beat down on the brim of her bonnet and she pulled it off, lifting her face to the sky.

"*Foxes and hawks!*" she said. "*Voles and mice and rabbits.*" Her world would have everything she loved best. "*Rocks, crags, linnets, curlews, dogs, cats!*" She broke into a run across the heath, shouting now.

"*Lightning and catastrophe!*"

Thunder cracked, and something bright knocked her off her feet.

"Oh!" She suddenly found herself in the mud on all fours. There was a black circle of scorched earth next to her and the smell of electricity in her nostrils.

She stumbled to her feet. The rain was harder now, not so pleasant as it had been a moment before. Thunder boomed, and another bolt of lightning struck a sapling just ahead, splitting it in two, making her scream.

"Help, someone!" She turned and started to run. Wind and rain drove at her, and she could hardly see where she was going. Ahead of her was a stand of trees, and she raced toward it as another flash blinded her. She ran straight into someone's arms.

Emily lifted her face to dark eyebrows and heavy, brooding eyes. "Rogue?" He was hatless and drenched with rain. "We must run or we'll be struck!" She tried to twist away, but he held her tight.

"It's no use running," he said. One hand was on her waist

and he moved the other to her cheek, drawing her closer. For a second, Emily thought he would kiss her, but instead he only stared into her eyes. His deep voice seemed to reverberate in her chest. "Listen to me. You made this place. You must make the lightning stop."

She gazed up at him, heart bumping. His hand was warm against her face. She felt that if he moved it, caressed her in any way or showed her any kindness, she would shake apart into a thousand pieces.

"*The storm is ended*," she said, pushing out of his grasp. The lightning abruptly stopped. She turned away and looked out over the hills. In all directions, clouds were scurrying away from them, like rabbits who had seen a wolf.

Emily wiped her face with her sleeve. "This is Gondal," she said without turning around. "It is a wild, lawless place, where ships are wrecked upon the rocks and storms rip the sky asunder . . ."

Thunder rumbled far away, making her give a little gasp. Rogue put a hand on her shoulder. "Yes, yes. I've had an adequate display of the storms."

Emily stiffened at his touch. "It is inhabited by only the worst criminals and scoundrels."

"I like it already. Did you make it for me?"

"Certainly not." She stepped away from his hand, but felt the weight of it on her shoulder even after it was gone.

"And yet I'm here."

She made no answer.

"Come, come. Aren't we friends now?"

She turned to face him. "Friends? You had your hands around my sister's throat. And a knife to mine."

He shrugged. "That was in another world, far away. If you will forgive me my many crimes, I will graciously agree to forgive you."

"Forgive *me*?"

"That's right, little goddess. When we see each other in Verdopolis, we can renew hostilities, if we wish."

"There is no more Verdopolis," she said a little sadly. "The other Genii have vowed to abandon it. I fear they mean it this time."

"Indeed? Well, all the more reason." He turned and walked away from her down the hill, lifting his arms to the sky. "A new beginning for a new world."

Emily followed after. Now that the rain had stopped, Gondal began to blossom and burgeon before her eyes. The grass grew greener, and the stand of trees ahead of them burst into pink and white bloom. One tree towered over the others; it seemed too big and old to belong to such a young world.

"This way!" she said, pushing past him. The ground was spongy and waterlogged under her feet.

Before she could reach the tree, its blossoms began to fall, white petals drifting toward her like snow. She laughed, turning to Rogue in wonder, and saw that the heather was blooming behind him—tongues of purple fire spreading over the hills.

"I can't tell if it's spring or summer," Emily said, petals swirling around them, getting stuck on their clothes and wet hair. "Everything is happening at once."

Rogue raised an eyebrow at her and shrugged. "Such things are beyond my understanding."

I've done it, she thought. *I've made a world. And it will be so much better than Charlotte's.*

"Apple?" Rogue asked. He ducked under the tree's spreading branches, beckoning her to follow.

It was a different place there—dark and holy and still. Emily felt the urge to whisper. It reminded her of her father's church, but it smelled like green moss and blossoms and turned earth. All around them little green apples were swelling and turning red. Rogue pulled one from a branch and tossed it at her.

Emily took a bite. Crisp and sweet. "Just imagine," she said. "The taste of this apple came from my own brains. I'm really quite brilliant, aren't I?"

Rogue grinned at her and took a bite of another apple, wiping juice from his chin. "A Genius."

"Now, don't this bring back memories?" said someone. From around the tree slid the figure of an old man not five feet tall. His face wore a sour smile.

"S'Death," Emily said. "What are you doing here?"

He made a sweeping gesture with his arms. "I have come to see this new-made world."

Emily knew the character from Verdopolis and was vexed by the interruption, but Rogue only laughed and slapped his friend on the back. "In a world of scoundrels and thieves, I suppose we must expect Mr. R. P. King."

"Scoundrels and thieves?" S'Death repeated. "Well, I never. You'll pardon me, miss, if I say you don't look the part of neither. Isn't this chit a bit young for you, Rogue?"

Rogue put his arm around Emily's shoulder. "This chit, as you call her, is one of the Genii. She is the goddess who has pulled this new world from the black ether of nothingness."

"The black ether of nothingness. You don't say." S'Death raised an eyebrow in doubt, then glanced out over the green and purple hills and shrugged. "It's very pretty, I suppose."

"Pretty!" cried Rogue. "It's miraculous."

"To be sure, to be sure. Far be it from me to criticize a goddess…" He paused.

"But?" said Rogue.

"Well, if I might inquire: What are the likes of you and I to do in this land of only wicked scoundrels?"

Emily stepped forward. "*You*, Mr. King, may go to the devil." Both men chuckled at this. "*He* is Alexander Rogue, highwayman and thief, leader of bandits, wickedest of them all."

S'Death snorted.

"What?" Rogue said. "You don't approve?"

"In the name of murder, you sweet babies, you can't have a world with just thieves and blackguards. You've got to have a few cullies."

"Cullies?" Emily asked, unfamiliar with the word.

"Dupes, sapheads, people to rob, my lovely," S'Death said with a leer. "Victims of our wicked outrages."

"That's true, you know," Rogue said. "Do make us a few cullies, Genius." He slapped Emily heartily on the back as he had slapped S'Death. She didn't like it. "And make them rich and fat, while you're at it."

Emily lifted her chin. "The Genii do not take orders." But at that moment a man riding a white donkey came up over the hill in front of them.

"Drink to the maiden of bashful fifteen. Now to the widow of fifty . . . ," he sang. "Here's to the flaunting, extravagant queen and here's to the housewife that's thrifty." He was obviously drunk. The donkey stopped at the top of the rise, panting. It was a very small donkey to be carrying such a large man, and the beast was further burdened by a dozen saddlebags that looked suspiciously like they might contain gold coins. The man shook his reins, but the donkey only lowered his head and began to crop the grass.

"Let the toast pass. Drink to the lass. I'll warrant she'll prove an excuse for the glass."

"Exactly," Rogue said with a laugh as the song continued. "He's the very thing."

"A bit *too* on the mark, if you ask me," S'Death murmured.

"Don't be such a crosspatch." Rogue reached into his jacket, pulling out a pistol that hadn't been there a moment before. "Look, the lady's thought of everything."

"No!" Emily cried, grabbing his arm.

Rogue furrowed his brow, not understanding her displeasure. "I'm going to shoot him. Isn't that what highwaymen do?"

"Not in cold blood," she insisted. But wasn't he right? Wasn't that exactly what highwaymen did?

Rogue lowered his pistol. "Well, S'Death, we are on the horns of a dilemma. On the one hand, I am becoming rather fond of this fetching little goddess. On the other, it seems a bad precedent to set, letting her get her own way so early in our acquaintance."

S'Death sucked his teeth, nodding. "Add to that, the cully is so clearly meant to be shot."

"Here's to the wife with a face full of woe! Here's to the damsel that's merry!"

S'Death winced at a sour note. "If only to stop that caterwauling."

"I've got it," Rogue said to her. "Tell me the name of one of the elder Genii—who he is in Verdopolis and how I may recognize him—and this cully may go on his way."

"Certainly not."

"But you yourself said that they have abandoned Verdopolis. What does it matter now?"

That was true enough, and Emily didn't want the cully to die. She didn't know why the idea of shooting him bothered her so much. It simply didn't seem right. There was something innocent about him, in his white tunic on his white donkey. It would be murder, the first murder in her pristine new world, and that would be a grave thing, not to be taken lightly.

"All right," she said with a shrug. "Since it doesn't matter." She smiled. "Tell me, Rogue, didn't you ever suspect that Lord Thornton Witkin Sneaky was more than he seemed?"

"Thornton? Never!" said S'Death in amazement. "And he a fellow redhead!"

Rogue said nothing, but as Emily watched, his face hardened to a look of pure malice. It frightened her. He looked more like the old Rogue, the one soured by drink and wickedness. "I counted him among my friends," he said.

"Never trust anyone, that's the lesson here," said S'Death.

"Well, that's that, then," said Rogue. He turned and lifted his pistol. A shot cracked. The singing ended. The cully slid off the donkey and fell to the ground with a thud.

"You've killed him!" Emily cried.

The white donkey brayed pitifully. All around her, the leaves on the tree grew brown. Red apples shriveled and shrank.

"For a Genius, she's a bit dim," S'Death said, chuckling.

Rogue turned to her, his face no longer quite so hard. A curl of smoke rose from the pistol in his hand. Rotten apples fell from the tree, splatting at her feet. "Poor little girlie," he said, and there did seem to be genuine pity in his voice. "I told you you'd get your fingers bit."

S'Death's chuckle had turned into a full-blown howl of laughter. He pulled out a handkerchief and wiped his eyes. "Oh, the look on her face."

Emily backed away. She wanted to scream. She wanted to tear both their eyes out. But hadn't she said she would make a world as wild as the fox?

She held out her hand, palm up. "Take me back," she said. And then she was sitting on her stone by Sladen Beck again, cold and shaking, a heavy rain pelting down.

BRANWELL

I T MIGHT HAVE ONLY BEEN THE RAIN.

It droned against the roof above him, against the window glass, sometimes harder, sometimes softer. Like breathing. In, out. In, out. Branwell glanced at his reflection in the mirror propped against the chair, then lifted his paintbrush.

In, out.

It might not have been the rain, though. It might have been someone breathing. It might have been someone breathing just behind him, just outside the mirror's frame.

No.

Yes.

The breath was labored. Rattling. It hurt. It was fought for. Last breaths.

In, out. In, out. The rain grew harder. He didn't turn around.

Every stroke he added to the canvas was a disaster. The figures of his sisters were all right—Charlotte looked rather pretty—but his own face was distorted. Bloated. His brush made staccato jabs against the palette.

A cough.

Was it a cough?

In, out. In, out.

"If I turn around, will you be there?" His voice shook.

Thunder rumbled in the distance. The rain was like fistfuls of shot hurled against the house.

"Thirsty," someone said—or didn't say. Branwell winced.

In the mirror, a flicker of movement. Without thinking, he wheeled around.

His paintbrush dropped to the floor. All sound stopped, even the rain.

"Elizabeth."

She wore a white shift. The urge to take her in his arms was as strong as the urge to run, and so he did nothing.

"You are so small." She had been his older sister once, but he had grown. She had not.

Elizabeth's shoulders rose and fell. Her mouth gaped. She could barely stand.

"Why is it always you and not Maria?" he asked, tears in his eyes. "She's the one I want to see." It occurred to him that perhaps his question contained the answer.

"Banny."

Her hand, heartbreakingly small, reached out to him. He'd forgotten the smell of a dying person. Sweet. Horrible.

"Would you get me a drink of water, Banny dear?"

His heart lurched. It was the last thing she'd ever said to him—her dying words.

"Branwell," said a voice through the door. Charlotte's voice. "Will you go and look for Emily? She's out on the moor in this rain. Papa is growing worried."

Branwell didn't take his eyes from Elizabeth's face. "Coming," he whispered.

ANNE

"WE HAVE BEEN FRANTIC," ANNE SAID, holding open the back door. "Papa and Branwell are out looking for you."

In the doorway, Emily looked hunched and small. She wore no cloak, and her clothes were wet through.

"Heavens above!" Tabby said, coming into the kitchen. "Get her in. Get her in!" Tabby bustled Emily toward the stove. It had already been stoked for the eventuality of wet people and for the making of beef tea, which Tabby believed could cure all ills. "Where's her bonnet, I ask you? In her hand, where it does no good." Emily's bonnet was, in fact, dangling by its strings from her fingers. "Now don't you touch her, Anne. You'll get those bandages wet."

"I'd like to help," said Anne, who was standing aside while Tabby peeled off Emily's clothes.

Tabby only blew out her cheeks and shook her head. "Why, Jasper Pheasant's got more sense 'an you chicks. One gets herself burned, t' other don't know enough to get out of the rain."

Anne felt a little stung by this. Tabby had treated her like a baby since she'd come back from Verdopolis, hardly letting her near the stove. Charlotte had told everyone that Anne burned her fingers while making gingerbread. No one questioned this, even though there was no gingerbread to be seen, and none of her siblings seemed to give the lie a second thought. It was only Anne who felt mortified by it, who hung her head whenever anyone asked after her hands. She remembered how shocked she had been when Papa had called Charlotte a liar at the breakfast table, but now she began to wonder if lying hadn't become a bit too easy for her siblings. They were beginning to remind her of the stories in her Sunday school book about wicked children who came to bad ends.

"Rub yourself all over with them towels, now," Tabby said to Emily, "while I tell Charlotte and Miss Branwell you've returned."

"I don't want to see them," Emily said. She was down to her shift now, and she hugged herself in front of the stove, her head lowered, a curtain of wet hair obscuring her face. "Tell them I am going to my room."

"Not dripping all over my floor, you're not."

When she was gone, Emily grabbed Anne by the arm. "I've done something terrible," she said. She lifted her face, and Anne was shocked by how very pale and harried she looked.

"Are you ill? What's happened?" But even as she asked, the truth began to dawn on her. "Oh, Emily. What have you done?"

"Something is gone!" There was anguish in her sister's voice and in her eyes. "Something was ripped away from me. Oh, Anne, am I ugly? Is my eye still blue?"

"Calm yourself!" Anne fumbled with a towel, managing to wrap it around her sister's shoulders. "I don't know what you're saying. You look exactly as you did before."

"Take care of your bandages."

"Never mind that. Sit down. You're shivering." She steered her sister toward a chair.

Emily sat in silence for a few moments, staring straight ahead, her breath in shallow gasps. "I felt well when I was in Gondal," she said after a while, "but the moment I crossed back home . . ." She took Anne's bandaged hand, looking up at her. "When I crossed back home, I felt something leaving me, draining away from me. I was so tired, I could hardly make the walk from Sladen Beck."

Anne forced herself not to wince in pain as her sister squeezed her fingers tight. "You've done it, then? You've made a world?"

"Yes. And I paid a price. I paid a price, but I don't know . . ." She blinked back tears and looked to the floor. "He wasn't worth it, whatever it was."

"Rogue? You saw him?"

Emily nodded, and her story spilled out. Old Tom. Her bargain. Her world. Anne could hardly believe her sister's foolishness.

"I shall never go back," Emily said. "I can't. Rogue was too wicked." She looked up at her again. "But what did I pay? It was something, something important, I know it. Oh, Anne," she cried. "What if it was my soul?"

CHARLOTTE

HARLOTTE'S MIND WANDERED ALL THROUGH evening prayers. She jumped at every sound and twice caught herself chewing her nails, a habit she had broken herself of years before. Even Tabby remarked on her nervousness, and, before Charlotte went upstairs, made her down some of the beef tea she had made for Emily.

She'd heard the laughter once more that afternoon, but a fierce wind had arrived with the rain, battering the house and whistling around the chimney, and she told herself it was only its blowing she had heard. If it weren't for the broken mirror in the bedroom, she might have been able to convince herself she had imagined that awful woman as well, but every time she saw its empty frame, she knew with a sinking feeling that it wasn't true.

When she tried to tell Branwell what had happened, he only snapped, and Charlotte didn't wish to burden the girls. And so, with no one left to confide in, she found herself standing in front of her father's door.

"Come in," he called, when she had worked up the courage to knock. He was sitting in a high-backed wooden chair loading his pistols for the night. "And how is dear Emily?"

Emily. Wandering about in a rainstorm. Making everyone sick with worry. *Dear Emily is as selfish and thoughtless as always,* Charlotte thought. "Recovering well."

He motioned her toward the chair opposite, and she sat down. Beyond him was a small mirror over a chest of drawers. She dreaded seeing a glimpse of that woman's face in its depths, and yet Charlotte's eyes were drawn to it again and again throughout their conversation.

Papa looked up at her expectantly but resumed his task when she didn't speak. He detached the ramrod from the barrel of one of his guns and used it to tamp down a round ball and some paper wadding, the pistol's one shot. Then he primed the pistol with powder from his horn and set it carefully on a side table next to its mate. He looked up once more, but still Charlotte couldn't find words. *I am hearing voices. I am afraid of mirrors. I made a bargain with a creature out of one of Tabby's stories, and now I might be lost.* How did one begin such a conversation?

"Ha, ha, ha, ha, ha."

Charlotte froze. The windows rattled like something trying to get in.

"There are demons on the wind tonight," Papa said. He didn't mean this literally—he was a modern man—and yet he touched the nearer pistol when he said it, as if part of him believed there was something real to fear.

Charlotte made an attempt at a smile. "Yes. Aren't there." The awkward silence dropped over them again.

Papa gestured to the two weapons. "You know, every night I load these, and every night they go unfired. And yet in the morning when I awake I feel as if I have left my family unprotected, as if something has been taken in the night."

Charlotte blinked in surprise, sure he had divined that all was not well in his home. Guilt sliced through her. She and the others kept so much from him.

"I worry," he continued. "About you and the girls. About Branwell. He took it very badly when you were away at school, you know. His nerves. Soon you will leave us to make your living, and I fear for what will happen to him when he is parted from your influence."

"My influence?" Charlotte gave a short laugh. "He pays no heed to me, I assure you."

"He worships you—no, do not frown. He might not show his feelings, but they are there. Remember when he walked all that way to visit you at Roe Head School?"

Charlotte had to stop herself from rolling her eyes. "Yes, yes. Forty miles. A very long way." Papa often brought up this incident as proof of Branwell's affection for her.

"But you are not here to speak of him," he said, as if reading her thoughts.

"No."

Part of her longed to tell her father that she was in trouble, that she'd been a fool—she even took a breath to do so—but for some reason the words died on her lips. Her father seemed to see this. Charlotte shifted in her seat, reading the disappointment on his face.

"I have made many mistakes in the raising of you children, I'm sure, but I hope I have always been . . . approachable." He smiled. "You have a way of peering at a person that can be very disconcerting, my dear."

"Forgive me, but I've never heard you admit to a mistake before."

He gave a wave of his hand. "You are grown now. A child should always believe that his father is all-knowing."

Charlotte wasn't certain she agreed with this. "Papa," she asked, "why did you allow Anne and Emily and me to read whatever we wanted, to expand our minds, when in the end there is nothing for a woman to do? No suitable employment to challenge such a mind?"

She surprised herself with this question, and she could see

that her father was surprised as well. "Should I have raised my daughters to be stupid?"

"No. Perhaps. I don't know." She could hardly express what she was trying to say. "If I'd never known there was more to life, it would be easier to be content with what I have."

The chair creaked as he sat back to consider her words. "It was Maria who guided my ideas on education, I suppose," he said finally. "I saw that it would be a travesty not to nourish such an intellect, regardless of her sex."

"Maria?"

"She was an extraordinary girl, you know. A shining girl."

"Yes."

He smiled thoughtfully. "By the time she was eight she was reading the newspaper cover to cover and could talk like a grown man on all the topics of the day."

In truth Charlotte remembered Maria's sweetness more than her intelligence. She was one of those people who seemed never to be cross or impatient. A shining girl indeed.

"She would be married now," Papa said.

Charlotte smiled thinly. Her father never mentioned marriage in regard to his living daughters—perhaps he didn't wish to raise their hopes—but on the rare occasions that he spoke about Maria, it was a matter of course. She would be married. She would be happy.

Papa took off his spectacles and rubbed the bridge of his nose.

When he looked up at Charlotte, there was a vulnerability in his face that she had never seen before. "You would tell me, wouldn't you, if there was anything I should know?" The quaver in his voice embarrassed her.

"Of course." She said it quickly, wanting to placate him.

"Perhaps I am a fool to think there is something wrong, but when a man has lost his wife and two of his children, he begins to feel that everything he loves might slip through his fingers." He so rarely spoke of these losses that to bring them up seemed to break a long-standing taboo. "This feeling that all is not well in my house—I've had it before, you see. I don't believe in premonitions, but when you were small and the four of you girls were at that terrible school, I had a powerful presentiment that my family was in danger."

And yet you ignored it, she said to herself, and was surprised by the anger behind that thought.

He looked up at her. "I was so proud of you for going back. But Roe Head School wasn't like . . . that place, was it? I made quite sure it wasn't before I let you go."

That place. The Clergy Daughters' School at Cowan Bridge. The Brontës might say Maria's and Elizabeth's names only rarely, but that name was *never* mentioned.

Why didn't you make quite sure that Clergy Daughters' was a good school before you sent your children off to die there?

"Are you certain there is nothing you wish to tell me?" There was a pleading tone to his voice that she could no longer bear.

"Nothing, Papa." She stood up abruptly. "And now I must be off to bed." She leaned over and gave him a kiss.

It occurred to her that she had never believed, even as a child, that her father was all-knowing. She had never really forgiven him for what happened to Maria and Elizabeth. None of them had. And so a gulf had grown between them.

What hard and wicked children we've become, she thought as she softly closed his door.

CHARLOTTE

T HE SOUND OF LAUGHTER WOKE CHAR-
lotte from a deep sleep. "Ha . . . ha . . . ha." She
sat up, gripped by an unnameable fear. Next to
her in the bed, Emily was sleeping soundly. *I'm
imagining things,* Charlotte told herself. But she lit a candle from
the rushlight that was still burning on the table and carried it
out into the hall.

She went to each door and listened carefully: Anne and Aunt
Branwell's, Papa's, Tabby's. She stayed outside Branwell's door for
a long time, but all was quiet except for the low sound of the
wind sobbing and moaning around the house.

She was about to turn back to her room when a sound from
downstairs made her stop. Was someone there? A robber? Surely

everyone in Haworth knew that the parsonage had nothing to steal. Swallowing her fear, Charlotte cupped her flame to keep it from going out and started down.

On the stairs she stopped again, listening. The dream she'd been having came back to her, adding to her growing unease. In it her dead sisters had returned, but only Charlotte seemed to think this was remarkable. They sat on the sofa in the dining room, drinking tea like honored guests, looking exactly as she remembered them, and yet as the conversation wore on, she saw that they were changed. Their hair was elaborately curled and their dresses were too fine, as if they belonged to a different family now. Their talk was vain and shallow. They had forgotten what they once cared for.

In life they had been Charlotte's older sisters, but she was older than they were now, while they remained eleven and ten, just little girls. But no little girls should wear such wicked smirks upon their faces. There was no warmth in their eyes.

Charlotte shuddered as she got to the bottom of the steps. Quickly she strode down the corridor, but when she got to the dining room door, she hesitated, her hand on the knob, half believing that she would see them there, sitting on the sofa, drinking tea from the best cups. She felt her heartbeat quicken. *Don't be foolish*, she chastised herself. She opened the door. Inside all was dark, but there was something . . .

"Branwell!" she cried, nearly dropping her candle. "You gave me such a start." She lit a candle that was sitting on the dining room table and brought her own over to him. "What are you doing here in the dark?"

Branwell was in his nightshirt, the red blanket wrapped around his shoulders. His bare feet were up on the sofa, something never allowed. In his arms he cradled a large brown bottle. "What do I appear to be doing?" he said, and he took a drink.

Charlotte noticed that a second, empty bottle lay on the floor beside him. "You're drinking the beer!" Aunt Branwell made her own beer and kept it under lock and key in the storeroom.

"Very observant."

"But why?"

"Because we have no gin."

"Oh, Banny." She sat next to him on a cane chair, setting the candleholder on her knee. "Where will we hide the bottles? How did you get Aunt Branwell's key?"

"Stole it from her reticule."

"Oh!" She put her hand to her mouth. "What will Papa say?"

Branwell started to laugh. "What will Papa say? That seems to me to be the least of our worries." His laughter petered out, and Charlotte saw that his face in the dim light was tense and careworn. "You understand, don't you? I couldn't sleep with all their . . . What I mean is . . . Are you seeing things yet?"

Charlotte took a moment to answer. "Seeing and hearing."

Branwell nodded. "It will grow worse."

She wasn't alone, then—there was some relief in that, at least—but she was vexed he hadn't confided in her. "Is it because we've stopped crossing over? You warned me there would be consequences for abandoning our worlds, but I didn't know . . ."

"That we would go mad?"

Charlotte's grip tightened around the candleholder. "I am being plagued by illusions of some sort—I am *not* going mad."

Branwell shrugged. "Is there a difference?"

"Yes!" Outside, the wind whipped rain at the windowpanes. "Because *he* is sending them. It's not fair. We never said we would cross over forever. That wasn't the bargain."

"I don't think Old Tom cares."

"Hush," she warned, although she knew perfectly well that her younger sisters were fast asleep.

"Afraid he'll appear if we say his name? Old Tom, Old Tom, Old Tom." Branwell took another drink, grimacing at the taste. "He never does. That's part of his cleverness. If he doesn't show himself, it makes the bargain seem less real. But it is, it is real."

"So he plans to harass us until we break down and cross over to Verdopolis again?"

Branwell nodded. "I think so."

Charlotte sat back in her chair. Branwell said nothing more, so for a while she sat in the semidarkness, watching him drink. The wind was like a dissonant kind of music, made with flutes or organ pipes.

"We won't do it," she said finally, straightening up. "We won't cross over. We'll simply go about our lives and ignore whatever minions he cares to send our way."

"Charlotte," Branwell said quietly, almost sadly, "it's only a matter of time. The voices. The apparitions. I cannot hold on forever."

She felt a lump coming to her throat. "If we continue to pay the price for crossing over, we'll die young. It's as simple as that."

"I know."

"For God's sake, Branwell. Ignore them. We have our whole lives ahead of us."

"Lives of torment."

"Oh, stop whining!" she shouted. She jogged her candleholder as she said this, spilling wax onto her knee, which she struggled to brush away. She lowered her voice. "I cannot bear to hear you complain about your poor life. At least you'll be an artist. You'll be doing something fulfilling. If I had your advantages and expectations . . ."

"They come at a cost, you know, my *advantages and expectations*."

"Yes, I do know," she snapped. She was thinking of his paints, of Mr. Robinson's two guineas a lesson.

Branwell crossed his arms protectively around his bottle, looking wearied by her anger. "You are so lucky that no one will ever ask you to *be* anything."

"What in heaven's name does that mean?"

"It means that I see," he said. "I see that you are as good as I am or better at everything I do. I see that it is unfair that you will probably never be a painter or a writer or anything else you want to be because you are a woman. But what would you like me to do about it, exactly?" He turned his head away from her, still hugging the bottle.

Charlotte had never heard such an admission from her brother. She was on the verge of putting her hand on his shoulder, but a moment later, his tone turned petulant.

"And why have you never tried to see things from my perspective? You do understand, don't you, that if Father died tomorrow, we would be homeless? The parsonage belongs to the church, not to us. It would fall to me to support you girls."

"God help us, then," she muttered.

"Yes!" he cried. "Now you understand. God help you indeed." He sat up on the sofa, shifting so that he and she were facing each other. "Charlotte, do you know why Father and I chose painting as my profession? Do you?" He shook his bottle at her to emphasize his words, and she could hear the beer sloshing inside. "Because we quite simply could not think of anything else. Oh, I can write Greek with my left hand and Latin with my right, but I haven't been to school as you have. I haven't learned anything systematically. Do you know how difficult it is to make a living as a portrait painter? Mr. Robinson is a great artist, and for God's sake, the poor man is reduced to teaching me!"

He sat back again, slouching sulkily. Charlotte went through a hundred arguments in her mind, but could think of nothing that would rouse her brother from his despondency. The wind didn't sound like music to her now, or even like laughter. It sounded like the low cries of something truly damned, something that suffered endlessly with no prospect of God or salvation.

"What exactly do you see in your visions?" she asked quietly. "What could be so terrible?"

"It's wrong to call them visions," Branwell said. "They're as solid as you or I."

"Fine, but what do you see?"

Branwell looked at her with pain in his eyes but didn't answer. In her stories, Tabby always said it was the see-er who chose what form Old Tom's minions would take. What could plague Branwell so?

A thought occurred to her. "Is that why you walked such a long way to visit me that time? Because you were seeing things then, too? Because you were being hounded by visions—or whatever you'd like me to call them—and wanted to confide in me?"

Papa had mentioned the incident just that evening. Branwell hadn't written to her; he had simply arrived at her school one day, dirty and perspiring, rudely demanding to see her. When Miss Wooler pulled her out of class, her first thought had been that someone must have died, but all he did was accuse her of breaking her promise to quit Verdopolis.

"I thought . . . I hoped . . . that you were seeing things, too," he said. "But I could tell that you weren't, simply by looking at you."

"Because I was writing and crossing over and you were not."

"Yes."

She winced, understanding now why he still held a grudge about it. The truth was, she had broken her promise before she even arrived at the new school. She'd been in the public coach on her way from Keighley to Roe Head. The farther she'd traveled from home, the more fearful she'd become. It was as if she were reverting back to the terrified child she had once been, and the more she tried to tell herself that Roe Head School would be nothing like that other place, the more she shook with dread. Then she thought of Zamorna. She didn't cross over to him then, of course—there was an elderly lady sleeping across from her, and the coachmen might have noticed her absence as well— but she scribbled the beginning of a story in the margins of a book. It had soothed her. It had made her feel that Zamorna was there with her, keeping her safe.

At school she crossed over briefly whenever she felt lonely or homesick, telling herself that since she wasn't crossing to Verdopolis, she wasn't really breaking her promise. The story was a romance about Zamorna and his mistress Lady Helen Victorine, and it took place on the Scottish highlands. Charlotte didn't use Rogue or any of their other characters. Branwell arrived at the school around the time the poor Lady Helen was dying in childbirth.

"I'm sorry," she said. "I wish you'd told me what was happening to you."

Her brother only shrugged and took another drink. Suddenly

she felt that his hopeless mood would infect her if she stayed another minute. She stood abruptly.

"I'm going to bed. Take the empty bottles to your room when you're finished. We don't want Tabby to find them in the morning."

BRANWELL

SHE WAS WAITING FOR HIM WHEN HE GOT BACK to his room. Elizabeth. She was sitting on his bed, hair and nightdress drenched in sweat. Her cheeks were hollow, but they were pink and rosy, and he remembered how this had fooled him when he was young. Consumption often gave its victims a deceptively healthy glow. Elizabeth had the glow to the end.

Branwell stood in the doorway for a moment, candle held aloft. Then he shuffled in, shutting the door behind him. He had his two empty bottles under his arm, and he put them carefully at the bottom of the wardrobe before coming to stand in front of her.

"Have you something to say to me?" he demanded, trying to sound brave.

His dead sister took a breath, but instead of speaking, she quickly pulled a handkerchief from her sleeve and began to cough into it. Branwell's whole body tensed. A consumptive's cough was wet and deep and painful, and it never seemed to end. It came back to him now, the days and nights of listening to that sound. He remembered thinking he'd almost rather strangle his sisters in their beds than hear it a second longer—and he remembered the weight of guilt that had fallen on him for having such thoughts.

"God help me," he said, and he sat down at his desk, setting his candle in front of him. He was dizzy and queasy and the beer in his stomach felt like lead, but he hadn't managed to get drunk, which had been his intention.

After a while the coughing stopped, but the exertion of it seemed to have left his sister tired, because for a while she bent panting over the handkerchief. Then she wiped her mouth and sat up, looking over at him. There was a smear of blood on her chin.

"Maria is the one everyone talks about," Branwell said. "'Maria loved to read the newspaper and spoke fluent French. Maria was like a mother to us.' If I remember you for anything at all, it is for being her sister—so why are you the one who haunts me?"

Elizabeth stared at him but didn't answer. The smear of blood on her chin made him want to look away. He wished she would wipe it off, but he couldn't bear the idea of asking her to. She slid off his bed, padding toward him on bare feet. He shrank away, but she only took the candle from his desk and brought it to the various paintings on easels around the room, examining each one in turn.

"Please. Won't you leave me alone?" he asked. He wanted nothing more than to go to sleep, though the thought of lying in the dark listening for his sister's wheezing breath was intolerable.

Elizabeth turned to him, frowning, her large eyes sunken in hollow cheeks. Still she didn't speak. She might have been pretty before her illness, but Branwell couldn't remember. He tried to think what she had been like, but she'd been so quiet and shy. Nothing came to him. In life she had followed behind Maria like a shadow, and when Maria died she had followed then, too. He did remember that when the girls went away to Clergy Daughters' School, Papa hadn't paid the extra few pounds to have her educated as a governess. He'd paid for the others, even Emily, and she was only six, but Elizabeth hadn't been clever. She hadn't been anything. At least, she hadn't been anything that anyone would ever know now.

"I'm sorry," he said, tears smarting his eyes. "I do wish I'd known you better."

Elizabeth was rifling through his paint box on the floor. Some of his mixed pigments had been preserved in glass cylinders for later use, and he saw her open a cylinder and cover a brush with dark paint.

"What are you doing?"

Without a word, Elizabeth went to the group portrait and began to paint with long vertical strokes.

"Stop!" He ran to her, but it was too late.

"It's better this way," Elizabeth said without turning around. She was covering him up, painting him out of the picture.

"I suppose . . . it is."

He should have seen it before. Without his own figure, the painting of the three girls looked well balanced and well executed. Without him, the painting was complete. Elizabeth turned and handed him the brush.

"If history remembers you for anything at all, it will be for being Charlotte Brontë's brother."

He gasped, stung by the words, but it was odd that as soon as he heard them, he knew they were true. Like a prophecy. Like a curse. After a moment, they made him feel . . . relieved.

"Yes," he said.

Branwell went back to his desk and took out a bottle of ink and a sheet of paper. He began to write.

CHARLOTTE

EMILY WAS AWAKE WHEN CHARLOTTE RE-turned. She was sitting up in bed, holding her knees, eyes shining in the candle's light. "Listen to the wind," she said. "Open the window, Charlotte." At that moment, a gust shook the house, making the window-panes rattle in their casings.

"What! I'll do no such thing, Emily Brontë." Charlotte blew out the candle and climbed back into bed. "Open t' window, the girl says, when the whole house is a'wuthering!" Charlotte and Emily both giggled at this imitation of Tabby's Yorkshire dialect.

In the dimness, Emily's moon-white face seemed to have a faint light of its own. How pretty she was, Charlotte thought, even with her hair a mess and her nightdress slipping off her shoulder. At other times she might have felt envy, but not tonight.

Tonight all she felt was a wave of love for her odd, wild younger sister. Whatever happened to Charlotte and Branwell, at least Anne and Emily had been spared their fate. That was something to be grateful for.

"Go back to sleep, my dear," she said, but as they lay back down, Charlotte knew that sleep was far away. Fear was pressing on her. Fear for herself and for her brother. Fear for what would come next. Branwell had said that Old Tom's harassment would grow worse, but how much worse? Would she hear things and see things all her life? Would she end her days in a madhouse, or locked in an attic somewhere, unable to tell the difference between fantasy and reality?

"Do you remember our bed plays?" Emily asked.

"In the Happy Village? Of course."

When they were little, Charlotte would sometimes cross them over to a secret world that Branwell and Anne knew nothing about. At bedtime, she would whisper stories into Emily's ear. One minute they would be lying sleepily in each other's arms. Then Charlotte would make the smallest movement with her hand, just the suggestion of holding out her palm, and the next minute they would be falling through fluttering white sheets, down and down until they reached a funny little village populated only by fat babies.

This was around the time that Charlotte and Branwell were founding Glasstown, so during the day there were wars raging and political intrigues brewing and love affairs smoldering, but at night, in the Happy Village, nothing very dramatic ever happened. There was a fat baby mayor and a fat baby dressmaker and a teashop where all the fat babies gathered to eat their bread and jam. They needed a lot of attention, these babies; Charlotte and Emily were often in demand to solve their disputes and dry their tears and change them in and out of their fine baby clothes. Now that she thought about it, it was a ridiculous place—Branwell would have teased her mercilessly had he known about it—but nothing bad could ever touch them there.

"I wonder what happened to all our baby friends," Emily said.

"It's not as if the worlds go on without us when we're not there."

"Don't they?"

Charlotte thought of dozens of abandoned babies growing sullen and resentful in her absence, hoarse from crying, tracks of dried tears on their stony faces. "What a horrid thought."

"Oh, I expect they've simply gone to sleep," Emily said. But that was too much like dying for Charlotte's taste. The wind picked up, wailing mournfully. "Or perhaps that's them now, crying on the wind."

Charlotte shivered in her bed. "Don't. It's too morbid." The howling grew louder, human but inhuman. Something wild calling for its lost mate. "Besides, it sounds more like a wolf to me."

Emily said nothing to this at first. After a while, Charlotte began to wonder if she'd drifted off, though it seemed impossible, with the wind so fierce. "That's not a wolf," Emily finally said. "It's a gytrash."

Charlotte froze, remembering the stories Tabby used to tell about the black dog with glowing eyes that roamed the moors.

"Open the window, Charlotte." Emily's voice had a pleading tone, like the pleading of the wind. "I want to hear him better, but I don't want him to see me. I don't want to give him the satisfaction."

Charlotte's mouth went dry. She knew it was nonsense, but she had the most illogical feeling that if she did go to the window, all her worry, all her dread, would coalesce into some black and threatening thing, howling up at them from the ground below. Another great gust battered the house, and Emily threw off the covers.

"Don't!" Charlotte grabbed her sister's wrist, but Emily pulled away and got out of bed. For a moment, Charlotte was afraid to follow, afraid of what she would see. Emily stood at the window, looking down. Charlotte rose from the bed and joined her.

And then she saw it, just beyond the stone wall, eyes red as coals. The black dog. Charlotte felt the horror of it through her body. It shouldn't be real. It shouldn't be in their world.

"I knew he'd come," Emily said.

Charlotte couldn't take her eyes from the dark thing below. It opened its jaws impossibly wide, letting loose a bloodcurdling howl. She gasped. So much seemed to be contained in that sound—anger, longing, sorrow—that she took a step back, but Emily pressed herself even closer against the window glass.

A chill traveled the length of Charlotte's spine. *There is something a little pagan about Emily,* she found herself thinking. If Emily had lived a thousand years ago, she might have poured out blood onto an ancient altar and been buried in a grave of heather and thistle, and her ear never would have missed hearing the word of God.

But then her sister turned to her with wide eyes, looking very young and lost, and Charlotte chastised herself for thinking Emily Brontë was anything but a good parson's daughter.

"It's Rogue. He's crossed over to find me."

"No." Charlotte's heart twisted as the realization dawned on her. "No, you foolish girl. That is one of Old Tom's minions, if I ever saw one. Have you made a bargain? Have you made a world and left it without my even knowing?"

Emily turned back to the window. "I'll tame you yet, old dog," she said. "I'll put a collar around your neck. Go and bite someone else." The eyes of the gytrash seemed to glow brighter for a moment, then it turned silently and leapt away.

"Please, Emily," Charlotte begged. "This is a mistake, isn't it? I've worked so hard to keep you safe. It's . . . It's . . ."

Emily didn't look at her. "I should have listened. I'm afraid I have been very wicked."

"Wicked?" Charlotte hissed, taking Emily by the arm and pulling her around. "Stealing currants from the kitchen is wicked! Letting one's mind wander in church is wicked! This is evil, Emily. It is unconscionable. It's . . ."

Charlotte fell to her knees, and a strangled cry rose from her throat, as full of sorrow as any wolf's howling.

EMILY

HARLOTTE, GET UP!" EMILY CRIED. HER SIS-
ter was on her knees with her hands pressed over
her face. "Are you ill?"

Charlotte lifted her head. "I'm trying to prevent
myself from slapping you! From throwing you out this window!"

Emily backed away. She had never seen her sister so distraught. Not Charlotte. Not the girl who made such tiny perfect
stitches, who never slept late in the morning, who never had a
hair out of place.

"Wake Branwell," Charlotte ordered. "Now. We must discuss
this."

Emily nodded and dashed out into the hall. There was no
answer at her brother's door. She opened it and saw a candle
burning on the desk, but no Branwell.

"He's not in his room," she said upon her return.

Charlotte had lit a candle of her own and was standing at the washbasin, wiping her face with a cloth. She swore, and Emily gave a little start. Branwell swore often—mostly to shock them, Emily believed—but Charlotte never did.

"He must still be downstairs," she said, taking up the candle. "Follow me." Her brusque tone was somewhat reassuring. Emily had often wished her older sister would be more passionate, but now she only wanted her to be herself again. She fetched the other candle from Branwell's room and followed her down the stairs.

"He's been at the beer," Charlotte warned, opening the door of the dining room. "Pray he's not drunk."

The room was dark, but as they entered, the yellow glow of the candles illuminated a body curled up on the sofa, covered by a red blanket.

"Branwell Brontë," Charlotte said sharply. "Wake up." She turned to Emily. "Pick up the bottles, please. There are at least two."

Emily got down on her hands and knees to peer under the furniture. She saw Branwell's blanket and a pair of bare feet hit the floor. Charlotte screeched.

"Oh!" cried Emily, scrambling away on her knees.

The person who had arisen from the sofa was not their brother. It was a woman. In the dimness, Emily couldn't make out the details of her face, but her dress was torn and dirty, and a mass of matted hair fell down her back. Emily's first thought was that some lunatic had taken refuge from the storm in their dining room, but then the woman opened her mouth and began to laugh. There was something preternatural in the sound, something not of this world. It seemed to mix with the wild wind that screamed and sang outside.

Charlotte shrank away, candle shaking in her hand. Emily wanted to go to her, but fear froze her to the spot.

"Get back," Charlotte said. "Begone!"

"Sister," the woman replied, her voice laced with false sweetness, "do not cast me out into the cold." She raised her arms to Charlotte as if for an embrace.

"You are no sister of mine."

"Don't you know me?" She stepped forward as Charlotte backed away across the floor. "I am Maria. This is what you've always wanted, isn't it? I lived. I am grown to womanhood."

"No!" Charlotte's voice was high with fear. Emily's eyes darted back and forth between the two. "My sister is in heaven."

The woman laughed again. Emily tried to think why the sound filled her with such dread. It made her want to run to the safest place she knew—but the safest place Emily knew was her own bed, with Charlotte beside her.

"What did you think it was like to be haunted?" The woman dropped her too-sweet tone, her voice thick with anger now. "Did you think I would wear white and float by your window?" She was much taller than Charlotte, and she seemed to loom over her, over the whole room.

Charlotte was visibly shaking, but she took a step forward. Emily was impressed with her bravery. "You are not a ghost. You are not my Maria. You are some creature of Old Tom's. He has created you to plague me."

"*You* created me," the woman insisted, and her tone was so firm it seemed to brook no argument.

"Go up to your room, Emily," Charlotte snapped, but Emily stayed where she was, staring at the strange apparition.

Then her curiosity overtook her fear, and she stood, leaving her candle on the floor. The woman had called herself Maria, but was this their sister's face? It was so gaunt and misshapen, so sallow in the flickering light—and yet it *was* familiar. Her unkempt hair was the same chestnut shade as Anne's, and her eyes, though lit with madness, were gray like Charlotte's.

Charlotte edged protectively in front of Emily. "I know what you want, creature. You want to hound me back to Verdopolis— but I shan't cross over."

"Insipid place, Verdopolis," the woman said. "I prefer to be with you." She grinned widely, showing yellowed teeth. "In the bosom of my family."

"I tell you, you are not my family! Maria was a shining girl, a sweet and mild and brilliant girl." Charlotte's voice quavered, but she pressed on. "If she had lived, she would be nothing like you. She would be happy. She would be married."

"But, Charlotte, my dear, I am married. To Zamorna."

Charlotte frowned and raised her candle to peer at the woman more closely. "Ridiculous. Make up your mind. Are you my sister or my heroine?"

"You made me live again in Verdopolis, but only half of me."

Emily saw it now. The resemblance to Mary Henrietta Welles-ley. This woman had looked familiar not because she reminded Emily of her eldest sister—whom she could barely picture—but because she was like some horrible, twisted version of Charlotte's duchess.

Maria—if Maria it was—held out her arms and made a par-ody of a fine lady's curtsy. "When I return to Verdopolis, this self will be nothing but a fading nightmare. I shall wear my pretty clothes. I shall sigh." Maria put the back of her hand on her fore-head. "I shall face my troubles with *insufferable* forbearance." She stepped toward Charlotte again. "But I will know in my bones that a part of me is missing." She jabbed Charlotte in the shoul-der with a dirty finger. "There is no room for imperfection in Verdopolis—but where do you think we go, all the imperfec-tions that you squirrel away? Down to the basement?" She jabbed Charlotte again. "Up to the attic? We are knocking, sister. Let us out!"

Charlotte had backed up into Emily, and Maria began to cir-cle around them both, the candle on the floor casting strange shadows on her face.

"Emily, go to your room," Charlotte said again.

"You have made a prison for me in Verdopolis, but I have no blood there." Maria's voice was choked with resentment. "There is nothing under my skirt! That's not truth. That's not life. No wonder I can never coax a spark out of Zamorna."

"Stop it!" Charlotte cried. She was hanging onto Emily's shoulder as if she needed it to keep her standing.

"Why are none of Zamorna's wives angry at his infidelities?" Maria said, close enough for Emily to smell her sour breath. "Wouldn't you be angry, sisters? Wouldn't you want to stab him in the throat with a pair of scissors?"

"Emily!" Charlotte said into her ear. "I am telling you for the last time. Please go to your room."

"I won't leave you with her!" Emily hissed.

Maria turned abruptly and sat on one of the dining chairs, her knees pulled up and her calves showing. Now Emily could see how thin she was—a frail creature lit with rage. Her feet were black with dirt.

"Let me tell you the worst part," Maria said, lowering her voice. "The unforgivable part. Come closer." She beckoned to Emily with a crooked finger, and Emily did take a step, though she was aware of Charlotte behind her, trying to hold her back.

"When Charlotte is done with her heroines," Maria said, picking idly at a scab on the top of her foot, "when she is done with us, she lets us waste away on velvet sofas, dabbing at our brows with silken handkerchiefs"—she looked up—"and yet she knows better. I wasted away, and it was not so pretty."

"Emily, look away from it, please," Charlotte said behind her. Her voice sounded weak and breathy. "Be careful."

"She's not an 'it.'" Emily couldn't help but give the person before her the same pity she would give an injured animal.

"How dare she?" Maria's voice was piteous now, though full of madness still, and her eyes were full of pain. "How dare she make my death ethereal and touching? Death is an ugly thing. How could she make it . . . presentable?"

Emily stepped forward again. "She knows better now, my dear." She tried to make her voice calm and soothing. "You must forgive her. You must leave us."

Maria smiled, and Emily suddenly knew how foolish she had been to get so close. A hand flew out and caught her by the wrist. "Where shall I go?" Maria said, her fingernails digging deep into Emily's wrist. "Charlotte has made no other place for me."

Emily pulled away, creating an angry scratch across her forearm. Maria threw back her head again. "Ha . . . ha . . . ha . . ." A slow, mirthless sound, hardly a laugh at all.

"Help me," Charlotte whispered.

Emily wheeled around to see her sister teeter and sway, then collapse onto the floor.

"Charlotte!"

Emily knelt and took her sister by the hand, but Charlotte's face was slack. She had fainted. When Emily glanced up, Maria's chair was empty. Without Charlotte's mind to create her, she was gone.

BRANWELL

A GROUP OF MEN—FLASHMEN, THIEVES, AND other unwholesome sorts—lounged by the entrance of the Elysium Club, playing games of dice on upturned barrels. Their presence wasn't unusual—wealthy members of the club often had need of such men when there were dark errands to be run—but the way they all looked up when he passed and followed him with their eyes made Branwell uneasy.

Inside, the secret meeting rooms looked seedier somehow. Tarnished. The velvet curtains were dingy with tobacco smoke. The mirrored bar no longer gleamed. Branwell assumed this was his mood coloring the story. At the back of the room, Rogue sat at his usual table with S'Death and Zamorna's young friend, the Viscount Castlereagh. The three had obviously been playing cards, but the game was over now. As Branwell drew closer, he saw that S'Death was tallying numbers in his little black book. The viscount looked on nervously, cheeks flushed with too much wine.

"Why, Castlereagh, have you won again?" Branwell said, slapping the young man on the back. He knew the answer already.

"I'm afraid not," the Viscount Castlereagh replied. He was trying to speak lightly, but there was a quaver in his voice. "I was just explaining to the earl that I can't pay him at the moment. I'll have to go to my bank when it opens. I . . . I don't know what induced me to bet so much on that last hand. I've lost a terrible amount . . ."

Rogue sighed, stubbing out his cheroot. "Listen to him moan. You won Thursday night, didn't you?"

"Yes, but hardly enough to pay back what I owe you and S'Death—Mr. King, that is. I fear I shall have to liquidate some of my assets . . ."

Branwell caught a look that passed between Rogue and his right-hand man. "Tut, tut, we can't have that. S'Death will lend you the money, won't you, old fellow?"

S'Death grinned like a skull, and a paper was produced. Poor young Castlereagh signed it without reading it. "You've been so kind. I hope you don't hold any grudge against me because of my friendship with the Duke of Zamorna."

"Nonsense," Rogue said with almost-believable geniality, helping Castlereagh to his feet. "Our rivalry has been much exaggerated." He gave Castlereagh a little push toward the door. Branwell took the vacated chair as Castlereagh staggered out to find a carriage for hire.

As Rogue sat down again, his expression turned to storm-cloud black. "That horse-leech!" He banged his fist on the table, so hard the barman looked over. "He acts the go-between for Zamorna and my wife, and he thinks I don't know it. Does he take me for a fool? Does he think I have no spies?"

"Don't fret," S'Death said, leaning back with smug satisfaction and patting the paper in his breast pocket. "We shall own him by the end of the month."

"It's his pretense of friendship I cannot abide." For some reason Rogue glanced at Branwell when he said this. "At least with Zamorna I know where I stand."

A waiter came to the table, distributing three glasses and leaving a bottle. Branwell poured them all a brandy, though the thought of drinking turned his stomach. He was still feeling the effects of his aunt's beer, and he was tense and agitated from all he had just seen back home. He wished he could forget Elizabeth—paint over the image of her the way she had painted over his. Usually coming to Verdopolis helped him shed his real-world cares, but now he kept expecting to see her gaunt face peeking out from behind the velvet curtains or reflected in the mirrored bar.

"Well," he said, forcing a brightness into his voice that he didn't feel. "What is the next part of the plan? How shall we use Castlereagh to our advantage and bring Zamorna down for good?"

A look of anger Branwell didn't understand crossed Rogue's face. It chilled him to the guts. He was already accustomed to Rogue's younger appearance and his larger frame, but this new malignity in his eyes made Branwell uneasy.

"You tell us, Lord Thornton. You are the architect of all our schemes."

"Well, I don't know about that," Branwell said with a nervous laugh. He glanced at both men, but they picked up their glasses and avoided his eye. "Have I done something to offend you, sirs?" He, too, picked up his brandy and took a sip for form's sake.

Rogue began to shuffle a deck of cards that had been lying on the table. He dealt a card each to himself and S'Death, leaving Branwell out of the game. When he spoke, he addressed his remarks to S'Death alone. "Have you ever noticed, old fellow, that there are plenty of flashmen in Verdopolis, but no brothels?"

Branwell choked on his drink and felt a blush rise to his face.

"I'm too old for that sort of thing," S'Death said. He squinted at his card. "I'll take one. What are the stakes? You know I don't play for sport. My filly, Bess, for your new stallion."

Rogue nodded, agreeing to the wager. "Think on it, though." He dealt S'Death another card, this time faceup on the table. "The term is used to mean a bully for a prostitute, am I right? There were four flashmen by the door when I came in, but

I have walked the streets of Verdopolis up and down and found neither whore nor brothel."

"Is that how you take your exercise?"

"No jokes, man. How do you explain it?"

"Well, don't ask me." S'Death waved a hand to the exit. "Go ask *them* their place of business if you're so interested." He tapped the table. "Another, please."

Rogue turned up one more card. "I *have* asked them," he said. "And they only look at me as if they don't know what I'm talking about." He looked to Branwell. "What do you make of that, Thornton?"

"I don't know!" Branwell insisted, hot with embarrassment. Truth be told, he *had* thought of making such a place. But if Charlotte found out, he'd simply have to take a shovel to the graveyard and bury himself, because he'd never be able to look her in the eye again.

"Look at him blush," said S'Death. "I do believe you're embarrassing the lad."

"Doesn't it concern you that we are living in a universe created by adolescent virgins?" Rogue asked. "Makes it difficult to be a dissolute reprobate, don't you think?" He picked up his brandy, then frowned at his glass and threw it across the room, where it shattered against the bar. "I can't even get drunk."

A cruel leer spread across S'Death's face. "And what sort of seventeen-year-old boy with the power of creation at his fingertips *doesn't* make a brothel? That's what I'd like to know."

"What . . . what do you mean, power of creation?" Branwell sputtered.

"Oh, pity us both, S'Death!" Rogue said, voice raised. "It's bad enough we have to live in a child's fantasy world—but we have to live in a child's *censored* fantasy world!"

"Stop!" Branwell cried. "What are you saying? What is the meaning of this?"

Rogue and S'Death shared a glance, the same wicked look of conspiracy they had given each other regarding Castlereagh. "Lady Emily told us," Rogue said. "She told us that you are one of the four Genii and that S'Death and I have been your dupes for all these years."

Branwell's stomach dropped. "Genii?" he repeated. Why would Emily tell them that? Alarmed, he tried to take control of the story. *"With that Rogue began to laugh merrily, and he and S'Death admitted that their words had been in jest,"* he murmured under his breath.

Rogue's eyes widened and he drew back as if in fear or disgust, pointing at Branwell. "Did you hear that, S'Death? He tried to make us laugh, like jesters in his little play."

S'Death nodded. "I heard it. Chills the soul, I won't deny it." After a moment he looked again at his down-faced card. "No more for me."

"You're very cavalier," Rogue said, but he glanced at his own card and turned up one more from the deck.

S'Death shrugged. "What can we do but play the hand we're dealt—so to speak?" They both chuckled as Branwell gaped.

"*S'Death suddenly remembered that a poor young widow who lived in one of his tenements was late with the rent,*" Branwell said. "*He leapt to his feet and looked at his watch, realizing that if he didn't act immediately, he would have to wait until tomorrow to throw her out onto the street.*"

S'Death leapt to his feet and looked at his watch.

"Be strong, old friend!" Rogue said. "He's doing it again. You are being manipulated!"

"I know it," S'Death said. "And I curse him for it—but it doesn't make the lady any less real, does it? You know how uncollected monies nibble at my soul!"

"Think, man! When have you ever forgotten a debt?" Rogue said.

"Never!" S'Death said. "And I can't begin now. Boy! My hat!" With that he ran out of the room as fast as his short legs could carry him.

Rogue glared at Branwell with fury in his eyes—and a touch of fear, too. Then he reached across the table, turned over S'Death's hidden card, and gave a bitter laugh. "Thirteen. And I had quince. I would have won that filly." He pulled a silver case out of his jacket pocket and lit another cheroot. For a while they sat in silence as he puffed at it thoughtfully.

"What are you going to do?" Branwell finally asked. "Now that you know."

"At first I thought I would kill you immediately." Rogue grinned. "Then I thought I'd kill you slowly."

Branwell shivered. There was something truly depraved about that smile. He glanced to the door, but he didn't think running was an option. It occurred to him that he could simply hold out his hand and disappear, but then, he knew he wouldn't be able to stay away forever. Sooner or later, he would have to come back. Elizabeth would see to that.

"There's something I want to say." Branwell tried to master his fear. "There's something I want you to know." He took a deep breath, forcing himself to look directly into Rogue's dark eyes. "I want you to know that I never considered you my dupe. All those times I confided in you, all the things I said to you over the years, they were all true. I want you to know that whatever happens, I consider you my dearest friend, and I always will."

"My, my. That's quite a confession." Rogue flicked an ash into the ashtray. "Truth be told, I do still consider you a friend, in spite of everything." He narrowed his eyes. "But perhaps that's only because you have willed it so."

"No!" Branwell insisted. "It's not a true friendship if you have no free will." He held out his hand. "Please. Shake hands with me. I wish us to be friends, but I do not demand it."

After a moment's consideration, Rogue reached across the table and shook the offered hand. Branwell felt a surge of relief, but Rogue tightened his grip and yanked him close.

"Remember, boy, you did make me the type of fellow who would stab his dearest friend in the back and sell his clothes to the ragman."

Branwell smiled weakly. "Yes. I suppose I did."

"Still." Rogue let him go and sat back. "I don't think I'll kill you." Then he added quickly, "But it's not because of Lady Emily. I won't have you thinking that!"

He stared at the table, frowning silently. A waiter came and cleared it, but Rogue didn't seem to notice. He was distracted by his thoughts, and Branwell was afraid to interrupt him.

"Just now, before you came, I think that I was dreaming of her," Rogue said finally. "I dreamt she was the moon and I was howling for her. Did she will that? Has she put this ache in me? Or has she given me a choice as you have?"

Was he still referring to Emily? Branwell wondered. He couldn't be. Not the Emily who was always bringing home injured animals and who still sometimes forgot to comb her hair, not the little sister who spent half her waking hours in a daydream.

Rogue sat up, seeming to come to himself. "If I thought you were the true architect of my fate, I wouldn't hesitate to kill you—if the Genii can die, that is, which I think they can. No. There's someone else, isn't there? Someone else who is behind all of Zamorna's successes."

"I don't know what you mean."

"Come, come. Admit it. I've thought hard on this. I have met three Genii so far: you, Lady Anne, and Lady Emily. None has any love for Zamorna, and yet he is so clearly the hero of this place. There is a fourth Genius. The most powerful Genius."

Branwell felt a twinge of annoyance at this. Charlotte was no more powerful than he. "Certainly not."

Rogue stood up. "I have no patience for argument. Bring this Genius to me."

Branwell hesitated. "I don't know that I can . . ."

"These are my terms. Bring him to me, and I'll let you live." Without saying good-bye, he turned away and began to walk to the door, but he had only gotten a few steps before he turned back, a finger raised.

"But do not tell Lady Emily that I showed you mercy."

ANNE

SOMETHING HAD HAPPENED IN THE NIGHT.
Anne knew it. The animals knew it. Earlier that
morning, Jasper Pheasant had refused to come out
of the peat house, and now the finches, Rainbow and
Diamond, were chattering in their cage. Snowflake was sitting
in the cold fireplace swishing his tail back and forth, and no one
dared remove him, not even Emily. Perhaps the animals were
only remembering last night's storm—it had strewn litter across
the yard and flattened all of Charlotte's flowers—but Anne was
convinced it was more than that.

"*Attention s'il vous plaît*," said Aunt Branwell.

"*Je . . .*," Anne began, her voice a hoarse whisper. "*Je . . .*" Her
face grew alternately hot and cold. She knew the answers, but
it was difficult for her to think extemporaneously at the best of

times, let alone now, with the world so obviously upside down and no one to tell her why.

"Remember your verbs," Charlotte said. They were in the dining room. Emily was on the sofa next to Anne, and Charlotte was perched on a chair in front of them, an open French book before her. She was so pale today, and Emily kept giving her such worried glances. How could Anne possibly concentrate?

"*Je . . . coupée ma . . .*"

Charlotte and Emily both winced.

"*Non!*" Aunt Branwell was standing at the dining room window, looking out at the wet yard. "*Je me suis coupée. Il s'agit d'un verbe réfléchi.*"

"I'm sorry," Anne mumbled.

They never knew when Aunt Branwell would decide it was time for an *examen de français*, but she seemed to have a hound's ability to sniff out the worst possible occasion. Now she gave a frustrated hiss, but it wasn't directed at Anne. "Where is that boy?"

Branwell had gone to Verdopolis in the night and hadn't returned, something he'd never done before. They knew he was still there, because his story paper was still upstairs, writing itself. The last time they had looked at it, he'd been in the Elysium Club, to Charlotte's great vexation. The rules of crossing over had been established long ago: Never miss meals; never stay too long; always be in your bed in the morning. The four Brontës hadn't kept their worlds a secret all this time by being careless.

At breakfast, Charlotte had made up a story about his having a headache and taking an early walk on the moor, but now morning was wearing on to noon. They couldn't make excuses for him forever, and Aunt Branwell's patience was growing short. Anne saw her sisters catch each other's eye and then glance away. Their very faces made her sick with dread. They were worried about something—afraid about something—and it was more than Branwell.

"I expect he's met up with Papa and Grasper, and they have all gone visiting," Charlotte said.

"Yes," Emily quickly agreed, though under other circumstances, she would have giggled at the idea of Branwell visiting parishioners with Papa—listening to their aches and pains and offering up opinions about wool carding and the Reform Act.

"But he knows how I worry about him!" Aunt Branwell said, still at the window.

"I'm sure Emily's *récitation en français* will divert you." Charlotte turned to Emily. "It is memorized, isn't it?"

Emily stared blankly. "Not . . . quite."

"Your students are ill prepared, Charlotte," Aunt Branwell snapped. "I fear I shall have to give a bad report to your father." It wasn't like her to speak so curtly. It occurred to Anne that perhaps she, too, could sense the tension in the house, the dark cloud that seemed to hang over them, and was reacting in the only way she could.

"Yes," Charlotte said, closing her book with what seemed

like relief. "I suppose you must." This lack of concern at Aunt Branwell's pronouncement was yet another clue that all was not well.

Aunt Branwell turned to her. "I do not enjoy having my time wasted—"

"Someone's coming through the cemetery," Emily interrupted, nodding to the window.

Aunt Branwell rushed back to her post. "Branwell?"

All three sisters went to stand beside their aunt at the windows. Anne saw immediately that the person on the path was not her brother. It was Tabby, coming very fast with a basket over her arm.

"I've never seen Tabby run before," said Emily. "Something's happened."

"Oh, the poor boy must have fallen in the mud somewhere, or been taken ill," Aunt Branwell said. "I knew it. We must send for Dr. Hartley in Keighley. I don't like that Dr. Kent."

Anne put a hand on her aunt's arm, worried that she was becoming overwrought. Aunt Branwell nodded, trying to smile.

"Quite right, my dear," she said in response to Anne's gesture. "We have no idea what Tabby will tell us."

She allowed Anne to lead her to a chair, and a moment later, Tabby burst through the front door and into the dining room. Her face was as red as beets, and it took her a moment to catch her breath.

"Do not spare us," Aunt Branwell said. "Is he"—she closed her eyes—"dead?"

"Not dead," said Tabby, still panting. "But terribly mauled, he was." She shook her head. "Terribly mauled."

The sisters all looked from one to the other in confusion. Aunt Branwell sat forward, clutching the arms of her chair. "Mauled? By what?"

"A dog. A black dog with glowing eyes, or so he says." Tabby put a hand on the doorframe to steady herself. "Nay, it's like one of Mother's stories come to life."

"Poor Branwell," said their aunt. "He must be out of his mind with fever."

Tabby looked up. "Branwell? Why, it weren't Branwell who were attacked."

"What? Who, then?"

"'Twere Michael Redman."

The room was silent for a moment. Then Aunt Branwell said imperiously, "Who in the name of heaven is Michael Redman?"

"He's the butcher boy from Stanbury."

Anne had read in books about a person's face turning "all colors of the rainbow," but she had never seen it before. First her aunt seemed to grow pale and almost greenish, but then the color rushed back and she grew an alarming pink. "And you have no news of Branwell?"

Tabby looked a bit sheepish now. "Nay, miss."

Aunt Branwell took a breath to speak, but Charlotte, perhaps fearing Tabby was about to be unfairly excoriated, interrupted quickly: "Allow Anne to take you to your room, Aunt. You've had a shock."

Ten minutes later, Anne was standing in the middle of the tiny bedroom, not knowing what to do for her aunt, who was clearly distressed. Anne was as shy with her as she was with other people, but nevertheless there was an intimacy between them. The two had shared a bedroom for a long time, and so Anne knew her aunt's many vulnerabilities. She'd seen her without her false curls. She'd seen her in her underclothes. She knew the sound of her snoring.

Aunt Branwell gave a peevish sigh. She was lying on the bed, facing the wall.

Anne coughed. "Would you like some . . . tea?"

Her aunt didn't answer. Anne wished she could straighten something, but the room was so plain and austere that there was nothing to straighten. A Bible and a few of Aunt Branwell's things lay on the dressing table. The only picture was a sentimental seaside scene hanging next to the mirror. It had been there for years, but it had never occurred to Anne before that it must remind her aunt of Penzance. She winced with guilt. Elizabeth Branwell had given up her life and all her friends in the south to help care for the young Brontës.

"I expect that even you know where your brother is hiding," Aunt Branwell said without turning around. "And why." She sighed again when Anne failed to answer. "Your father was right. You children are very secretive."

"Would you . . . May I get you some . . ."

"I'd like to be alone now, please," her aunt said.

Anne went out into the hall, closing the door quietly, and heard her sisters murmuring in the children's study. Annoyance washed over her. She entered without knocking and found Emily and Charlotte bent over Branwell's desk, heads together like coconspirators. They were reading Branwell's story paper.

"Where is he now?" Emily asked.

"He's traipsing around the streets of Verdopolis," Charlotte said. "I shall murder him."

"Our actions have begun to harm others in an unconscionable way," Anne interrupted. She hadn't rehearsed this comment and was pleased by its firmness and its coherence.

The strength of Emily's reaction surprised her. "Oh, do you think he'll die?" There were tears in her eyes.

"Who?" Anne asked.

"Michael Redman!"

Anne was at a loss. What did the butcher's boy from Stanbury have to do with anything? "I was speaking of Aunt Branwell and Papa."

"She's right," Emily cried, taking Charlotte's arm. "What if the gytrash bites Papa? He could be in danger!"

"Calm yourself," Charlotte said.

Anne frowned at her sisters in turn, considering all she knew and trying to fill the gaps in her knowledge with intuition. Emily had told her about making a bargain with the mysterious Old Tom; she knew Tabby's stories well; she knew her sister had vowed not to go to Gondal again.

"The gytrash," Anne said finally. "Did he come for you? Is he one of Old Tom's minions?" Charlotte's eyes widened.

"Don't be surprised," Emily told her, wiping her face with the back of her hand. "Anne always knows things without being told."

Charlotte peered at Anne through her spectacles, as if considering her in this new light.

"But, Anne." Emily came to her and took both her hands. "The gytrash was Rogue. I'm sure of it. Old Tom may have sent him here somehow, but the creatures haunting us are our own characters, come over to this world."

Haunting *us*? Anne glanced at Charlotte.

"The gytrash wasn't some apparition. It was real and solid," Emily continued, becoming emotional again. "It can do terrible damage. I told Rogue to go and bite someone, and he did! Poor Michael."

Anne fished a handkerchief from her pocket and handed it to her.

"You mustn't blame yourself," Charlotte said. "I am at fault."

"Stop saying that, Charlotte," Emily said, blowing her nose. "You are too saintly. I can't bear it."

"It is her fault," Anne said.

Her sisters both looked up in surprise. Emily put her arm

through Charlotte's, and Anne saw that something had brought them closer in the night. She bowed her head, but she didn't mean to take back her words. Aunt Branwell had called them all secretive—and it was bad enough that they were so with the adults, but the Brontë siblings had been secretive with one another, and this, Anne was sure, had led them to disaster.

"It's time to tell us everything, Charlotte," Anne said, hardly believing her own nerve. "It's time to tell us the price you pay for crossing over."

ANNE

"I HARDLY KNOW WHERE TO BEGIN," CHARLOTTE said.

There weren't enough chairs for all of them, and it had seemed somehow improper to sit on Branwell's unmade bed, and so they elected to sit on the floor, as they often had when they were children. Anne was glad she had swept the day before.

"I was wearing my black dress with the tight collar," Charlotte said. "I remember that." Idly she pulled at the neck of her dress. "And it was autumn, so Elizabeth must have been about four months gone and Maria five . . ." She frowned. "That means I was only nine years old, and Branwell only eight."

And I was five, Anne thought. Her clearest memory of that

time was of Charlotte and Emily's return from Clergy Daughters' School. While everyone else was mourning the loss of two sisters, in her little mind she had gained two. Suddenly she had a pair of fascinating playmates instead of only Branwell, who was so loud and wouldn't let her touch his toys.

"Branwell and I were just getting to know each other again," Charlotte said. "We'd been separated for a year, and that's a long time for children. I found him very arrogant, but very clever. When I mentioned that Maria had told me stories at school, he positively hounded me to tell them—he became quite desperate. You know how he can be. When I relented, he hung upon my every word as if he were hearing Maria's voice from beyond the grave." She paused. "Then came a day when we were outside at the stone wall . . ." Her voice trailed off.

"You were at the stone wall," Anne prompted.

"Please understand." Charlotte looked at them now with remorse in her eyes. "The world was so gray to us then. We missed Maria and Elizabeth so terribly, and we were so young . . ."

"Go on."

Charlotte nodded, pushing up her spectacles. "One day I caught Branwell in the yard, holding out a shilling in his hand." She held out her hand palm up, a gesture Anne knew well. "He explained he was calling for Old Tom, and it became a great game with us. We'd promise all sorts of things. *Old Tom, Old Tom, I'll give you all my hair. I'll give you all my teeth. I'll give you my firstborn child.* We offered more and more, but nothing ever happened. It became a dare of sorts. Who had the courage to promise the most?"

Anne shivered. She had expected something like this, but actually hearing the story was like hearing about babies playing with sharp knives.

"Then I had an idea. A bargain Old Tom wouldn't refuse. I even wrote down the words, so that they would be perfect. Branwell was very impressed and called them 'fine poetry.'" Charlotte looked at Anne and Emily again. "You must understand that I only half believed what we were doing!"

"What was the bargain?" Anne said firmly.

"I won't hold out my palm now," Charlotte said, and she sat on her hands, as if afraid they might hold themselves out of their own accord. "We stood with our backs to the parsonage, and we said . . ." She took a deep breath. "We said, 'Old Tom, Old Tom, listen please. We ask passage between our mundane world and sunlit places far from here. In return, we offer our days—one for every crossing.'"

Anne felt her heart sink.

"At first nothing happened, and we thought we'd failed again, but Branwell said we should tell a story, to make that sunlit place real. I started telling a story I'd cobbled together from *Gulliver's Travels*, and then . . ." Charlotte stared at the center of the room as if she could see something now. "We saw a ripple. A crack in the world. And beyond the crack was something very bright. I knew, I knew with certainty, that the story I was telling lay just through that strange door—a whole world. We still had our hands out . . ." She lowered her head. "How awful to hear myself say these things aloud."

"One day," Emily said. "One day from the span of your life every time you go to Verdopolis or any other invented world?"

"Two," Charlotte said, barely audibly. "We have to hold out our hands to go back as well."

Emily seemed to wince. "And you never saw Old Tom at all?"

"Never."

Emily pulled thoughtfully at her lip, considering what she'd heard. She looked very solemn, but this was no surprise to Anne, who knew what she had bargained. *How many days?* she wondered. *How many years?* If Emily had promised as many days as Charlotte and Branwell had lost, all for just one crossing to Gondal, and if she had paid this price a second time to cross home, how much of her life had been sheared off already?

"How dare you, Charlotte!" Anne said. "The days God gave you. The *life* God gave you. Have all Papa's sermons fallen on deaf ears? What were you thinking?"

"We were children!" Charlotte said.

Anne was so angry that her words seemed to speak themselves. "When you made the bargain, yes, but you have been crossing over for *years*, and every time . . ."

Anne had never felt this way before. She suddenly knew what it meant for one's blood to boil. She stood up—she had to—and began to pace the room.

"I . . . I . . . I can't believe I thought you were the sensible sister!"

"A long life of drudgery stretched out before me," Charlotte cried. "Making it shorter didn't seem like such a sin."

"Oh!" Anne flung up her arms, knocking Branwell's Martin canvas right off its easel. She ignored this and continued her attack. "You would rather die than be a governess? It's not prostitution, for heaven's sake!"

Charlotte gaped, and Emily, pale and stricken as she was, stifled a giggle.

"I shudder to think where you learned of such things," Charlotte said, standing.

"The Bible," Anne snapped. "Allow me to recommend it to you."

Good heavens, Anne thought. *What am I saying? Where are these words coming from?*

"You are overwrought, my dear," Charlotte told her, brushing off her skirts.

Anne could feel that Charlotte was now trying to take back the position of seniority she had lost by being scolded, but Anne felt that she had hours more of scolding to impart—a lifetime of unsaid words.

"It seems an appropriate moment to become overwrought. I'm sorry you disagree."

"Let me assure you that this can all be put to rights," Charlotte said.

"Indeed?" She didn't think Charlotte could return what Emily had lost, but she found that, angry as she was, she didn't have the heart to tell her elder sister about Emily's bargain.

"We must cross over one more time."

Anne's mouth dropped open, but no sound emerged.

"Emily and I have discussed this," Charlotte said. "It has been decided."

"Are you . . . are you quite . . ." *Do not leave me, words*, she thought. *I need just a few more.* Anne picked up Branwell's painting and set it back upon the easel, trying to calm herself. "Are you quite mad?"

"Emily will not pay for the crossing. I will cross her over to Verdopolis, as I have before." Anne found this little consolation. "We have no choice. We have an idea for how to stop Old Tom's minions, but we can only do it from inside the invented worlds."

Anne took a deep breath. "No," she said. "No. I don't want any part of it. I won't go."

Charlotte and Emily shared a glance. "We are not asking you to, my dear," Charlotte said.

BRANWELL

RANWELL HELD OUT HIS HAND, PALM UP-
ward, ready to go home. He closed his eyes, but
when he opened them, it was the rich oak paneling
and velvet curtains of the Elysium Club that he
saw, not the plain white walls of his bedroom. He squeezed his
eyes shut and tried again. Something was pressed into his outstretched hand. This time when he opened his eyes, the barman
was standing at his side.

"The Earl of Northangerland said that you would cover the
bill, sir."

Branwell stared at the slip of paper. "Put it on my account."

"Yes, my lord. It's only ... my lord's account is rather high ..."

"What the deuce ... ?" No one had ever asked him to pay a
bill in Verdopolis before. He patted his breast pockets and found

them empty, but this was no matter. "*The barman had forgotten,*" he said, "*that Lord Thornton had paid the bill in full with his gambling winnings.*"

He waited for this change in the plot to take effect and for the barman to slink away, but instead the man's face grew stony. "My lord cannot drink free forever."

Branwell sputtered. "I beg your pardon. Do you have any idea who I am?"

The barman shrugged. Branwell noticed with embarrassment that the few patrons left in the club were glancing toward him and whispering among themselves. "I will send payment today."

"See that you do."

Branwell stood up, cheeks burning. "And then I will see to it that you are dismissed!" He crumpled the bill and tossed it onto the table, then strode to the exit with as much dignity as he could muster. Laughter erupted behind him as he went out the door.

Outside, morning had dawned, bleak and overcast. What time was it back home, he wondered? Was it morning there as well? What would Father think if his bed were found empty? He stood in the cobblestoned street with his hand outstretched, trying one more time to will himself back to the parsonage. His head ached, probably from the beer. Was that why he couldn't concentrate? He had never thought much about how he returned to his own world. A scene would come to an end, he would hold out his hand, and he would find himself home again. If crossing over was like calling a door, then going home again was like pushing a door away—a simple gesture of the mind that he had done a thousand times. But now, he couldn't seem to manage it.

"Watch out below!" someone called.

Branwell looked up to see a servant emptying a chamber pot from the window above him. He leapt away to avoid its contents, stumbling to his knees and twisting his ankle in the process. "In the name of murder, madame!" he shouted up to her. "There is a gentleman below!"

The servant, a sour-faced woman in a dirty cap, spat and closed the shutters with a bang. Perhaps Charlotte was right and Branwell had gone a bit too far when creating the seedier side of Verdopolis.

He decided to go to Sneaky Hall, reasoning that if he went to sleep in his character's bed, he might—with any luck—wake up in his own, and so he started down toward the valley where the wealthy neighborhoods were, limping as he went. It should have been easy enough to find his way. The huge Tower of All Nations was always visible, dwarfing everything else around it. All Branwell had to do was make his way toward this landmark, and yet it appeared to be getting farther and farther away from him. The streets twisted and turned. Instead of growing more refined, the city grew rougher and dirtier as he went. He reached a dead end in a deserted laneway and stopped.

"Old Tom!" he yelled to the sky. "I did what you want! Now send me home!"

Of course there was no response. He turned and walked on

for what seemed like an hour, then for what seemed like another. Drying laundry crisscrossed the narrow streets above his head, and groups of grubby children loitering on corners whispered to one another. Branwell knew that he had made these places, but nothing was familiar. He thought of what Verdopolis had been when he and Charlotte first created it, when it was Glasstown—a glittering, perfect place. How had his creation wandered so far from that ideal? He had wanted Glasstown to be a monument to his sister Maria. With nothing more than a hand mirror and light from a window, she had taught him that even the deepest sorrows could be lessened by looking at something beautiful—but somehow he had allowed ugliness to spread across her city like a stain. Up ahead at a cross street, a hackney coach was passing.

"Stop!" Branwell called. "Driver!"

The coach drove on, but Branwell chased madly after it, wincing with every step. Finally he managed to grab the driver's coat. "Please stop!"

The driver pulled at the reins and stopped his horse, but he scowled down at Branwell from his perch and pointed his whip threateningly. "I am engaged, sir!" he said. "Do not detain me."

The coach's curtain was lifted, and a figure, white and ghostly, peered out at him through the glass. The door opened.

"Come in if you must, Lord Thornton," said a woman's voice. "But I fear our errand will take you far out of your way."

Branwell climbed in with relief, and the conveyance drove on.

Two women sat on the seat opposite, both in veils that covered their hair and face, but he had recognized the voice of the one who had spoken. It was Mary Henrietta, Zamorna's wife. Her white gossamer gown seemed to take up most of the room in the coach. The other woman wore a simple dove-gray dress and veil. Branwell decided that this must be her maid, Mina Laury.

"I cannot thank you enough, Duchess," Branwell said. The white figure made no response. "What brings you to these rough neighborhoods? And why are you not in your own carriage?" Mary Henrietta's equipage with its four chestnut stallions was a well-known sight in Verdopolis.

She was silent for a moment. "I did not wish to call attention to my errand. In fact, I hoped you would not recognize me. May we rely on your discretion?"

She unwound her veil now, and Branwell's breath caught in his throat. There was a tragic poignancy about Charlotte's heroines that always clawed at his heart. Her pale skin and bright hair were luminous against the dark interior of the carriage, and she wore a diamond pendant at her throat that glittered like a star. *Charlotte's going to kill her off*, Branwell thought with certainty. *They're always at their most beautiful right before they die.*

"You may rely on me completely," Branwell said.

Mina put a warning hand on her lady's shoulder. "This man is no friend to your husband, milady."

"If your husband was not my enemy before," Branwell said, "he would be now, after his behavior toward you, Duchess." He was not usually so gallant when playing Lord Thornton, but the words came from his heart. Mary Henrietta deserved better.

The lady lifted her chin proudly. "I suppose all of Verdopolis speaks of my shame."

"The shame lies entirely with Zamorna."

She frowned and fingered her pendant. It seemed to glint with its own radiance, the diamond's facets refracting beads of light across the roof of the coach. He found himself wishing she didn't have to die. Why Charlotte was driven to kill off heroines again and again was beyond him. It was as if all their beauty and goodness only served to make their eventual sacrifice more heart wrenching—and he didn't care to have his heart wrenched.

The duchess gave a long sigh. "An affair with my stepmother." She leaned her head against the window of the coach. "I try not to care so very much, but Zamorna is my all. I shall die without his love."

Branwell knew her words should seem ridiculous—they were typical of Charlotte's highly charged romantic dialogue—and yet he found himself moved by her suffering and angry at her fate.

"Why anyone would spare so much feeling for that over-dressed tin soldier I have no idea," he said.

Mary Henrietta's expression turned icy, and Branwell knew he'd gone too far by insulting her husband. He tried to stammer out an apology, but she only rewound the gauzy veil about her head. "I have been too talkative. Do not let my conversation trouble you, sir."

After a somewhat uncomfortable pause, Mina pulled open the drawstrings of a reticule and took out a small prayer book. She lifted her veil to speak. "Would you care for something to read? I fear we must journey a while longer."

Mina was looking rather too lovely as well, though in an innocent-country-girl sort of way; she'd probably be for the block, too. Often Charlotte killed off her women in pairs, the heroine taking a faithful friend or dutiful servant with her somehow, just to make things more tragic.

Branwell refused the offer of the prayer book and fell to looking out the window instead. They seemed to be on the outskirts of the city; Verdopolitan buildings were beginning to give way to rolling countryside. *What am I still doing here?* he wondered. His eyelids fluttered, then shut.

He was still in the coach when he awoke, but he was alone. He climbed out. The driver was not in his box, but Branwell saw Mary Henrietta ahead of him, with Mina at her side. They were standing atop an arched bridge that spanned a dark river. He recognized the place from Charlotte's stories. Normally it was picturesque, with gliding swans and low-bending willows. Now the swans had disappeared, and a stiff wind made the willow branches whip frantically. Mary Henrietta's unwound veil streamed out behind her, undulating gracefully as she stared into the fast-moving water.

"Don't!" Branwell called, knowing what she planned.

She turned to him. "I must! I am compelled!"

"Suddenly Mary Henrietta realized the folly of her actions and came back to the shore," Branwell said—but Mina and Mary Henrietta stayed exactly where they were.

This was where the Duke of Zamorna had proposed marriage; it was only fitting that Mary Henrietta would end her life at the same spot. Branwell looked around, wondering if Charlotte was hiding somewhere, directing events unseen. This was her story—wasn't it?—so why was it progressing without her? Events seemed to be moving forward with a horrible inevitability.

"Please, Your Grace," he said, coming toward her across the bridge. "I would do anything to divert you from this fatal course of action."

Mary Henrietta's face was deadly pale, but a smile twitched on her lips. "He has hidden his good manners very well up to now, has he not, Mina? Lord Thornton, I thought you were nothing more than a lackey for my wicked father."

"Your goodness and beauty can melt the hardest heart," Branwell said, stopping in front of her. It was sugary dialogue worthy of Charlotte, but he didn't care.

Mary Henrietta turned to lean against the iron railing of the bridge. Her diamond pendant hung from her neck over the water. "Not Zamorna's heart."

The pendant caught the light, and Branwell was suddenly reminded of refracted colors scattered across a white wall. His sister. His sister and the mirror.

"Maria?" he said without thinking.

Mary Henrietta looked up as if she recognized the name.

Branwell looked to Mina Laury. "Elizabeth?"

The maid frowned at him, but didn't answer.

"Why have you used these names?" Mary Henrietta asked.

Mina took a step forward, squinting at Branwell as if recognizing something in him she hadn't seen before. "I am reminded of a dream," she said. "You were in it, Lord Thornton, and I . . . Did I ask you for a drink of water?"

Branwell jerked back, seeing in Mina's plump and healthy features the gaunt face that had haunted him the night before. What did it mean?

"I . . . ," he faltered.

"It is no matter," Mary Henrietta said, and she set a hand on Mina's shoulder as if to climb up onto the iron railing of the bridge.

"No! I implore you! I . . . I order you!"

"Order?" Mary Henrietta stopped, raising an eyebrow at him.

"Indeed," Branwell said. "I order you." He drew himself up, throwing his shoulders back. "Prepare yourselves for a shock, ladies. I tell you that I am not Lord Thornton Witkin Sneaky, rich young reprobate, but am in fact one of the four great Genii. As your deity—as one of your creators, in fact—I do decree that you shall not die today."

Mina and Mary Henrietta stared at him for a full half minute, their eyes wide. Then Mina put her hand over her mouth. Mary

Henrietta turned away, her shoulders shaking. A peal of laugher escaped Mina's lips. In a moment, the two women were clutching each other, laughing so hard that tears streamed from their eyes.

"He orders us," Mina said through her merriment.

"One of the four great Genii," Mary Henrietta said, burying her face in her maid's shoulder. "Oh my."

"I assure you ladies . . . ," Branwell began, but the two women only laughed harder.

Heat rose to his cheeks in spite of the cold wind. In the end there was nothing for him to do but wait until they had gathered themselves. After a while the laughter died down and Branwell, with all the dignity he could muster, stepped forward and gave Mary Henrietta a handkerchief.

She took it gratefully and dabbed her eyes. "Lord Thornton, I must commend you. Never has tragedy been averted in so ridiculous a manner."

"Milady!" Mina said. "Is it true? Is tragedy averted?"

"It is." Mary Henrietta stepped toward Branwell and gave him a gentle kiss on the cheek. "I hear and obey, oh great Genius," she said softly. "I find I am in no mood to die today." She turned toward the hackney coach.

The missing driver appeared from behind a tree, threw the end of a cigarette to the ground, and climbed atop the conveyance. Branwell watched the two women walk toward it, arm in arm. He wanted to call them back, or join them, but he was afraid he would somehow ruin what he had just accomplished.

"That was well done," said a voice behind him.

He turned. It was Charlotte in the guise of Charles Wellesley. Emily was beside her, dressed in the same scarlet gown with red roses he had seen her wearing at the party.

"Did you see?" he asked, delighted with himself. The embarrassment he had felt a moment before was melting away, replaced by a giddy joy.

"We read. Your story papers continue to write themselves back home. Emily and I followed along, waiting for the right opportunity to join you."

"They were going to die. I changed their fate."

"Yes." Charles Wellesley's eyes were dark blue—not his sister's eyes at all—but he found great pity in their depths. "Your will changed the direction of the story, just like Anne's when she set fire to Wellesley House. We must all be so strong willed or we shall lose control again."

"I'm sure I could do anything now." He wanted her to share his elation, but she looked so grave. "I saved her."

"Yes. You saved her," Charlotte said. "But now she has to die. Banny, they all have to die."

CHARLOTTE

THE DUKE OF ZAMORNA SAT ON A GARDEN bench, gazing at the blackened ruins of Wellesley House. Charlotte stood behind him in the shadows. She had planned out the scene carefully. In a moment, the Viscount Castlereagh would arrive and give the duke some incredible news. This was to set the stage for Zamorna's death, for the death of every character in Verdopolis, for the death of all the invented worlds.

The reasoning was sound, she tried to tell herself. Three characters had crossed over to the real world—Mary Henrietta, Rogue, and, she had learned from Branwell, Mina. Perhaps every Verdopolitan character had this potential. The solution was to end them all—was it not? What else could the Brontës do but create a last, climactic scene of death and devastation?

Even now, Emily and Branwell were with Rogue—at least she hoped they were—setting up the villain's participation in the final carnage. Branwell hated the idea—they all did—but it was this or let a gytrash loose in Haworth; it was this or be haunted by her dead sister for the rest of her days.

She opened her mouth and tried to say the words that would set the current scene in motion. They stopped in her throat. Zamorna, still on his bench, looked neither right nor left. He had no thoughts, as Charlotte had not given him any. He was as lifeless as a rag doll, left by a child.

Why didn't you live? she wanted to say. If left alone, Mary Henrietta and Mina would have some conversation or activity—and Rogue would probably devise some new way to take over the world—so why did Zamorna only sit?

It couldn't be a coincidence that it was also these same three characters who had crossed over to her world. Zamorna hadn't haunted her. Perhaps he couldn't. Perhaps it took some sort of intention to be able to cross over, and he had no intentions of his own. She couldn't help but think that if she'd been able to grant her hero one true emotion, he might have come to life.

"Why didn't you love her?" she asked, coming up behind him on the bench. "Why didn't you love your wife?"

"Ah, little brother, how you cut to the heart of the matter. I wish I knew." Zamorna showed no surprise at her appearance and moved over on the bench to make room. "You seem troubled."

She sat down beside him, her boy's legs not long enough to

touch the ground. The scene in front of her was one of desolation. There was nothing left of Zamorna's great mansion but charred beams and collapsed chimneys. The bench where they sat and the bush of white roses next to it were the only remnants of what was once a magnificent garden.

"Of all your wives and mistresses, I thought Mary Henrietta was the one," Charlotte said.

Zamorna gave her a brotherly pat on the knee. "As did I. But perhaps the Red Countess . . ." His voice tapered off. Even he seemed to realize that his affair with Rogue's wife was not likely to end in happiness. "I suppose I have yet to find my equal."

"Your equal!" Charlotte cried. "I assure you, brother, Mary Henrietta exceeds you in most virtues. Goodness, charity, fidelity, piety, loyalty . . . Who among the nobility do you think could rival her in any quality you'd care to name?"

Zamorna pulled one of the white roses to him, inhaling deeply. Then he let it go and sighed as if even its lovely fragrance bored him. "Perhaps my equal is not to be found among the nobility."

"What are you suggesting? An affair with a servant? Will you be seducing your wife's maid next?"

Her voice was mocking, but as soon as the words were out, Charlotte found herself considering the idea. Perhaps someone innocent and fresh like Mina Laury would make him fall in love. But no, it was too late for any of that. In his very next scene, Zamorna would die.

"Why not?" he said. "If two souls meet, what does it matter? If I could find my equal, I would love her, be she poor and plain."

Charlotte's heart skipped a beat. "Poor and plain?" she said with a nervous laugh. These were two words she often used to describe herself. "I doubt such a woman would keep you interested for long."

"Just because she is poor and plain doesn't mean she is soulless and heartless."

Charlotte's heart lurched again. Zamorna could never love someone so like herself, could he?

She allowed herself to wonder what it would be like to play a heroine, to kiss and be kissed by the Duke of Zamorna himself. She found that she longed to try. She longed to wear beautiful gowns and flutter beautiful eyelashes, to wrap her snow-white arms around his neck—but she had the most terrible fear that if she did, she would change back to herself in mid-kiss like some horrible, twisted version of *The Princess and the Frog*. Zamorna was so arch and condescending. How would he react? He had never seen a woman as ugly as herself.

"Sometimes I almost dream of her, you know," Zamorna said. "My perfect woman. I wish I could invent her like a character in a story. She would be vexing and challenging. A strange elfin thing who'd be as clever as I. Not pretty, perhaps, but stark and austere."

Charlotte felt tears sting her eyes. Her beloved character did have thoughts of his own. And they were of her—or someone like her.

"Will you listen to a fancy, brother? I often imagine that she is just around the corner listening to all I say."

"Perhaps that's true," Charlotte said, struggling to keep her voice steady. "Perhaps she hides."

"I wish she wouldn't. I wish she'd know I wanted to meet her."

Oh, Charlotte thought. *If only I'd been brave and created the story I wanted. If only my stories had been a little more true.* But it was too late now.

It occurred to her that perhaps Zamorna had never found a true and vibrant life of his own because she hadn't wanted him to find happiness with a woman other than herself.

"*Suddenly, hoofbeats were heard upon the road,*" Charlotte said. "*At the blackened gate the Viscount Castlereagh dismounted from his thoroughbred and ran through the ruined garden to his friend.*"

"Zamorna!" Castlereagh cried. "I bring incredible news!" He stopped in front of Charlotte and Zamorna, breathing heavily. When he had caught his breath he went on. "All of Verdopolis is abuzz with it. A new country has been discovered, called Angria, and you are to be its king! They say the Genii have already built its capital city on the banks of the Calabar River. Your coronation is tomorrow at St. Michael's."

Zamorna did not remark on any of the oddities and inconsistencies of this announcement. He did not ask what he had done to deserve the honor. Nor did he ask why a king of Angria would be crowned in a Verdopolitan cathedral, nor why he must be coronated so soon, nor how such an event could be planned in only a day. Charlotte did not put these questions in his head, and so he took the news as a matter of course. The fact that this new country did not exist, he would not live long enough to learn. Charlotte hoped that Branwell and Emily would have as easy a time getting Rogue to come to the coronation—where tragedy awaited them all.

BRANWELL

ONCE, WHEN THEY WERE SMALL, BRANWELL and Emily went for a walk with Nancy, who was their servant before Tabby came, and they were caught in a terrible downpour. They took refuge in a lonely farmhouse on the moor, its owner so surly and ill-tempered that he almost didn't let them in. It was a filthy place. Branwell had been as much afraid of the scowling farmer as he was of the violent storm that raged outside, but Emily seemed to enjoy herself. She made repeated attempts to pet the farmer's two liver-colored hounds, though they bared their teeth whenever she came near.

Suddenly there had been an enormous explosion, greater than any thunderclap. The whole cottage shook. A collection of pewter plates and pitchers fell from their shelves, crashing to the floor.

"The end times are upon us!" Nancy cried, putting her arms over her head.

Emily bolted to the door. "I must see!" she said, her eyes shining with excitement. "I must see the four horsemen and the lamb-horned beast." Young as she was, she knew the stories from the Book of Revelation, and she took Nancy's words to be the truth.

Branwell tried to stop her from going out, but she slapped his hands away. She ran outside, while he clung to the doorframe, reaching to her and calling her name.

From that day to this, Branwell had carried a picture in his mind of that small girl, pelted with rain, squinting up into the black clouds. He never forgot the look on her face when she turned to him: The disappointment there was unmistakable.

Later they found out that a bolt of lightning had caused a pocket of marsh gas to detonate—a freak occurrence, but not unheard of. Out on the moor the explosion had caused a landslide that sheared off part of a steep hill. The whole family had gone out to see it a few days later, and their father lectured them about the awesome power of nature. Branwell's eyes kept slipping back to Emily. She looked so sweet and modest, following with interest all that Papa said—but Branwell had seen another side of her. He'd seen the girl who was just a little disappointed when the end of the world didn't arrive.

"We're committing a murder," Branwell whispered now.

"I know," Emily replied.

"Of someone . . . someone who I think we both love."

"Yes."

They were in the sitting room of a rough-stone house, standing in front of a huge fireplace. Branwell had made reference in some of his stories to a "hideout" in the countryside outside Verdopolis, where Rogue and S'Death sometimes retreated, but he had never set a scene here before. In faded sofas or high-backed chairs, half a dozen examples of the criminal class sat sharpening swords and long knives, giving off a clear impression that they were getting ready for some great mischief. These men ignored Emily and Branwell for the most part, though some occasionally looked up from their work to give them a sly glance or a knowing leer.

"He says I'm to wring your pretty necks if you don't talk," said S'Death, entering the room from what appeared to be the kitchen.

"We'll tell him what he wants to know," Branwell answered, shielding Emily with his body and forcing a boldness into his voice that he didn't feel. "But it's for his ears alone."

S'Death gave a sullen grunt and told them to wait.

When he was gone, Emily ran her finger along the mantel of the fireplace, seeming unsurprised by the thick layer of dust she found there. Above the mantel was an impressive gun collection, with fowling pieces and horse pistols hanging on pegs all the way up to the ceiling. At the far end of the room, shelves of pewter plates and tankards sat row upon row. Two liver-colored hounds lay in the corner, licking themselves. Branwell wondered if she recognized Alexander Rogue's hideout for what it was, or if she'd forgotten that day in the rain. Then it occurred to him that this might be as much her creation as it was his.

"Look," she said. "It's Gondal." To the right of the fireplace was the only painting in the room, a dark landscape in a small, rectangular frame.

"Oh," Branwell said, stepping up to it. He had only just learned his little sister had made a world, and he was curious to see it. At first he was rather disappointed. "It's . . . a moor."

And a more desolate moor one could hardly imagine. He would never have chosen such a subject for a painting—or for a world. There was nothing to be seen but gray hills and gray sky. A rock. A leafless tree. The more he looked, though, the more he began to admire the mood of the place. There was a bleak beauty about the painting. He decided that he'd be very proud to show such work to Mr. Robinson someday—but a moment later he saw that this painting could not exist in life. The clumps of wild grass swayed in the rough wind, and the clouds moved across the sky. He felt that he might reach his hand through the frame and travel to this stark place.

"I wish I were there now," Emily said, and Branwell was struck by the longing in her voice.

"Why?"

She needed no time to think of an answer. "I'm more myself there. He is, too, I think."

Branwell was a little annoyed by this, knowing she meant Rogue. He and Charlotte often borrowed each other's characters, but Rogue was different. He was just beginning to realize that Emily was responsible for all the recent changes in him. The terrible truth was that she'd made him better.

He looked away from her, crossing his arms and frowning at the painting. "Reminds me of *Rob Roy*. You've been reading Sir Walter Scott."

"I have. He is my second-favorite author."

"Who is your favorite? Let me guess. Byron?"

"No." Emily laughed. "It's you, of course."

He saw that she was quite serious and felt touched.

"You made Alexander Rogue," she said.

"Almost," he said quietly.

The words of Elizabeth's ghost came back to him: *If history remembers you for anything at all, it will be for being Charlotte Brontë's brother.* Not only Charlotte, perhaps. He and Charlotte had been fighting all their lives over which of them was the most brilliant Brontë. It would serve them both right if it was neither of them.

"Banny?" Emily said with hesitation. "Would it be all right if I played the next scene just Rogue and me? I . . . I want to say good-bye to him."

"Yes," he said, after a while. "I don't mind." Though he did, a little.

EMILY

MILY AND ROGUE STOOD ON A RISE ABOVE the hideout. The sky was gray. A damp wind blew through the yellowing grass. All around them were green hills as far as the eye could see.

"Reminds me of your Gondal," Rogue said. It reminded Emily of home. "I thought you said you hadn't made this world."

Emily was still warm from the walk. She had tried to steel herself as she climbed the hill—Rogue was dangerous, a mad dog that needed putting down—but now, seeing his face . . . Why did his rough face claw so at her heart? She smiled at him. She couldn't help it.

"I didn't make this world, but there are some things I can do." She closed her eyes. "*All around them, foxglove swayed in the breeze.*" When she opened her eyes again, Rogue had drawn very close and was staring down at her. His eyes made her breath catch. "My favorite flower," she explained, wanting to step away but not wanting to seem afraid.

Rogue raised an eyebrow. "Deadman's bells," he said, using the country name. "Poisonous, I believe."

Emily broke free of his gaze and looked around her. Taller than the tall grass, the stalks of foxglove teetered in the wind, each flower as white as bone. She frowned. "I'd meant to make them purple." Tabby always said the white ones meant a death.

All at once, the enormity of what she was doing fell over her. She was setting the stage for Rogue's death—for the death of Verdopolis—and she felt crushed by the weight of it. A raw wind whistled through the grass, making her shiver.

"Fitting," said Rogue. He looked out over the green landscape and took in a deep breath. "Everything becomes a bad omen at a time like this."

Emily swallowed. Did he know what was coming? "What do you mean?"

"After all these years, do you think I can't feel it? You Genii have something terrible in store."

She didn't ask him to explain further, fearing what he knew. She rubbed her arms against the chill. Almost out of earshot was a high tinkling sound, like very distant music. Emily couldn't identify it, but for some reason it seemed terribly mournful against the low keening of the wind.

"Once, years ago, I stood in front of a firing squad and knew

I was going to die," Rogue said, his gaze still fixed on the distant hills. "I knew it. There would be no last-minute reprieve for me, no rescue by my men."

"But you were wrong," Emily said. "I know the story."

"I was wrong because the gods changed their minds." He turned to face her. "You won't change them this time, will you?"

Emily was taken aback by the directness of the question and by his gaze. He knew. He knew exactly what she and her siblings planned. "Would you be truly . . . distressed not to exist anymore?" As soon as the words were out she knew it was a stupid question—but then, Rogue wasn't a real person, after all. At least, that's what she tried to tell herself.

"Distressed?" he spat. "I'm not being snubbed by the duchess at the ball, my dear. I'm being murdered by my makers! Wouldn't that *distress* you?"

"It's not murder!" she insisted.

"What would you call it?"

"You're not alive. You are a story. We made you up."

Rogue pounded his chest with his fist. "I *feel* alive. I don't *feel* like a story any more than you do!"

"I'm sorry," she said, tears stinging her eyes.

"It's true, then?" he asked. "They're killing me off?"

Emily nodded, and he turned abruptly, rubbing a hand through his hair. She braced herself for a volcanic burst of fury, but his voice, when he turned back to her, was soft and full of pain. "Can't you stop it? Can't you save me?"

Anger she could bear, but the look of suffering on his face sent guilt stabbing through her body.

"You think we are all-powerful, but we are at the mercy of something else," she said. "All this . . ." She lifted her arms to the scene around them. "All this comes at a price. If I were the only one to pay it, I would do so gladly, but I am *not* the only one."

Now his anger came. "What the devil are you talking about?" he shouted. "I don't understand a word—but it doesn't sound like a justification for my death!"

"You must die, or you shall continue to torment me. Don't you remember coming to my world? You howled up at my window!"

He started, and she thought perhaps he did remember, but then he pointed a finger at her face, making her take a step back. "It is you who torments me, girl!" He fumbled for something in his jacket pocket, took it out. "Look at this!" He thrust something under her nose. "Why do I carry this? Why can't I get rid of it?" In his hand was a plait of hair tied with a scarlet ribbon. It was hers. He had cut it with the stiletto during the party at Wellesley House. "You'll have me writing poems next."

"Oh," she said. "You kept it."

"You have done this to me, and yet I know you will betray me. I can feel it. You gave me a heart only to break it!"

Emily stared dumbly at the plait. She touched the place where it had been. "You . . . feel something for me?"

Carefully he put the braid back in his jacket pocket. "I believe you know that I do," he said, with a fiery glare in her direction.

It wasn't true. She hadn't known, and she hadn't made him care for her, though she couldn't deny that she'd wanted it to happen.

"I suppose you will enjoy weeping for me," he said, "the way women enjoy weeping over a sad book. Will my death be touching, goddess?" She hated the bitterness in his voice. "Will there be a moral lesson?"

"Don't. Please don't," she said, as a sob escaped her. "Do you think I want you to die?"

"Don't cry, for heaven's sake," Rogue said. "I have a heart of stone, remember. I am unaffected."

Emily tried to stop, but a tear was running down her cheek now. It would be so much easier if he hated her. And if she hated him.

"I only laugh when women cry," Rogue insisted. "Ha!"

Emily's breath stuttered and hitched as she tried to steady it.

"Oh, gods help me," Rogue said in frustration. "I am slain already." The next thing Emily knew, she was in his arms.

Emily didn't come from a family that embraced very often, but being held by Rogue was like something she had been waiting a long time for without knowing it. Something in her body that had been held tense relaxed. She cried harder. The wind all around them was like a song, a melancholy song, and the faint tinkling sound made it all the more sad. She pressed her cheek against Rogue's black waistcoat.

"I'm sorry I shot that cully," Rogue said softly. "In Gondal,

I mean. And I've never been sorry for anything before. It's a strange feeling." Emily laughed a little through her tears. "You're not reforming me, are you? Making me see the error of my ways? I'd rather die than be that kind of story."

"Never," she said. "You are irredeemable."

"That's a relief," he said, gently smudging away one of her tears with his thumb. "It will be all right. You'll see. We'll run away to Gondal, just you and I."

"Yes."

"I know it's those others who are to blame. Not you." He took her by the shoulders. "That's why I needed to know who they were. That's why . . . You'll tell me, won't you? You'll tell me the name of the eldest Genius, the one who's truly behind what happens in Verdopolis. Lord Thornton promised me a name."

Emily hesitated, wiping her face with the back of her hand. "Perhaps we could go to Gondal. Perhaps we could go now." She meant it. She didn't care how many days she lost. At that moment she was willing to go and never come back.

"Not yet," said Rogue. His grip on her shoulder tightened. "The name first."

There was something in his eyes she didn't like, and there was the hint of a threat in the tightness of his grip. Emily remembered how he'd tricked her before, in Gondal. Was he really sorry he shot that cully?

"Can't you guess?" she asked.

"No tricks," he said. His voice had a hard edge.

Emily couldn't believe she'd been willing to run away to Gondal with him only moments before. She had to remember—she'd said it herself—Rogue was irredeemable.

"If you had the power to make a world," Emily said, "wouldn't you make yourself the hero of every story? Wouldn't you make yourself the richest, the handsomest, the most dashing—the most fascinating man in Verdopolis?"

Rogue's eyes hardened to obsidian. "Zamorna," he breathed.

"Of course."

He let go of her shoulders and turned away. "It's so obvious. I should have known. And they say he's to be king of some new country."

"Yes," Emily said softly. "If he lives through the coronation day."

"He won't," Rogue said. "Not if I have anything to say about it."

The wind gusted, bending the white flowers all around them, and the dissonant tinkling sound she'd heard before grew louder. The foxglove. That was where the sound was coming from. The deadman's bells were all ringing, ringing, ringing—a death knell for her beloved Alexander Rogue.

ANNE

"I HOPE THEY DO NOT MISS THEIR TEA," PAPA SAID.

Anne didn't know what to say to this, but he didn't seem to expect an answer. She pulled a skein of red yarn from her workbasket and began to wind it into a ball. This was awkward with her bandages, but she needed something to do. She was on the sofa, and her father sat opposite her on the wooden chair. Everything was strangely ordinary. Snowflake and Grasper sat in their respective baskets, eyeing each other with suspicion. In the kitchen Tabby and Aunt Branwell were arguing over how many walnuts to put in an apple pudding.

"Let me," Papa said, taking the yarn from her lap. "Don't look so surprised, my dear. Your mother taught me the skill." He held the yarn between his two upright hands, letting it out gradually as Anne began to wind. "It doesn't hurt your burns?"

"Oh, no." Anne's fingers were still a little stiff, but she wasn't in any pain. "I'm sure it will do me good." It was so unusual to have Papa to herself. He was almost always shut up in his study at this time of day.

"I expected to look in on Branwell's painting or look over Charlotte's lesson plans . . . They left no word as to their return?"

"No," she murmured.

"Nor Emily?"

She shook her head.

"Strange that they should go for such a long walk today, of all days." He nodded to the windows spattered with rain, but Anne knew he meant something more. He meant, *Where have my children truly gone?* He waited as if expecting her to say something, then sighed. "You look tired, my dear."

"I am, a little."

Anne had been counting the minutes since Charlotte and Emily crossed over, and her nerves were frayed. She dreaded being asked a direct question about their whereabouts; she'd even hidden their boots so Aunt Branwell wouldn't ask why they'd gone without them in the rain. *What an excellent criminal I am becoming,* she thought with dismay. For a while they wound yarn in silence.

"Do you remember the painted mask I once had?" Papa asked.

She shook her head.

"Years ago, when Maria and Elizabeth were still alive, it

occurred to me that my children were growing shy, that they did not speak their cares to me, and so I contrived a method for hearing their thoughts. I sat them in a circle and had each wear the mask in turn, and I asked them questions. You were too little, I'm afraid, and didn't wear it, but with the others, it worked wonders. They lost their fear of speaking when they had that mask on, and I learned many instructive things about my children's character and intelligence.

"A parent shouldn't have to resort to such means, but my children had no mother, and men are never taught the art of raising children. I have had to make it up out of my own head, and I suppose I have done it very badly."

"Not at all, Papa!" Anne insisted.

"I wonder. If I had you wear that mask today, Anne, would you find the courage to tell me what is troubling you?"

Anne would very much have liked to confide in her father, but where in the world would she begin?

He leaned over and whispered in her ear. "I will tell you a secret, my dear. All my children are shy. They have simply learned the art of wearing masks."

Anne looked up at him. "All except Branwell."

Papa laughed. "Especially Branwell. What do you think his arrogance is? Just a mask he wears to help him be the person he wants to be—though now I think he finds he cannot take it off as easily as he put it on."

It was an interesting idea. Anne had often wondered if Charlotte pretended to be Charles Wellesley sometimes, even when she was not in Verdopolis. Perhaps that's how she found the courage to go to school again—by wearing the mask of someone else until she became that someone else. A clever trick.

"Charlotte does it, I think," she said.

"Yes. She wears the mask of the dutiful daughter." It wasn't what Anne had meant, but she didn't interrupt. "It hardly ever slips, but when it does"—he leaned back in his chair—"Charlotte will never forgive me."

"No," Anne said quietly. "I suppose not."

He fixed her with a piercing gaze. "Now, any other of my children would have denied that, denied they even knew what I was speaking of. But not you."

Anne felt herself blush. She had strong memories of the ugly black wreath that had covered the parsonage door when Maria and Elizabeth died, of crying bitterly not because she missed them, but because everyone else's tears made her feel so bereft. Her memories of Maria and Elizabeth themselves were much more vague—but she'd always known that their ghosts persisted.

"Honesty is one of your great strengths, my dear. Never forget that." Anne wasn't sure she deserved such praise. Perhaps she only lied less because she said less. "If you could choose any mask to wear right now, what would it be?"

Anne lay down her yarn. "I suppose if, as you say, I would

grow into this mask, then I would make it of my own face . . . but a braver, better version of myself."

"And what would this braver Anne do?"

The answer came quickly, as if it had been there all along. *I'd save them*, she thought.

CHARLOTTE

THEY WOULD ALL DIE TODAY.

Every important person in Verdopolis was crammed into St. Michael's cathedral for Zamorna's coronation—artists, politicians, the wealthy elite—row after row, all wearing their finest clothes: the men in morning coats, the ladies in bright colors and elaborate hats. Charlotte stood at the back of the cathedral with about a dozen others who would also be part of the ceremony.

"We're here," Branwell said, coming up beside her. Lord Thornton was a peer of the realm, and so he was dressed in an ermine-trimmed robe and coronet.

"Emily, your dress!" Charlotte said.

Emily's dress had turned an inky black, and its velvety black roses left a trail of petals behind her. She looked down at herself distractedly. "Oh. I'm sorry, Charlotte. It simply . . . happened."

"I suppose no one will notice in this crowd. What of Rogue? He'll be here?"

"He won't be able to resist," Branwell said, "and I have an idea for how he'll make his entrance. I think you'll both be pleased." Charlotte nodded, though Branwell's face was grim and she herself was full of misgivings.

"Find our seats, will you, Branwell?" Emily asked. "I'll join you in a moment."

Branwell gave them both a look, but he nodded and made his way down the aisle to the front of the church.

"I'm worried about him," Emily hissed when he was gone. "I'm afraid he's not ruthless enough."

Charlotte didn't know how to answer. "Are you?" *Am I?*

Emily caught up Charlotte's hand and held it tight, her expression fierce. "I saw. I saw what haunts you." As she spoke her dress changed from black to vivid red again. "I'll be ruthless. I'll be . . . the lamb-horned beast!"

Charlotte found this a little alarming, but she didn't pull away. Instead she nodded. "*A great cheer rose up,*" she said, still looking into Emily's eyes.

Immediately they heard the roar of the crowd outside. Emily smiled and gave Charlotte's hand a final squeeze, then disappeared down the aisle. The wooden doors of the cathedral swung open, and Charlotte caught a glimpse of waving crowds, of red banners flapping, of a dozen white horses pulling a golden coach. Someone came up behind her.

"Into your place, Charles! Into your place! We've rehearsed this a dozen times!" It was the Viscount Castlereagh, also in peer's robes. Above his ermine collar, his ashen face glistened with sweat.

"Why, Castlereagh, you look terrible. Is all well?" She knew that it was not. Castlereagh and his troubles were instrumental to her plan.

The viscount turned away, shaking his head furiously. "It's nothing," he insisted.

Trumpets sounded and the Duke and Duchess of Zamorna entered together. Mary Henrietta wore a dress of pure white velvet embroidered with diamonds, and Zamorna was in the uniform of a Verdopolitan general, with gold medals on his chest and a long sword at his side. Slowly they passed, walking down the aisle toward a raised dais at the front of the church. Six maids of honor and six handsome noblemen carried the trains of their crimson mantles. Mina Laury was among them. This wasn't quite appropriate, as she was only a servant, but it seemed fitting. Charlotte waited patiently among the many peers and knights and clergy members who would follow slowly behind them.

"More," Charlotte whispered. "He deserves more." This was her hero's final scene. Her Zamorna was about to die. From the galleries above their heads, choirs of children appeared and began to sing, tossing white rose petals down on the assembly.

"Still more," Charlotte whispered.

The twisted columns around her stretched as the great cathedral grew larger and more magnificent. Gilded paintings of saints and angels appeared on the ceiling. A second gallery of singing children appeared above the first. The crowd responded with exclamations of wonder.

"Did you see that?" said a bishop standing next to her.

"Surely the Genii are among us today," said someone else.

"I pray not," the viscount muttered. "There are enough here already to witness my shame."

The never-to-be king and queen took the changes to their world as a matter of course as they glided serenely down the aisle. Charlotte wondered how Branwell planned to have Rogue enter and ruin the scene. Was the villain hiding somewhere already? Would he swing down upon them like a pirate on a rope?

An old archbishop with a crosier and golden robes was next in line to follow after the couple, and then it was Charlotte's turn to join the procession. She traveled the length of the red carpet at a snail's pace. When she reached the dais, Zamorna and Mary Henrietta were already seated on their two golden thrones, their trains artfully arranged on the steps in front of them. Above them, a stained-glass window threw down shafts of colored light, making the diamonds on Mary Henrietta's gown glitter and Zamorna's medals glint and shine.

On either side of the dais sat the peers of Verdopolis who had not been in the procession—the counts and dukes and viscounts who were Charlotte's favorite characters. Zenobia, the Red Countess, was frowning in the front row of the right side. Her death would be by poison, Charlotte had already decided.

Branwell and Emily were sitting next to the countess, and Charlotte moved discreetly to stand beside their chairs. The wizened archbishop shuffled forward to a spot in front of the dais and faced the crowd. In a loud voice he declaimed, "I hereby present unto you the undoubted sovereigns of Angria. Are you willing to do them homage?"

This was the first part of the ancient coronation ceremony, the recognition, when the people would acknowledge Zamorna and Mary Henrietta's right to rule. As was the tradition, the assembled crowd enthusiastically shouted their approval of the king and queen.

"Honestly?" the archbishop said. "These two? You are willing to do *them* homage?"

A murmur rose from the crowd. Zamorna sat forward in his throne.

"What is he doing?" Charlotte whispered over Emily's head to her brother. Branwell said nothing, but she noticed he was muttering to himself.

The archbishop hobbled over to a group of young page boys who held the crown jewels on velvet pillows. He picked up the Angrian scepter and faced the crowd again. "I simply wish you to be quite certain," he said, straightening up. His voice seemed more youthful now.

"What is the meaning of this?" sputtered the Earl of Scadding, standing from among the peers. "They have been recognized by us all."

The archbishop raised the scepter, at the top of which was a ruby as big as a man's fist. "Then you're all a bunch of jackanapes!" He brought the scepter down with a crack upon the floor. The crowd gasped. The ruby came loose, and the archbishop picked it up. He polished it on his robes like an apple, then slipped it into the folds of his clothes.

"Ladies and gentlemen, there will be no coronation today!" He pulled off his miter and his white hair came with it, revealing dark curls underneath.

"Rogue!" Zamorna cried.

"Father!" said Mary Henrietta, clutching her breast.

"Husband!" cried the Countess Zenobia in the seat next to Branwell.

Rogue tore off his false white beard and shed his robes, revealing his usual black attire and a large cutlass at his waist. Branwell flashed a smile at Charlotte, who nodded in approval. They were working well together, she thought, like the old days. She could hardly tell which parts of the scene were hers and which were his, and Emily, who was nervously clenching and unclenching her fists, seemed to be, if not contributing, at least successfully keeping herself from causing chaos.

Charlotte turned her attention back to what was happening on the dais. Her own part was coming up—Mary Henrietta's death scene—and she wanted the dialogue to be perfect.

"Guards!" Zamorna shouted. "Take him! And evacuate the building!"

"I think not," Rogue said. With that, every clergyman in the room tore off his robes as well, revealing Rogue's accomplices, dastardly highwaymen all, their knives and cutlasses gleaming. "No one leaves the church until this business is done."

Charlotte was surprised to see S'Death among the miscreants—he was a little old for armed mischief—but Branwell must have had some business for him later. The old man took a seat among the spectators with a dagger across his knees, watching the events unfold like a man at a play.

"You give me no choice," Zamorna said, ripping the velvet mantle from his shoulders and standing to his feet. "I should have known you would not grant me the perfect happiness of this day. Your obsession with me would not allow it."

"I?" Rogue said with a sneer. "Obsessed with you? You are married to my daughter and sleeping with my wife. Who is obsessed with whom, I ask? You'll be courting my old mother next!"

"Devil!" Zamorna shouted. He drew his sword.

"Please stop, both of you," Charlotte murmured under her breath.

"Please stop, both of you!" cried Mary Henrietta, falling to her knees and holding out her arms beseechingly to them both.

"*Can't you see that if you proceed in this deadly course...*"

"Can't you see that if you proceed in this deadly course, I will lose either a husband or a father this day?"

She was so lovely, Charlotte thought, so ethereal—but Charlotte couldn't lose her nerve now. "*Take pity, gentlemen.*"

"Take pity, gentlemen!" Mary Henrietta clutched at Zamorna's leg. "To lose either of you would break my heart in twain."

Zamorna broke from her grasp and leapt down the steps. He and Rogue circled each other in front of the dais, both their swords drawn. Again and again their weapons clashed, sparks flying. At first the bulkier Rogue seemed to have the advantage, but Zamorna's blows were quicker, and he moved with great agility over the dais steps. Soon his sword shot out, drawing first blood. Rogue cried out and clutched his arm.

"Oh!" Mary Henrietta moaned, wringing her hands at the scene below her.

Zamorna pressed his advantage and aimed a killing blow.

"Husband, I beg you!" Mary Henrietta cried.

She flew down the steps and hurled herself in front of her father. Beside Charlotte, Emily's dress went dead white. Branwell winced. *Stop, stop, stop,* Charlotte wanted to say, but all she could do was grip the back of Emily's chair as Zamorna's sword, meant for Rogue, pierced Mary Henrietta's breast.

"No!" Zamorna cried. His sword clattered to the floor.

Mina, who had been standing at the side of the dais, rushed to her mistress, kneeling at her side. "We must take her to a doctor. Quickly!"

Zamorna knelt as well, gathering Mary Henrietta into his arms. "Oh, my dear, speak to me."

How dare she? How dare she make my death ethereal and touching? Death is an ugly thing. The words rang in Charlotte's memory, but she pushed them aside.

"Stop it," Rogue said to Zamorna, his expression black. "Stop pretending to be shocked by this turn of events. Gods, if I had known . . . Oh, you fiend. This was your plan all along."

"What?" Zamorna said, looking up, his face spattered with blood. "You say that I meant to harm her? My wife?"

"Only a villain like yourself could harbor such a thought," Mina said, tears flooding her eyes. "She was hurt trying to save you!"

"Of course he meant for this to happen. He's orchestrated everything, down to the color of the blood against her gown. Oh, you do look tragic, Zamorna, with my dying daughter in your arms. What a sense of pageantry you have."

"You're mad," Zamorna spat.

Mina, assisted by some of the noblemen and ladies who had been trainbearers, took the unconscious Mary Henrietta from Zamorna's arms and carried her away, though Charlotte knew that no one could save her now. Zamorna let out a fierce howl as he watched them go.

"For pity's sake, stop this playacting!" Rogue said. "I cannot bear it." He turned to the crowds of spectators, who sat in frightened silence. "You sheep who sit there in your silks and satins, you call me a scoundrel—a murderer—but by the gods, do you not see how this . . . this Bluebeard dispatches his wives and lovers when he grows bored with them? Does it not chill you to the core?"

"I?" Zamorna asked. "A murderer? My previous wife died of a wasting disease. You claim I caused that as well?"

Rogue continued to direct his comments to the crowd, though he pointed at Zamorna. "Oh, his women may die of illness or accident, but *he* is the architect." Rogue turned to face him. "You will fool me no longer, Zamorna of the Genii."

For a moment all Zamorna could do was stare at Rogue with wide eyes. Then, still on his knees, he began to laugh. It was choked, half-mad laughter that twisted Charlotte's heart. "You believe I am one of the Genii?" he said. "You believe I know why these things happen? Why anything in Verdopolis happens?" He laughed again, so hard that tears sprang to his eyes. "I am nothing but a bobbing cork on a tide of events. I have no sail, Rogue. No rudder." He caught his breath and wiped his face, leaving a streak of blood. "If it's true the Genii caused this . . . then they are very cruel indeed."

The truth in his words rang clear like the peal of a bell. Charlotte felt that Rogue must have heard it, and indeed, he frowned and turned in a circle where he stood, squinting at the peers and spectators. His eyes stopped at Emily, who sat staring at him in her white dress like a frightened little dove.

"One of you, do something!" Emily hissed. "Distract him. He suspects that Zamorna speaks the truth."

Charlotte nodded. "*My love. Do not grieve . . . ,*" she began.

The Countess Zenobia now leapt from her chair next to Branwell and flew to Zamorna's side. "My love. Do not grieve," she said. "We can be together now. I will divorce my brutish husband, and we shall be happy." She tried to stroke his cheek.

"Do not paw me, woman!" the duke said.

The countess gave a cry and stepped back. "Zamorna! What is this? I see all affection extinguished from your eyes."

Zamorna gazed into the distance. "I realize now . . ." He stopped and bit his lip. Branwell and Emily looked over at Charlotte.

"*I realize now that it is my own wife I love,*" Charlotte murmured.

"I realize now . . . ," Zamorna began again. A realization seemed to dawn as he spoke. "I realize now that I have never loved anyone."

The countess blanched, staggered, and fell swooning to the floor. No one in the crowd had the sense to help her, and so the poor woman lay unaided in a heap in front of the dais.

"'I realize now that I have never loved anyone,'" Rogue mimicked, his voice full of scorn. "And yet we all know you'll be writing poetry to the chambermaid in an hour."

Zamorna's face turned to stone. "Enough talk. You will die this day, Rogue." He stood.

"Hold, Zamorna. Hold," Rogue said. "I am not your enemy."

Zamorna picked up his sword and held it aloft. "I beg to differ."

"Wait!" Rogue put down his own sword and held up his hands. "I begin to smell his plan. This is a death scene, and not just for Mary Henrietta."

"Pick up that weapon!"

"Listen to me very carefully," Rogue said, "for our very lives depend upon it. I have met three of the Genii. At least two are with us in this cathedral." The peers and spectators began to murmur at this, and even Zamorna glanced quickly around. "I thought you were the fourth, the eldest one, but now I see that I was wrong."

Zamorna seemed to hesitate, and Rogue pressed his advantage. "The others . . . perhaps they are his pawns, I don't know, but the fourth means to make us kill each other. I'm certain of it. Think, man! Who's ever heard of this Angria place? And why should you be king of it? All this, it's just a stage for us to die on!"

Zamorna lowered his sword. *The plot is getting away from us,* Charlotte thought. This was just like the party at Wellesley House—but she could not let that happen again. "*Do not blame the gods, as it is I who am to blame,*" she murmured.

"It is I who am to blame!" the Viscount Castlereagh cried, stepping forward. "Zamorna, hear of my degradation! I was foolish and gambled away my vast inheritance until there was nothing left." He pointed to Rogue. "This nefarious creature, this devil in human form, threatened to ruin me unless I helped his men gain entry to the cathedral. My family honor, my mother's home—all would have been lost if I had not complied. It is because of me that Mary Henrietta lies at death's door." He pulled a knife from his robes. "I have betrayed you, and I know of only one remedy."

"No!" Zamorna and Rogue shouted together, but the viscount plunged the dagger between his ribs and buckled to the ground.

"My friend!" Zamorna cried.

Castlereagh, on his hands and knees, coughed a spray of blood. He held out a hand to Zamorna. "Forgive . . . me," he moaned, and with that he fell dead.

We've gone too far, Charlotte thought, sickened by the sight of the blood pooling around Castlereagh's body. *Zamorna was right to call us cruel.*

"What could be clearer?" Rogue said. "The Genii hunger for our lives today."

"You corrupted that poor young man," Zamorna said darkly. "Ruined him. Not the Genii, but you."

"Yes," Rogue agreed. "But what is worse, the man who does evil things, or the god who watches them for sport?"

"My husband is right," said the Countess Zenobia. She had recovered from her faint and now sat upright on the floor. In her hand she held out a green vial that glittered like a jewel. "I found this on my person, but I've never seen it before. I think . . . I think I was meant to end my life with it." She stood, brushing off her peer's robes. "But why should I do that? We've had a few dances, Zamorna, you and I. A few kisses. But you never loved me." She set the green vial on the first step of the dais. "You are not worth dying for." She straightened, and with her head held high, strode away down the center aisle of the cathedral.

"I begin to see why I married that woman," Rogue said. "Well, Zamorna, are you with me or against me? Shall we forge a truce?"

Zamorna considered this, his sword still lowered. After a moment, he seemed to come to some steely resolution. "A truce. Yes. But not with you." He turned to the crowd. "Genii! Wherever you are! For many years I have lived a charmed life, but now it seems you desire my end. If that is your final say, stay silent, and I will lift my sword against Rogue. He and I shall kill each other as is your will. But if there is some other path we might take, show yourselves now, and we shall find it together." His eyes searched the crowd.

Charlotte hesitated. She saw that she was standing at a forked road. She could stay silent, or she could step forward. It came to her with perfect certainty that if she did nothing, her story would roll on, no matter what Rogue did. The two heroes would kill each other. The plot would stay in her hands. It would be a tale of bloodshed and meaningless death, but it would be hers. But if she tried to change things now, take the fork she hadn't planned on, there was no telling where her story would end.

"Emily," Charlotte said softly, putting a hand on her sister's shoulder. "It's me. It's me who's not ruthless enough." Emily turned, her eyes wide.

Before Emily could stop her, Charlotte stepped forward. "I am here," she called. "I am the fourth Genius."

BRANWELL

OU, BROTHER? YOU ARE . . . ONE OF THE Genii?"

Zamorna's face was white with shock. Branwell had never seen him react in a way that wasn't wooden, but now there was something more vivid about him than before, more real.

Charlotte came forward to stand in front of the two men. She was still Charles Wellesley, and her slight boy's frame was dwarfed by Rogue's bulk and by Zamorna's willowy height, but she held her chin high. Branwell could only hope she had some plan, now that she had scuppered the previous one.

"Let me say . . . ," she began, looking up at them, but Zamorna held up his hand.

"No!" The word echoed through the cathedral. "I want no words from you."

"Seize this boy!" Rogue called to some of his men. "Quickly, now!"

Charlotte looked back to Branwell in panic as two of Rogue's cutthroats grabbed her by the arms. "Zamorna!" she said. "I took you at your word. You said you wished to find some compromise—a second path!" The duke only turned away in distaste.

"She's got no plan at all," Branwell hissed.

"We should run," Emily said, but it was too late.

"Over there," Rogue called, pointing. "Lord Thornton and the girl in red—white—the one in plaits. They're Genii as well."

Peers turned to stare at Emily and Branwell, looks of fear or hatred on their faces. Branwell stood and tried to bolt up the aisle, but many hands reached out to stop him. In moments he and Emily had been half dragged, half pushed to the front of the cathedral. He saw that Charlotte was trying to turn up her palm and return home, but to no avail.

"What do you think?" Rogue said to Zamorna, his arms crossed. "Will we blink out of existence the moment we slit their throats? Even so, I'd say it's worth it."

Zamorna's face was sad and stony. "There is a better punishment," he said.

+++

There was rioting on the streets of Verdopolis. All around, Branwell could hear shouting and breaking glass. The three Brontës were being taken in a mob down a wide avenue that ran alongside the public park and led to the Tower of All Nations. It was a strange group: Verdopolitans still dressed in their coronation finery and cutthroats brandishing knives—people who under normal circumstances would have nothing to do with one another.

"The end times are upon us!" a drunken man cried at them from a park bench. He threw a bottle that crashed at Branwell's feet, making him jump.

"This is terrible," Charlotte said beside him. "Are we doing this?"

"I don't know." Branwell glanced at Emily on her other side. There was something quite disturbing about her dress. It seemed to be going scarlet again in places, but it was the scarlet of fresh blood, not fresh roses. She had been nowhere near Mary Henrietta, and yet she seemed to be stained, and she left a trail of blood and dead flowers as she walked.

"I believe we're all making these things happen," Branwell said. "All of us and none of us. Our characters, too, for all I know."

Charlotte turned away with a deep frown. "*Stop,*" he heard her say as they walked. "*Stop, stop, stop.*" There was no effect.

Ahead of them the great tower loomed, and beyond it, small fires had broken out over the hillside. *My city is coming to an end,* Branwell thought, but above the hills the sky was strangely beautiful. The stars were bright as polished diamonds, and the twilight was a shade of indigo he'd only ever seen in Verdopolis.

I made that blue, he thought. *I made this place. I will never write or paint anything to rival it.* But even as the words came to him, he saw: This was a child's world. He and Charlotte hadn't even tried to make it like Africa. The flora was pure Yorkshire, with the exception of a few palm trees. And the buildings—cobbled together from maps of London and a few John Martin engravings. Still, he loved it. He loved it.

Ahead of them at the end of the avenue, a man with a bucket of paint began to deface the Tower of All Nations with graffiti. A riderless horse galloped by. Somewhere a child cried.

"Charlotte," Branwell hissed. "This was your plan. Remember what you said about being strong willed and taking control of the plot?"

"You always said I kept too tight a rein on my stories," she said. "Perhaps that's why they didn't breathe."

"A little more rein might be required at this point."

"We deserve whatever our characters do to us," Emily said darkly, staring straight ahead. "For what we tried to do to them. For Castlereagh. For Mary Henrietta. For trying to kill our heroes."

"Don't say that!" Branwell said. "If you believe that, who knows what will happen!"

"Even if we don't say it, I think we all feel it," Charlotte said. She took him by the arm, looking up at him. Her eyes were ridiculously large and blue at the moment—Charles Wellesley's eyes. The boy had always looked to Branwell as though he'd been painted by the worst kind of sentimentalist.

"Will you change into yourself, for the sake of reason?" he implored. "I'm tired of talking to a ten-year-old boy."

"Yes, brother. Do turn back into your true self," said a voice behind them.

Charlotte dropped Branwell's arm and they separated immediately. He hadn't thought Zamorna could hear.

"He always was a little too articulate for a ten-year-old," Rogue said. "You should have realized."

"Yes," Zamorna said, "he was always present at the seminal events of my life—my great joys, my wretched lows. Strange I never wondered why."

"What will you do to us?" Charlotte asked, not turning around. Branwell could hear the fear in her voice.

"What *can* you do to us?" Branwell said, trying to sound defiant. "We are the Genii." He tried not to think of Anne's burned fingers.

"The worst punishments are the ones we devise for ourselves," Zamorna said.

Branwell didn't know what this meant, but it gave him a sinking feeling all the same. The fires were bigger now. He saw that they would soon envelop the whole hillside. From the indigo sky a star fell. Then another. And then all the stars began to rain down—dazzling streaks of white light. Branwell remembered the time with Emily when he'd thought Armageddon was upon them. Then, he'd been terrified, but in reality, the end of the world was only terribly, terribly sad.

"*Stop,*" he pleaded to no one. "*Stop.*" They all trudged on.

The man who'd been painting graffiti on the Tower of All Nations was gone, but he'd left behind some words in red, dripping paint. They said: *Mene, mene, tekel, upharsin.* These were the words that were written on the wall by the hand of God at Belshazzar's feast. They meant: *You have been weighed on the scales and found wanting.* Branwell was sure they were meant for him.

ANNE

NNE SAT ON THE FLOOR OF THE CHIL-
dren's study. She had taken up the secret floor-
board, and all her brother's and sister's writings
were laid out in orderly rows.

There is something I am missing, she thought.

She had tried ordering the papers by author, and then by date.
Now they were ordered by character—a line of Rogue stories, a
line of Zamorna stories, each going back in time to its beginning.
Newer characters like Castlereagh had shorter rows. She had
spent a good deal of time considering where a story with multi-
ple characters should be placed. There was something here. She
knew it. There was something in all this paper that would help
her siblings and herself, but she didn't know what it could be.

At the back of the cavity under the floor, Anne had found two flat boxes. She opened one now. Inside were twelve battered toy soldiers. She took one out, marveling that she remembered his name, could still distinguish him so easily from the rest, though to other eyes he might seem identical. It was Napoleon, Branwell's favorite.

She pulled out the others, laying them with reverence on the floor. They had given the Brontës something precious, these little men. They had inspired some of Charlotte's and Branwell's earliest stories.

Here was Gravey, Anne's favorite, so called because his face held a grave look. This one was Sneaky, because of his shifty eyes. This one was Butter Crashie, named for an unfortunate kitchen accident. And here was Charlotte's favorite, the Duke of Wellington.

After a while Charlotte and Branwell hadn't needed the little men for inspiration. In fact it became an embarrassment that many of their best characters could trace their lineage back to toy soldiers. Even Alexander Rogue, Anne now realized, had his beginnings in an English child's notion of Napoleon, the wicked and fascinating villain.

Anne stood and set Napoleon at the top of the row of Rogue stories, the Duke of Wellington at the top of the Zamorna stories. Then she opened the second box, which held a set of ninepins. These had been the ladies, but the ribbons and carefully fashioned paper hats that had distinguished one from the other were all gone now, so Anne didn't bother setting them out.

Still, she could see how the characters of Verdopolis had developed and changed from these humble beginnings. Some characters were really the same person, she realized. Mary Henrietta and Marion Hume were the same, she decided, and after some thought she put Zamorna's wives and lovers together in one row.

"What am I missing?" she said aloud. "What am I . . . ?" She stopped.

"No. Who?"

There was a character who didn't have a row. He was never the main character. He had no beginning as any soldier or ninepin. He hadn't grown and developed, but he had always been the same man with the same name. Since before Glasstown. Since the beginning. He was outside. Separate. It was as if . . .

It was as if the Brontës hadn't made him.

"He was always there, watching us," Anne said aloud. "The old fox."

Two papers sat on the desk, writing themselves, Charlotte's and Branwell's, but they had long since become unreadable. The tiny handwriting had covered the margins and was now crossing the page lengthwise, words weaving through other words, tangling into knots. Still, Anne understood what her siblings were trying to do, and she knew it was a mistake.

"You are fighting the wrong enemy," she murmured.

Anne sat down. Without any hesitation or ceremony, she held out her hand, palm up.

"Old Tom, Old Tom," she said. "I wish to make a bargain."

CHARLOTTE

CHARLOTTE HAD THOUGHT THEY WERE heading to the Tower of All Nations, but Zamorna stopped at a nondescript door along the avenue. The crowd behind them had grown. Many held lanterns, since night had fallen and even the stars were leaving the sky.

The building in front of Charlotte was identical to many others they had passed. She was sure she'd never set a story here. These places were simply pieces of stage setting for people to go by on their way to the tower. She was reminded of the white room she used to make for Emily and Anne. A blank. Something she'd never bothered to invest with any detail.

"I demand to know what you intend!" Branwell shouted. "You

will not treat your gods in this manner!" Charlotte couldn't help but love his puffed-up bravado at that moment.

Emily, in a dress that seemed to be drenched in gore, was staring at Rogue like a vengeful goddess, and she was having some effect. He tugged nervously at his hair and wouldn't meet her gaze.

Zamorna moved to face the crowd, leaving the three Brontës to be held by Rogue's cutthroats.

"None of us can truly understand the Genii," he shouted. "None of us can imagine what they fear."

"Drown 'em!" someone yelled.

"Burning oil!" shouted someone else. "They'll fear that!"

Charlotte took hold of Branwell's shoulder to steady herself. She searched the faces around her for kindness or sympathy, but found none, which seemed terribly unfair. *I've loved you all,* she wanted to tell them, but she was afraid this might be met with violence.

S'Death stood at the front of the mob, smiling fiendishly, clearly delighted by this turn of events. She amended her previous thought: She had never loved *him.* His grin widened as she caught his eye, and he seemed about to say something, but then he cocked his head. Had someone called his name? The complete shift in his attention reminded her of Snowflake when he heard a mouse in the grass. A moment later he was speeding off down the street, and Charlotte found herself glad he wouldn't be there to witness her end—whatever that end might be.

"Beyond this door is the worst place that the Genii can imagine," Zamorna said.

"And where's that, exactly?" asked Rogue, who was standing a bit to the side, arms crossed, out of the path of Emily's dagger stare.

Zamorna smiled grimly. "No idea."

Charlotte began to understand.

"Why, Duke, that is clever," Rogue said.

"Don't think, Charlotte," Branwell hissed beside her. "Don't think about anything."

But the worst place Charlotte could imagine was already taking shape in her mind.

"Don't," she pleaded. "Don't make me go in there."

"Were you laughing at me all these years, brother?" Zamorna asked, his face lined with sorrow. "Was I your clown, my trials and tribulations nothing but entertainment?" His famous basilisk eyes seemed to sear into her. She noticed he still had a white rose petal caught in his hair from the coronation, and she longed to reach out and brush it away.

"It was my favorite thing," she said, "my very favorite thing, to forget myself with you, to be completely lost in the scene."

"May you be lost again," he said. He turned the knob of the door and pushed it open. Rogue stepped up and took her roughly by the arm.

"*She went through the door and found nothing unusual inside,*"

Charlotte said, her voice high and tight as she was pushed toward the door. *Only an empty room. Only an empty room.*

"It's too late," she heard Emily say behind her, voice bleak. "We all know what's in there."

"Charlotte!" someone said in her ear. "Charlotte, can you hear me?"

She turned, but no one was there. It was cold, so cold that she could see her breath in front of her, and she shivered in her thin frock and pinafore. She was eight years old, standing in a long room with a low ceiling, and she was very hungry. In front of her, rows of neatly made beds lined the walls—neatly made except for one.

"Maria," she cried, running over. "Maria, get up!"

With difficulty, Charlotte's eleven-year-old sister raised herself to a sitting position. "Hello, dear one. Is it morning?"

"You know it is, Maria. All three bells have gone. You must get dressed." Charlotte pulled the sheet away from her sister's body.

"Please, dear. I'm too ill," Maria said, drawing it up again. Charlotte glanced over her shoulder. "For heaven's sake, Maria. Don't do this again. You can't be sick—your cheeks are too rosy."

But Maria lay back down, and Charlotte let out a little moan of frustration. At home Maria had been considered very capable; she could read at four, recite poetry at six, and speak French at eight. It wasn't until they came to school that Charlotte began to see her many flaws. She was always being scolded for her untidiness and her poor spelling and her unladylike handwriting. All the accomplishments Papa had praised her for seemed unimportant to the teachers at Clergy Daughters'. In fact, Maria was by far the most unsatisfactory student here.

"Please," Charlotte said. "We shall all be punished for your laziness if you do not get up, and I'm so hungry."

"Tell Miss Evans that I am ill," Maria said. "She is kind. She will understand."

Charlotte began to tear up now. Miss Evans might be kind, but she had little authority over the other teachers. "I can't believe how selfish you are! You know I couldn't eat the beef last night because it was spoiled, and if we are punished this morning, it will mean no breakfast!"

Maria sighed. "Hush," she said. She sat up again and slowly, very slowly, swung her legs over the edge of the bed. "I'm getting up. See?" She sat for a moment breathing heavily. "And you will have my porridge this morning. If you share it with Emily."

"Emily doesn't need it," Charlotte said with disgust. Emily was the youngest at the school and so pretty with her curls and turned-up nose—the school pet. If she asked Cook for more porridge, she would probably get it. If Charlotte asked, she'd get her hand smacked for greediness.

Maria pushed herself off the bed and into a standing position. "Get my frock and pinny, dear. And a hairbrush, if you please."

Charlotte wrinkled her nose. Her sister smelled both rotten

and sweet, like bad fruit—but it was too much trouble to get her to wash, and by now the water in the basins would have been used by countless other girls. She opened the box at the foot of the bed where Maria kept her few belongings, pulling out a purple stuff frock, a white pinafore, and Maria's underthings.

She tried to hand them to her sister, but Maria wouldn't take them and didn't seem to see. There was something wrong with her balance; she seemed to sway like a sapling in a wind.

"For heaven's sake," Charlotte said, practically frantic now. "Will I have to dress you?"

And then Maria coughed.

It was a horrible, painful cough that seemed to rattle up from hell, shaking Maria's whole body. It didn't seem to end.

"Oh," Charlotte said.

Her sister doubled over, holding onto the edge of the bed to keep from falling, coughing and coughing. Charlotte could see the bumps of her bony spine poking through her shift. How thin she had become—a skeleton.

"Maria," Charlotte whispered. "There's blood on the sheet. You coughed blood."

Maria stared at the stain but didn't seem to see it.

"We must write to Papa."

"It's only a cold," Maria said, straightening slowly. "And this is the only school Papa can afford. We must be educated."

"If our father knew what it was like here, perhaps he'd say it was better to be stupid."

"No," Maria said. "This is the trial that God has given us. Besides"—she lowered her voice—"if we did write, I think they would only confiscate our letters."

"Brontë!" said a sharp voice from the doorway. "Late again, I see."

It *would* be Miss Andrews, Charlotte thought. She was by far the most heartless teacher at Clergy Daughters'.

"Forgive me, Miss," Maria said. "I'm getting ready now."

Charlotte quickly pushed the purple frock over Maria's head, not bothering to remove her night shift, then she fetched the hairbrush. Maria stood docilely, allowing Charlotte to tidy her hair as if she were a little child.

"I see the Duchess has found a servant to dress her," Miss Andrews said. Charlotte noticed she was carrying the birch rod she often used to discipline her students.

"Please, Miss!" Charlotte said. "My sister couldn't help being late. She is very ill."

"We struggle through adversity here," Miss Andrews said. "We do not cow to it. Please stand in the center of the room, Brontë."

"No!" Charlotte cried. "Tell her, Maria." But Maria had pushed herself off the bed and was shuffling to the middle of the room.

"Charlotte! Come away." Her sister Elizabeth beckoned from the door. "Come! There's nothing we can do." Little Emily was beside her, looking blankly at the window, as if there were something far more interesting outside.

Maria bent down into a low crouch, her back to Miss Andrews.

"Oh, Elizabeth! It's wrong!" Charlotte said. She desperately wanted to throw herself at the teacher, but she was too afraid of being beaten herself.

"Come to breakfast, Charlotte."

Charlotte backed toward her sisters, turning her face away as the first blow fell across Maria's back. Emily showed no reaction. Charlotte envied that. She wished she could simply depart, cut whatever fine string held her to reality and get lost in a dream that way.

The sound of another blow made her wince. Elizabeth put a hand on Charlotte's arm to lead them away, but as they went through the door, Charlotte heard a sound that was even worse than the *smack, smack* of the rod. Someone was laughing.

She wheeled around, enraged at Miss Andrews, but it wasn't she.

It was Maria, who held her sides and emitted a low, slow "ha . . . ha . . . ha," so divorced from any merriment that it could hardly be called laughing at all.

There was something awful in the sound. It was broken and hysterical. There was no hope in it. Charlotte turned away quickly, already telling herself that what she had heard could not have been real. She'd imagined it. Maria hadn't laughed. Who could laugh at such a moment?

On the stairway, students either smirked or gave them looks of sympathy, but no one spoke to them as they passed. The unfortunate Brontë family was a target of too much attention from Miss Andrews, and no one dared to be their friend. Elizabeth wiped away a tear. She'd been so pretty a few months ago, as pretty as Emily, but now she looked pinched and tired. Her cheeks were very pink, too, Charlotte noticed, but underneath, the skin was papery, stretched too tight over the bones of her face.

Charlotte felt her heart skip a beat. "Lizzy," she asked softly. "Are you ill, too?"

"Charlotte!" someone said in her ear. "Charlotte, can you hear me?"

And then Charlotte found herself alone. She had reached the bottom of the stairs and should have been at the entrance to the dining hall, but instead of tables, she saw a long, gray room with neatly made beds lining the walls. It was the dormitory, and her sister Maria was sleeping late again.

"Maria," she cried, running over. "Maria, get up!"

With difficulty, Charlotte's older sister raised herself to a sitting position. "Hello, dear one. Is it morning?"

"You know it is, Maria. All three bells have gone . . ." Charlotte frowned. Had she said that before? "You . . . you must get dressed."

Maria lay back down. "Tell Miss Evans that I am ill. She is kind. She will understand."

"I can't believe how . . . how selfish . . ." Charlotte couldn't go on. Her sister wasn't selfish; she was ill. In a week she would be sent home. Not long after, she would be dead. "Oh, Maria." She caressed her sister's cheek, felt how hot it was. If only she had felt it then. But wait. What was then and what was now?

"Charlotte!" someone called. "Listen to my voice!" She turned but could see no one.

Maria raised herself with difficulty. "Hush. I'm getting up. See?" She sat perched on the edge of the bed, breathing heavily. "And you will have my porridge this morning. If you share it with Emily."

"Don't," Charlotte pleaded. "Stay in bed. You must rest—you must!" She cast her gaze around the room, looking for help, and was surprised to find that she wasn't alone. A dim figure stood watching from the foot of the bed.

"Branwell?" she asked, squinting.

The figure became clearer, resolving itself into a boy. It *was* him. For a single moment, all Charlotte felt was delight. Her brother had come. He was going to save them all. And then another feeling overtook her gladness like a tidal wave overtaking a tiny ship. Anger.

"You can see me?" Branwell said. He ran to her, his face wet with tears.

"What are you doing here?" she asked coldly. She began to fully realize where she was—in Verdopolis still, beyond the door that Zamorna pushed her into. She had lost herself. "You were never at Clergy Daughters' School. This isn't the worst place you can imagine."

He wiped his eyes. "Isn't it?" His words were choked with feeling, but Charlotte remained unmoved.

She looked down at her frock and pinafore and tightened her fists, willing her clothes and body to change back to their true form. She stayed the same. If there was any body she hated worse than her own, it was this one. Her younger body. Her hungry body.

"How long have we been here?" she asked. "How many times have I replayed this scene?"

"Five? Six, perhaps? I don't know."

"And you were watching all along?"

"I tried to shake you," he insisted. "I tried to pull the stick out of that woman's hand, but there was nothing . . . I even tried to shield Maria with my own body, but the stick seemed to go right through me, and she was beaten just the same, every time."

Maria was standing now and began to cough. They both winced and stepped away. Branwell put his hands over his ears. "I couldn't do anything. I can't do anything. It just goes on and on. How can we stop it?"

"We, we, we," Charlotte said. "There is no we. Must you even steal my nightmares? You never saw any of this. You never saw Maria sicken, get worse every day . . ."

"I saw her when she came home!" Branwell said. "I saw her die. I saw them both die." He took a deep, gulping breath. "It was awful for both of us. Why are you so angry with me?"

"This is the trial that God has given us," Maria murmured.

The rage inside Charlotte crested to a peak. "I'm angry because Papa and Aunt Branwell never would have sent you here," she shouted. "Not to a charity school. Not the precious boy."

"I know that," Branwell said, his voice ragged. "I've always known that. Don't you think that might be hard to live with?"

Charlotte pressed her lips together, moved in spite of herself by the pain on her brother's face.

"This is the place where my sisters went and came back to die. I don't have to have been here for it to be the worst place I can imagine," he said.

"Brontë! Late again, I see."

Charlotte and Branwell both turned to glare at the figure in the doorway.

"Forgive me, Miss," Maria said. "I'm getting ready now."

"I can't bear to see her beaten again," Branwell said. "I can't bear to hear that laugh."

"I know, I know, but how can we stop it? This has already happened." She went to help Maria, who was struggling with her frock. "Look at her. She's so young. We had an eleven-year-old for a mother."

"We struggle through adversity here. We do not cow to it. Please stand in the center of the room, Brontë."

"What's wrong with you?" Charlotte cried at Miss Andrews. "We were children! You were meant to protect us!"

"Charlotte! Come away," said Elizabeth from the door.

Charlotte's eyes fell on the little girl beside her. "Emily?" Was that her, the real Emily, trapped here just as she and Branwell were? It must be. Charlotte came forward cautiously, as if approaching something wild. "Come back now, Emily," she whispered. "We need you."

Emily's mouth was open slightly, and Charlotte could see she had a tooth out. At six, she'd been among the youngest girls at Clergy Daughters'. Charlotte had always believed that she'd been spoiled at school, that she hadn't struggled the way Charlotte had, but this was contradicted by the thinness of her arms and the dullness of her eyes.

"Emily, can you hear me?" Charlotte said. Her sister's gaze was locked on the little square of window. "What are you thinking about, my dear?"

Emily turned away from her daydream, slow as a diver coming up from great depths. She blinked. For a moment Charlotte thought she hadn't heard, but then she said, "I'm thinking that if we only had a rabid dog for a pet, we could make him come and ... and tear out Miss Andrews's eyes!"

"Oh."

"Charlotte!" Branwell called.

Maria had gone to the middle of the room and was bending down for her beating. Branwell was beside her with his arms around her. Miss Andrews lifted her cane.

"*Stop!*" Charlotte shouted. "*This all happened long ago, and my sisters are dead.*"

The scene stopped. The pair were frozen, Miss Andrews's stick arrested just before it came down. Charlotte circled them— her sister cowering, Miss Andrews with a cruel smile upon her face. Branwell had his eyes squeezed shut, but he opened them when Charlotte put a hand upon his shoulder.

"Help me," she said. "I'm not tall enough."

At her direction, Branwell reached up, took the birch rod out of Miss Andrews's hands, and handed it to Charlotte.

She broke it with a snap across her knee.

ANNE

NO ONE HAD SEEN ANNE YET. SHE WAS SITting on one of the low beds, hands folded in her lap. She had not attended the Clergy Daughters' School at Cowan Bridge—she'd been too young—but she was surprised by how well the scene before her matched the picture in her mind. Bare walls. A dingy sky seen through a tiny window. And so cold. No one seemed to be dressed for the temperature—not her siblings, who were their proper selves again, and not the teacher, who stood like a statue in the center of the room, empty hands lifted above her head, a motionless child hunched before her.

Tentatively, Charlotte held out her hand, palm up. Nothing happened.

"Blast," said Branwell.

"You might have power over the story again," Anne said, "but *he* controls the doors."

Her siblings turned as one. She wished she couldn't read their faces so well, because the emotions that flickered across them— anger, sorrow, disbelief—threatened to make her lose her nerve.

I must wear a mask, she thought, *a mask of someone who is capable of saying what needs to be said.*

"Yes, I am here," she said curtly. "I had to come."

Charlotte crossed to her. "You made a bargain? How foolish! Now you are trapped just as we are."

"But *why* are you trapped, Charlotte?" Anne asked. She looked from one sibling to another in turn as they drew around her. "Think, all of you. If you are unable to cross back home, then Old Tom doesn't get his payment, so why hasn't he made a door for you?"

Charlotte hesitated. Emily and Branwell shared a puzzled glance.

"He wants more," Charlotte said finally. "He wants a higher price."

Anne nodded. "I think he's worried that we'll never come again, so he's going to try to get all he can." She looked calmly into her elder sister's gray eyes. "Is it your intention to come again?" She didn't like the answer she saw.

"I must summon him," Charlotte said, ignoring the question and holding out her hand, "if I'm able. I must offer him some- thing—"

"Don't!" said Anne. She leapt up and grasped her sister's hand. "Before we face him, we must be ready. Charlotte, listen to me very carefully. We must never come back here. We must arrange it so we never have to cross again."

Charlotte shook her head. "It's impossible now. I failed. I couldn't kill them."

"It's not impossible!" Anne said, her voice raising in pitch. "It can't be."

"They'll haunt us—" Emily began.

"Stop!" Anne shouted. "Listen to me, all of you. There are things you need to hear." *Braver, better Anne,* she reminded herself. "And our allies need to hear them, too."

"Our allies?" Branwell asked.

"We'll need help if we're to face Old Tom." Before they could question her further, she cleared her throat and said:

"Alexander Rogue, Earl of Northangerland, and Arthur Wellesley, Duke of Zamorna, fearing the end of Verdopolis, the Glasstown Confederacy, and the world, began to waver in their decision to dispatch the Genii. They resolved to rescue their makers from whatever terrible fate had befallen them, and so, full of apprehension, entered the mysterious door."

Anne's three siblings stared at her, then slowly turned their heads toward the narrow hallway, where two figures were indeed approaching. Zamorna cast his eyes about in wonder as he entered the room.

"It's uncanny, I'll give you that," Rogue said, giving Miss

Andrews a poke. "But is this the worst you can imagine? I thought we were sending you to the pits of hell." He rubbed his hands together. "Too cold for that, though."

"The pits of hell?" Emily said sharply. "And it took you this long to come for me?" Anne noticed that although she was now wearing her Haworth dress, Emily's hair was still in braided loops and scarlet bows.

Rogue drew himself up. "I'm not the rescuing sort."

"I don't understand," Zamorna said. "I see Thornton and my two cousins—whom I've been led to believe are Genii—but where is my brother, Charles?"

"I am the fourth Genius," Charlotte said, meeting his eye.

Zamorna gave a start of recognition. "But I know you," he said, taking a step closer. "I've imagined you." For a moment they held each other's gaze. A blush rose up Charlotte's neck.

"Take care," Rogue said, laying a hand on his arm. "Remember who they are."

"Yes." Zamorna's look hardened to a scowl, and Charlotte cast her eyes to the floor. "We may have come to save you, Genii, but you are not forgiven. Look at me still stained with my wife's blood. I cannot forget . . ." He stopped. His eyes had fallen on the still figure of Maria. "What is this?" He circled the strange tableau. "Is it Mary Henrietta I see? Is she a child?" His voice turned angry. "Who is this woman who threatens her?"

"Calm yourself," Charlotte said. "She is . . . a villain from another story."

Zamorna shook his head, still frowning at Miss Andrews. "When I crossed that threshold, I imagined many villains to vanquish, many trials to overcome, but this one poses no threat."

"No," said Charlotte. "Not anymore."

Anne gave a cough. "The two of you might help us in another way." All eyes turned to her again, and she fought to control her nerves. "That's why I've called you here." She moved back to one of the beds and sat down. "Rogue, if you will." She gestured to the bed opposite, inviting him to sit also.

You're doing well, she told herself. *Your mask is holding. Brisk, competent Anne.*

Rogue sat, the bed creaking. "You've called me, have you?" He didn't seem to like the suggestion that his presence here wasn't entirely his own idea.

Emily, Branwell, and Zamorna gathered around, while Charlotte perched next to Anne. The weight of all their attention made her courage flag. She looked up at Rogue, but she realized it was no longer easier to speak to him or to Zamorna than it was to speak to anyone else. They were real people to her now.

"You don't like me much, I think," Rogue said.

"No. I don't."

He smiled, amused by this response. "You should. We share a loved one, you and I." He gestured for Emily to sit down next to him, which she did with a lack of hesitation Anne found vexing.

"I may be brutal," Rogue said, putting a hand on Emily's knee, "but my one redeeming quality is that I'd never harm her."

"In the real world," Anne shot back, "I'm not sure brutal people can draw such clear demarcations."

"I'm not from the real world."

"Thank heaven for that."

He narrowed his eyes at her, and she narrowed her eyes right back at him, her annoyance making her brave. How could Emily see anything romantic in that brooding frown, those gleaming teeth?

"You bit someone," she said. "Do you remember that?"

His guilty look told her that he did. Rogue took a moment to answer, shifting to face Emily as he spoke. "Only vaguely. It was like a dream. A dream of death. You had abandoned me. I had no world, no story. There was a light . . ."

"A door," Emily said. "That was Old Tom opening a door, I think."

"I remember little else except the desire to find you." He smiled, and Emily sighed up at him.

Anne frowned at Charlotte, hoping her elder sister would say something about the warm looks they were exchanging, but Charlotte's attention was on Zamorna.

"Who is Old Tom?" Zamorna asked.

"We hardly know," Charlotte replied. "He creates magical doors, and we believe he opened one for Rogue to enter into our world. Now he's trapped us here in yours."

"Rogue has visited the world of the gods?" Zamorna said, amazed. "Could I do that?"

"We don't know for certain, but I believe you could now."

Anne tried to steer the conversation back to the plan she had begun to form when she was in the children's study. "Rogue, you say you plagued us because you had no world, no story." She looked around at her siblings. "But isn't that the solution? Once we get home, couldn't we write him a world without crossing over ourselves?"

Branwell had been leaning on the wooden box at the end of Anne and Charlotte's bed, but now he stepped in closer, excitement on his face. "Keep Verdopolis alive, but cheat Old Tom out of any further payments—is that what you mean?"

"Exactly!" said Anne. She had thought this the answer to everything, but the looks on her siblings' faces told her they didn't agree. Even Branwell's smile was beginning to fall.

"Old Tom wouldn't stand for that," Charlotte said. "If we're not crossing over, he'd still open doors for our characters to cross to our world. What would prevent Rogue and Zamorna and all the others from plaguing us then?"

"I would prevent it!" Zamorna cried. "I have no desire to plague anyone."

"I'm sure that Mary Henrietta, if she were here, would say the same," Charlotte said, "and yet she haunted me in a terrible way. I think she couldn't help it."

"Charlotte's right," Branwell said.

"No!" Anne said. "You are giving up too quickly. Your characters are not the true enemy. You must make some pact with them, some agreement. If you tell their stories fully, if you make them truly live on the page, perhaps they will not cross so often or so dangerously. Don't you see? You must try, at any rate." She could tell by the way her siblings failed to meet her eye that they were not convinced.

"I shall be honest, Anne," Charlotte said, after a pause. "If we write but don't cross over, the doors will still come. You wouldn't understand this, having no world of your own, but it would be a kind of torture for us. I for one don't think I could resist forever."

"Nor I," Emily said.

Anne felt her anger build inside her. They were still as reckless with their lives as they had always been—but she knew they would not be so reckless with each other's.

"Emily," she said, her voice clipped. "Tell Charlotte the price you pay for crossing over."

Emily hesitated. "Days. I told her. Days of my life, just as she and Branwell give."

"Tell her the exact words. Tell them both."

"I . . . don't think I remember them."

"I do." Anne took a deep breath. "'Everything my sister Charlotte and my brother Branwell have given in their years of crossing over, and everything they will give in years to come, this I offer, all at once, for one passage to my beautiful world.' Wasn't that it?"

Beside Anne, Charlotte stiffened. "Are you mad?" she said to Emily. "Is that what you promised?

"'Everything they will give in years to come,'" Anne repeated. "You see, Charlotte, you have no choice but to never cross again. If you do, you will be ripping days from her life as well as your own."

"What in heaven's name is the matter with you?" Branwell shouted at Emily. "How could you offer so much for one passage? Charlotte and I must have crossed a thousand times!"

"Emily," Rogue said gently. "Have you paid days of your life to go to Gondal? How many?"

"Very many," Emily said.

"But how can you ever go back if the price is so high?" There was a tenderness in his voice that surprised Anne.

"She can't!" Charlotte said, on the verge of tears now. "It would mean years!"

"And that debt will increase if you and I cross again," Branwell said.

"Yes, and *my* debt will increase if *anyone* crosses over again, including Emily," Anne said.

The room fell silent. The heat of everyone's emotions was so strong now that Anne imagined she could feel it radiating toward her in waves, making the mask she wore peel and crack.

Just a few more words, Anne told herself, *and then they will know everything and I can be invisible again.*

"This was my bargain," she said, her mouth gone dry. "I told Old Tom that I did not wish to live longer than my sister Emily." Emily's eyes widened at this, and Anne faltered but pressed on. "I told him to take as many days as lets me die within a year of her, and that if she ever crosses over again, he should add those days to my debt."

Anne knew Charlotte would be appalled, but the look on Emily's face was truly horrified, and Branwell had gone white as sheets on the washing line. Had they truly believed she would let them carry all the burdens?

"Why?" Charlotte finally said. "Why have you paid this price? You are as reckless and as foolish as Emily to make such a bargain!"

"Don't you see?" Anne said, her voice shaking. "I did it so you'd never cross over again. I did it because you're all too stupid to value your own lives! How many times have you vowed to never go to Verdopolis again, Charlotte, and how many times have you broken that vow? Well, now you *cannot* go, because every time you do, you will be bringing Emily and me closer and closer to our deaths."

"You had no right!" Emily cried, her face pink with anger.

"Emily . . . ," Anne began.

"You had no right to take Gondal from me. The days I gave, I chose to give." She stood, turning toward the door. "I can't forgive you. I won't!"

EMILY

MILY REMEMBERED WALKING IN THIS YARD, round and round and round. It was their daily exercise. She could see the tracks countless girls had worn in the dead grass. She remembered the craggy old tree in the center of this circle, how beautiful it was, and stark, with its wild, black branches—the only thing at Clergy Daughters' School that she had loved.

She left the school building and walked toward the tree. The anger she'd felt was already dissipating, being replaced by a hollowness inside her. As she walked, she hugged herself against the bitter weather. It wasn't snowing, but it was cold enough, and Emily had no coat. She closed her eyes, wondering if she could make one appear.

"*The great Genius conjured herself a coat out of thin air,*" she said aloud.

"Lady Emily!"

She turned to see Rogue coming toward her, holding out his own black jacket. The sight of him made tears sting her eyes.

"I can't go back," she called before he had even reached her. "She's made it so I can never go back to Gondal."

"Do you think I would have let you go?" he shouted. "When the price is years from your life?"

You couldn't stop me, she thought. No one could have but Anne. "But I want it," she said, her voice almost a sob. "I want it so badly. Even when I said I'd never go again, I always knew that I could change my mind, but now . . ." He reached her and set the jacket around her shoulders. "That place is my soul, I think."

"I know," he said softly. "It's mine, too."

Do you have a soul? she almost asked, but if she had one, surely Rogue did. Perhaps they shared the same soul.

"What you need to do," he said, "is kill me off."

"What?"

"When you get home to your own world, I mean. Write a story that ends me."

She gave a short laugh. "We've tried that."

"I won't resist this time. It will be doing me a favor, and you'll be less tempted to come, won't you?"

"I'm not going to kill you, you fool!" Emily pulled the jacket closer around her shoulders. "Besides, we don't know if we will

be able to summon Old Tom. We might all be trapped here."
She looked around the bleak landscape as if the old devil might
finally appear and open one of his doors, but of course he didn't.

Had Clergy Daughters' School truly been built on such a bar-
ren spot, she wondered, or was this simply how she remembered
it? Everything from the bare tree, to the pale grass, to the black
crows that wheeled around the chimneys of the school seemed
to echo the bleakness inside her.

She wondered if the Brontës might be able to turn this place
into a replica of Haworth now, with its own parsonage and its
own Papa, but it came to her how terribly empty and sad that
would be, and she realized that as much as she loved Gondal,
there was a place she loved even more. She wanted to be home.

Emily reached up to one of the low-hanging branches, and
where she touched, a bud appeared, pale and pink. The bud
grew, opening to blossom in moments. The petals fell. The fruit
swelled and turned from green to red. She picked it.

"Apple?"

He took it from her gravely, polished it against his waistcoat,
and put it in his pocket like a remembrance he wanted to keep.

"Please," he said. "I don't want to live in Gondal or Verdopolis
without you. I'll do myself in if you won't kill me."

"Don't say that!" The only thing worse than not seeing Rogue
would be knowing that he was dead and buried in some grave
she could never visit. "I'll do as Anne says. I'll write adventures
for you, and make you live." She smiled up at him, though she

didn't much feel like smiling. "And I'll write you vexing heroines to make you miserable."

Rogue drew closer now. He didn't touch her, but the nearness of his body made her heart beat a little faster in her chest. She put her hand against the trunk of the tree to steady herself.

"It's no use," he said. "I want no other heroines. I can only love you."

She reached out to brush her fingers against his black whiskers, feeling the jacket slip from her shoulders to the ground. "Listen. You will still love only me. And I will love only you. It's only that we'll have different names." Her voice started to break, but she pressed on. "Sometimes I'll be Augusta, queen of Gondal, and you'll be a dangerous highwayman. Sometimes we'll be Alexander and Zenobia, the young lovers. Sometimes . . . sometimes we will just be two lonely children roaming the moors together. But the 'he' of the story will always be you, and the 'she' of the story will always be me. Forever. For as long as I live. Can't you agree to that?"

He thought about this for a moment. "If you can."

Without another word, he leaned in and kissed her. Her first kiss. Her only kiss. Emily put her arms around his neck, knowing she could lose herself entirely in the feeling of warmth and happiness that flooded through her, but pulling him closer just the same.

CHARLOTTE

OOD GOD, THEY LOVE EACH OTHER, CHAR-
lotte thought as she watched Rogue and Emily
from the door of the school. *How did that happen?*
Emily had been to Gondal just the once, hadn't
she? Charlotte had spent years on the periphery of her own stories, but Emily had thrown herself in, body and soul.

"You're simply going to ignore that?" Branwell said behind her.
The kiss *was* going on for rather a long time.

"Oh, Branwell. Don't be such a prig."

"As usual, it falls upon me to be the sensible one."

He pushed past her and strode across the yard toward Emily
and Rogue.

Emily noticed them now and waved to her younger sister.
Anne dashed off, and the two met in an embrace in front of the

tree, Rogue and Branwell looking on. Emily's anger was like a quickly passing storm. Over the years, this had led Charlotte to believe her sister's passions weren't serious. She saw now that she'd been wrong about that.

Charlotte and Zamorna started toward the others across the hard ground. "I'd like you to know," he said, "that if I can do anything to help you get home, you have only to ask."

Charlotte knew what she must do and did not think he could help her, but the gesture touched her. "Then you are not angry with us any longer? You don't hate us?"

Zamorna hesitated. "I hardly know what I feel," he answered. "Or what I am. I have only just learned that all the days of my life were bought with days of someone else's. With my own dear brother's days. Except, of course, that you are not my brother." He shook his head. "All I can say is that it has made me think of how I've spent that time, and your sacrifice seems too great for the dissolute life I have led."

She stopped walking. There was a new warmth and intelligence in his brown eyes. It had been growing there ever since they were together in the garden. For a moment, she was at a loss for words, though she quickly regained her composure.

"My name is Charlotte," she said. "Charlotte Brontë."

Zamorna bowed. "A pleasure."

When she arrived at the tree, all faces turned to her, expectant, and Charlotte did not hesitate. In a loud voice she cried, "*The*

wicked Old Tom, knowing it was the last time he would ever open a door
for the Brontë siblings, appeared in person to negotiate his price."

Nothing happened at first. She glanced behind her to see if
anyone was coming out of the school, and when she turned back,
someone was leaning against the trunk of the tree, someone who
hadn't been there before.

"S'Death," she said.

"In the flesh," he said with a nod. He was wearing the fine
green velvet he had worn to Zamorna's party.

Emily, who was closest, gave a little scream and jumped away
from him.

"You?" Branwell said. Only Anne, standing off to the side,
seemed unsurprised.

"Yes, I." S'Death seemed offended at Branwell's disbelief. "Don't I look like all the stories? I could wear my red furs if
you'd prefer. Might be warmer."

Charlotte approached warily. "I see. You liked to keep an eye
on us, I suppose. But what are you?"

"Who's to say?"

"A demon? A fairy?"

S'Death looked at his fingernails and shrugged.

"Hold one moment," Rogue interrupted. "You are not who
you claimed to be, either? First Thornton and now you?" He
grabbed S'Death by the collar and shoved him roughly against
the tree trunk. "Do I have any true friends at all?"

"Now, old fellow," S'Death said.

"Tell them what they want to know!"

"I will! I will!"

Rogue let go, and S'Death harrumphed, yanking at the end of his waistcoat.

"I've had as many shapes as I've had names. I didn't always look like this, you know. Before you came, I wasn't much. Just the sound of wind on the moor."

"Before we came?" Branwell repeated. "We, the Brontës?"

S'Death rolled his eyes. "No, dimwit, you, the human beings—before you came with your axes and your bows and your telling stories around a fire." A smile cracked his craggy face. "Oh, the things you humans dream up. I can't think of nothing on my own, but you. They're almost real, you know, the things you dream. You're almost little gods." He thumped his chest with his fist. "You dreamed me up. Or anyway, you dreamed up different forms for me—fox, fairy, spider—a thousand more. Old Tom's the story they tell now, but there are plenty of good ones."

"You made Verdopolis?" Charlotte asked. "And all our places?"

"Nah," he said. "You done all that. All I done was give your stories a little push. It only takes a breath from me, a little whisper, to make them solid, to make a bubble where they can grow. A world. And then, for a price, you can go there, to that place you made. I poke a little door in that bubble, and I let you in."

He grinned. "It's been a long time since anyone's made worlds as rich as yours, though, a long time."

Charlotte stepped forward. "Please, let us go home. Take one more payment—but take it from me alone. A hundred days, will that suffice?"

S'Death seemed to think about this, puffing out his cheeks. "Nah. Not enough. Not enough by half."

"Right, then," said Zamorna. He brushed past Charlotte, took S'Death by one ankle, and, before the small man could protest, had him upside down and was shaking him back and forth like a terrier with a rabbit. Charlotte backed away with her hands up, and Emily laughed in surprise.

"Come, Rogue!" Zamorna shouted as he shielded his face from S'Death's free foot, which was kicking wildly. "Don't stand there like a toadstool, man! This is the villain we're meant to vanquish, or I'm the son of an ape."

"I've called you worse," Rogue muttered, but he grabbed S'Death's other leg.

Their gesture was a useless one, but it thrilled Charlotte none-theless, and as she watched, a wave of emotions swept over her. He was a marvelous character, her Zamorna. They both were.

"What shall we do, then?" Rogue asked his new ally. "Split him like a wishbone?" S'Death gave a squawk and thrashed harder.

"Wait!" Charlotte cried. "My dear duke." Zamorna looked to her. "Your Grace. Your motives are very admirable to me, but my siblings and I might be stranded here if you kill S'Death."

"That's right, that's right," S'Death shouted up at them. "I make the doors. There are no doors without me."

Zamorna and Rogue gave S'Death a shake to keep him quiet. "Lady," Zamorna said. Then more softly: "Charlotte. I won't pretend to understand all that I've seen, but you know I wish to help you. Tell us what to do."

"Allow him to stand," Charlotte said.

"You are certain?"

She nodded. With a frown Zamorna turned S'Death over and set him on his feet.

S'Death staggered for a moment, regaining his balance, then he glared at Charlotte, his red hair standing straight up. He had said that a fox was one of his forms, and she could see the fox in him now. There was a flash of yellow in the depths of his eyes.

"I warn you, Brontës," he said. "Don't try that again. You think this is our last bargain, but you will cross again to your worlds, and don't forget that I can raise the price whenever I want."

"If you believe that, then let us go home free of charge," Branwell said.

"Yes," Charlotte said. "Allow us to cross over, and keep collecting your price for the rest of our lives. You win."

She saw the doubt that crossed S'Death's face and smiled. "He knows we'll never come back."

"You will!" S'Death said. He jerked a thumb toward Rogue. "That one will haunt you. And now Zamorna will, too, though what form you'll give him even I can't guess."

"I assure you, I would haunt no one," Zamorna said haughtily.

"You couldn't help it," S'Death said. "You'd come in your

dreams. You'd long for your lost gods. I would open a door—out of the goodness of my heart, of course—and a part of you would slip through. There's always a part that thrives in their world, the ugly parts that can't breathe in Verdopolis, the parts they leave out. The shadowy bits." He chortled with laughter. "You see, Genii, I've tied you up well in my little net."

"But we won't be their lost gods," Charlotte said. "We won't abandon our characters again. We'll write worlds for them. We'll write them fully, with all their . . . bits."

She thought of Mary Henrietta, who had been the light side of Maria—the shining girl—and it came to Charlotte that she had given Verdopolis no room for darkness. For doubt. For shadows. That must change.

She glanced at Anne. "I'll tell the truth. They will live their whole lives in our stories, and we will leave nothing out."

"Didn't I already live fully?" Rogue asked Emily. "I crossed to your world. What shadowy bits did you leave out of me?"

Emily thought about this for a moment. "I think you could be wickeder," she said finally. "What do you think, Branwell?"

Branwell nodded slowly. "Yes. We've been holding back."

Rogue rubbed his whiskers thoughtfully, as if this were a challenge, and Charlotte saw Anne blanch at the idea of his being even worse.

"Don't get ahead of yourselves, Brontës," said S'Death. "We still have our . . . negotiations to complete."

Charlotte felt her anger rise. "Tell me, you old devil, just what do you do with our days? Do you add them to the tally of your own?"

"Not at all. A thousand girls have given me their beauty, and"—he put his hands on his cheeks and batted his eyelashes—"as you can see, it hasn't improved this face. As for your days, I will last as long as the moor, so far as I know, with or without them."

"Then why take them?"

S'Death leered, but when he caught sight of Zamorna's dark countenance, his expression sobered. "Honestly, I make bargains. It's what I do. It's what I've always done. Bargains and doors, that's all I make—that and a little mischief." He smiled again, as if that last part were a joke, but found no one to smile with him.

"It's our misery he wants," Emily said. "Our regret. The bargain doesn't really matter, as long as it's a bad one. For us."

He crossed his arms. "A bad bargain. That's a thought. Make me one of those, and perhaps I shall let you go home. But it must be very bad, for you've put me in a very bad mood."

"What else do we have to give?" Charlotte asked. "You have taken our days. Take all of mine, then, if it will save my siblings. Take all I have left!"

"No," S'Death sniffed. "It's not so many now. And the bargain isn't bad enough."

"Then what! What do you want! What could I give you that is worse than the knowledge that I have played a part in damning my siblings and myself to shortened lives? What could possibly be worse than what you have taken?"

But as soon as she said it, she did think of something worse. S'Death's eyes lit up.

"That," he said, pointing at her face. "That's what I'll take. Nothing less. Oh, I knew that there was one more bargain to be squeezed out of you all."

"No," Charlotte said, weakly. "Not that. I couldn't bear it."

But the look in S'Death's eyes told her it was the only way.

They were home. They were in the children's study, and Charlotte had only a moment to sigh with relief when she heard a gunshot.

Branwell was at his desk, and Anne was sitting on the floor. Both looked as dazed as Charlotte felt. Emily was the first to act, running to the door and throwing it open. The shot had come from the backyard. Tabby gaped as they came running down the stairs and crowded past her to the kitchen door; she must have been wondering where in the world they had come from.

Papa stood in the yard with his pistol at his side. It was dusk. Charlotte could see Grasper on the other side of the stone wall, his nose to the ground and his tail straight back. He lifted his head and barked when he saw them.

"Why, there you are," Papa said. "Your aunt is in a terrible state. I went out looking for you wicked children, but I see you came back while I was gone—and Branwell in his dressing gown already."

Branwell looked down at his clothes but could provide no explanation.

"What were you shooting at?" Anne asked.

"A fox just over the wall. A big one. I was afraid he was after your pheasant, Emily."

Jasper, the pheasant in question, was sitting in a tuft of grass by the near side of the stone wall, oblivious to the danger. Emily gathered him into her arms. "Did you get him?" she asked their father. "The fox, I mean?"

She and Charlotte shared a glance.

"I thought so," Papa said. "But Grasper can't seem to find a body. Perhaps not."

"It's just as well," Emily said, rubbing Jasper under the chin.

"You don't mean that," said Charlotte in surprise.

Emily looked at her and blinked. "A fox can't help being a fox."

"My aim was true, or so I thought," said Papa, squinting over the wall.

"I'm sure it was," said Charlotte.

"You've all missed your tea, but I will not let you miss your prayers."

"No indeed, Papa." Charlotte was surprised to hear the shaking in her voice.

A wave of love for her father crested over her. How selfish they all had been. Their father had lost two children already, and yet they had risked never coming back from their invented worlds. He would have wondered for the rest of his life what had happened to them.

"You should all be punished, I suppose, though you're all far too old for it." He hesitated. "How shall I punish you, Charlotte?"

Abruptly she threw herself into his arms. "Oh, Papa!"

"Oh!" Papa wrapped his arms around her stiffly as she began to cry. "Have you punished yourself already, my dear? That is always the way of it. The punishments you give yourself are so much worse than anything I would give you. Is that what happened?"

"Yes, Papa." She wiped her face. "It is."

CHARLOTTE

"EMILY BRONTË!" CHARLOTTE SAID, EMPLOY-
ing the same tone she used when Snowflake
jumped up on the kitchen table. She hadn't even
had to look over that time; she had caught a faint
shimmering in the air from the corner of her eye.

"I wasn't going to cross." Emily spoke without looking up, pen
scratching away, hair hanging down, obscuring her face. "I can't
help it if the door comes."

They were in the children's study, Charlotte at the window,
Emily at the desk, and Anne sitting on the floor. Grasper sat on
Emily's feet.

"She's telling the truth," Anne said. She was organizing Branwell's latest writings, tying them in ribbons or folding them up

into little tin boxes to be put back under the floor. "You needn't worry, Charlotte."

The study was very tidy today, with no easels or unfinished paintings to trip over. All of Branwell's work was on display downstairs. At that very moment, the great portrait painter William Robinson, who had studied with Sir Thomas Lawrence, who had painted the Duke of Wellington, was in the dining room viewing Branwell's efforts. Charlotte was sure that everyone else in the house found his presence as distracting as she did—keeping their voices low and their steps soft—everyone but Emily. Emily was lost in her writing, as she had been every day since they'd returned.

"Tell us what's happening in Gondal, my dear," Charlotte said.

Emily took so long to answer that Charlotte thought she hadn't heard. These days her pen moved at a rate she'd only seen during Branwell's periods of "scribblemania."

"The Gondals are discovering the interior of Gaaldine," she said finally.

Charlotte looked to Anne for explanation, but her youngest sister only shrugged. Anne was the only person allowed to read the Gondal writings, but even she didn't read all of them. Some Emily burned without showing another soul.

"These Angria stories of Branwell's are marvelous, Charlotte," Anne said, carefully tying the last stack of their brother's writings. "The city of Adrianopolis is even more opulent than Verdopolis."

"Yes," Charlotte agreed, still frowning at Emily. "Very impressive."

"I'm sure he's made it so as to tempt you."

Charlotte looked over at her younger sister now. There was a question in her words. Anne was asking when Charlotte was going to write again.

"You know, Charlotte, *he* will cross over to our world if you don't write about him."

"Branwell writes about Zamorna," Charlotte said, "so he has no reason to . . . come looking for us."

"I think he does. I think . . ."

"I'm going to take some of our old magazines to Michael Redman and his mother," Charlotte interrupted with a forced smile.

"In Stanbury?" Anne said. "But Mr. Robinson—"

"Is here for Branwell, not for me. I'll post some letters while I'm out."

Minutes later, Charlotte came down the stairs wearing her bonnet and struggling with the button of a glove. A drawstring bag containing two letters and some of her aunt's old magazines hung from her arm.

"Tabby!" she hissed. "You are quite incorrigible."

Tabby had her ear to the door of the dining room but straightened up as Charlotte approached, a guilty look on her face.

"Well," Charlotte whispered. "What are they saying?"

Tabby smiled and bent to the door again. "Nary a peep!"

Charlotte listened, too, but heard nothing, not even a footstep. They stood silent for a full minute, frowning at each other. Finally Charlotte said, "Are we certain that they're in there?"

She knocked gently. No response.

They opened the door to find the room empty, a note propped up on the dining table. *Have taken Branwell to the pub to discuss the artistic muse. W. R.*

"Oh dear," Charlotte said, looking at the paintings and sketches so carefully displayed around the living room. "And Branwell worked so hard. I do wonder if Papa's two guineas a lesson are well spent."

"I didn't like to say, but he stank of whisky, that Mr. Robinson."

Charlotte put the note into her bag. "Best to tell Papa that . . ." She changed her mind. "No. I suppose we shouldn't lie." She took the note out again, setting it back upon the table. She was done hiding things from her father.

Charlotte was halfway to Stanbury when she saw the shadow.

She was walking down a lane thick with blackberry bushes on either side. In the weeks since she'd made her final bargain, summer had turned to autumn. Now, though it wasn't yet cold, there was something on the breeze that promised winter, and Charlotte was imagining the lane around her as it would be then—leafless, snow-covered, and utterly silent.

She stopped at the base of a small hill for no other reason than to admire the slate blue sky and to take a long pull of crisp air. From over the hill ahead it came: a shadow that resolved itself into a great, black dog. Charlotte's first thought was of Emily's gytrash. Would Zamorna take that form, too? Her heart swelled at the thought, and she took a few steps forward to greet the creature.

"Pilot!" someone called from beyond the rise.

The dog, which was only a dog, turned and cantered back to its master, disappearing from sight. Charlotte's face burned with shame and disappointment. She'd wanted it to be Zamorna. She'd wanted him. Was this why she hadn't been writing? Because deep down she wanted Zamorna to cross over to her, no matter what the consequences? The truth was that she'd tried to write, had wanted to write, but no words came, and the only scene she could imagine was the scene that had played out between her and S'Death.

She was passing a stile that led into a yellow field and decided to sit down on it to rest, and think.

"I will be the last," she said aloud. There was great relief in letting these words out, even if no one could hear her. These were the words she would have said if Zamorna had come to her, the words she could speak to no one, but which were always on her lips. She realized she'd been longing for someone to talk to. Someone to tell. "I will be the last Brontë sibling."

She squeezed her eyes tight, but still the vision of S'Death rose up before her. He had reached out his hand, palm up, and though he hadn't spoken the words aloud, Charlotte had heard them clearly inside her head: *I give you back half the days I took from you, Charlotte Brontë, enough to outlive the others, enough to mourn them all. This is my bargain.*

It was their misery he wanted, that's what Emily had said. S'Death knew the guilt Charlotte would feel in taking such an offer, in getting such an unfair reprieve.

"How can I live with it?" she asked aloud. At first she received no response but the sound of crows cawing in the brambles. Then, a voice.

"Charlotte! Charlotte Brontë!"

Something thrilled through her, passing from her head to her extremities, sharp as an electric shock. "Zamorna, is it you?" She listened. The wind sighed. Had it been Zamorna, or someone else?

"Where are you?" said the voice, louder now.

"Oh! I'm coming!" she cried, and at that moment, without thinking about it, a door appeared in front of her like a fissure of light.

Charlotte stared at it. Slowly she turned her head this way and that, looking for a flash of red fox amid the green. She saw nothing, but he must be there. S'Death. Old Tom. He would always be there, waiting for a moment of weakness.

Charlotte fumbled in her string bag for a stub of pencil. Then, setting a magazine on her knee for a desk, she held her pencil poised over the back of an envelope.

"I will not cross," she called. "Do you hear, S'Death? I'm through with bargains."

She gripped her pencil more tightly, trying to think of a scene. Zamorna would be in Angria now. Branwell had made it a magnificent place full of perfumed gardens and alabaster towers. He'd made Zamorna king and Rogue prime minister, though their alliance was already showing cracks and wouldn't last long. Soon Charlotte would be drawn into that story again. Perhaps she would even try to do what she had never been able to do before and resurrect Mary Henrietta. It might work.

But for now . . .

She glanced up and saw that the door still hovered in front of her.

For now she wanted to write something else. She couldn't help but wonder what Zamorna would have been like if he had come up over that hill. What sort of man would he be in her world, if he had been born in Yorkshire? A little burlier, perhaps, a little shorter. His face not handsome, but dark, strong, and stern.

Though she did not look up, she was aware that the door was right in front of her now, almost touching the tips of her toes.

A warm breeze came from it, carrying the scent of unfamiliar blossoms.

"You have lost, Old Tom," she whispered without looking up. "I will use every extra day you gave me, and I will let none of them be miserable. I will make them a gift and not a burden. I will work and write and draw and study. And . . . and plain as I am, I will marry someone, and it will be for love. If I am to have a life of sorrows, I will not let them conquer me. I will be as brave as Emily, as honest as Anne, even as wicked as Branwell, if I must be, but I will be happy! Do you hear?"

When she glanced up, the door was gone, but Charlotte barely registered the fact. She had chosen her scene. It would be a simple one: a man and a woman in front of a fire. The woman would be herself, a plain Yorkshire governess. The man? He would be a little bit like her father, a little bit like Zamorna, perhaps a little bit like someone she hadn't even met yet. She wasn't quite sure. She might need some time to get the scene right.

What she did know is that she would be her true self in front of him. She would sit across from him by the fire and show him her sketches. She would be his equal, and in being so would make him live.

She set her stub of pencil on the envelope and began to write, knowing he was waiting for her.

Afterword

Although this book is entirely fictional, I have peppered it with references to many true incidents in the lives of the incredible Brontë family. Charlotte's and Emily's unhappy experiences at Clergy Daughters', for instance, were based in fact. Charlotte always held the school responsible for the deaths of her two elder sisters, and readers of *Jane Eyre* will recognize parallels between it and Lowood, the school where Charlotte's heroine suffers many abuses and deprivations.

All the major characters that the siblings write about in *Worlds of Ink and Shadow* were the Brontës' creations, not mine: Zamorna, Rogue, Castlereagh, Mina, Mary Henrietta, and even S'Death. I took many liberties with them, however, as I did with the imaginary worlds that were also theirs—the Glasstown Confederacy (with its capital city of Verdopolis) and Gondal.

The Brontë siblings wrote about these imaginary worlds well into adulthood. Much of Charlotte's and Branwell's early work still survives, written in tiny books or on small scraps of paper in cramped handwriting. Unfortunately, almost all of Anne's and Emily's Gondal stories have been lost, but it's clear that they used many of the same characters in their world, including Branwell's favorite, Alexander Percy, Earl of Northangerland, aka Alexander Rogue. Some scholars theorize that it was in these early writings that Emily began to develop Heathcliff, the famous romantic antihero of *Wuthering Heights*.

Although they died young, all three of the Brontë sisters became published authors, writing under the pseudonyms of Currer, Acton, and Ellis Bell. Only Branwell failed to live up to his potential, succumbing to consumption (tuberculosis) in his early thirties, brought about by his alcoholism and drug addiction. He is probably best known for the portrait of his famous sisters, painted when he was around seventeen, which hangs in the National Portrait Gallery in London. Over time his own figure, which he had painted out, has begun to show through.

Charlotte's first novel, *Jane Eyre*, was a runaway bestseller that caused a great stir in London, with many people speculating about the true identity of its author. Emily's novel, *Wuthering Heights*, was more controversial, loved by some, called "coarse" and "strange" by others. Today both, along with Anne's novels *Agnes Grey* and *The Tenant of Wildfell Hall*, are considered classics.

Sadly, Emily and Anne did not get a chance to enjoy their

fame. They, too, developed consumption and, in what must have been a terrible year for Charlotte, died within nine months of their brother. After the death of her siblings, Charlotte revealed to the public that she and her sisters were the famous Bell brothers, and the world marveled that these mild-seeming parson's daughters could create such passionate books.

Charlotte Brontë continued to write and publish, though none of her novels achieved the critical success of *Jane Eyre*. She married Arthur Bell Nicholls, her father's curate, but died a year later at the age of thirty-eight.

The Reverend Patrick Brontë survived all six of his children.

Acknowledgments

I am a slow writer, so by the time I've finished a book, my writing group is usually wholly sick of it. Thank you to Paula Wing, Hadley Dyer, and Kathy Stinson for never saying this out loud, and for the many years of critiques and encouragement. Thanks also to beta readers Georgia Watterson and Anne Laurel Carter.

I read many books on the Brontës while researching this novel, but I'd like to single out two that I referred to again and again: Juliet Barker's biography *The Brontës*, and *Tales of Glass Town, Angria, and Gondal*, edited by Christine Alexander. I'd recommend them to anyone interested in learning more about this extraordinary family.

Peggy Needham corrected my terrible French; Kate Blair weeded out all my Americanisms; and the wonderful Geoff Baines painstakingly helped me to put all of Tabby's speech into

Yorkshire dialect—and then had to be very patient with me when I took it all out again for readability, leaving just a hint of his work.

I received a grant from the Canada Council of the Arts to complete this work, for which I am very grateful.

Sarah Laycock and Ann Dinsdale of the Brontë Parsonage Museum answered all my questions and allowed me to conduct research among the rare and fascinating works in the parsonage archives.

Finally, this book would not exist without the support of four people who are so much smarter than I am: my Canadian editors, Hadley Dyer and Jane Warren (team Emily); my agent, Steven Malk, who has never failed to be there when I needed him; and my US editor, Susan Van Metre (team Charlotte), who was both patient and demanding, in exactly the right measure, and whom I hope to know for many years to come.